The Grandest Adventure

The Grandest Adventure

Writings on Philip José Farmer
1996–2018

Christopher Paul Carey

LEAKY BOOT PRESS

The Grandest Adventure: Writings on Philip José Farmer, 1996–2018
by Christopher Paul Carey

First published in 2018 by Leaky Boot Press
http://www.leakyboot.com

ISBN: 978-1-909849-61-7

Also by Christopher Paul Carey

To my friends Michael Croteau and Karl Kauffman,
who pointed me toward the future,
and to Phil, who welcomed me when I got there.

Contents

Foreword

Christopher Paul Carey saved my life. One day Phil Farmer, Chris, and I were floating in tubes down the Kickapoo River when suddenly mine sprung a leak. Without a thought for himself, Chris instantly—okay, fine, I made that up. But there is no question that when I found myself in over my head, Chris saved me.

You see, I launched a website about Philip José Farmer in 1996, which started by listing all his known books, then adding stories, poems, articles, reviews, speeches, introductions to other authors' books, convention appearances—pretty much anything I could find out about him went on the website. Eventually I added a section for fan fiction, fan art, and fan articles. Chris contributed three articles to the latter that were so good, so well researched, so well written, so *Farmerian* in their level of detail, I hesitate to call them "fan" articles at all.

The website continued to grow, and by the early 2000s, Phil, his wife Bette, and I had become close enough that Phil let me go through his files and sell photocopies of some of his unpublished manuscripts on my website. But each time I visited his home in Peoria, Illinois, I'd go through the files again and always find something I hadn't seen before. This occurred so regularly we started calling it "The Magic Filing Cabinet," a term coined by Chris in one of the essays reprinted in this collection. In 2004, another fan, Paul Spiteri, and I, convinced Phil to let us publish a fanzine dedicated to him, *Farmerphile*, where each issue would contain previously unpublished fiction and nonfiction by him, alongside articles about his work and life by his fans and peers.

This was a dream come true for me! Although I love to read and am an avid book collector, I know I'll never be a writer, so the closest I can come is to be a publisher. But then it hit me. Every issue would need an overall introduction as well as an introduction to each individual piece. The problem is that grammar and I had never seen eye to eye. From verb tense agreement, to dangling modifiers, to sentence fragments and run-ons, to comma splices, to semicolon misuse, to learning that the bleeping commas and periods go inside the quote marks instead of outside...my writing was a mess.

A week or two before we were going to press, Chris asked to see the first issue. He's never come out and said this to me, but he must have been horrified by what he saw. He immediately wrote back and offered to proofread the whole issue for us if we could hold off printing it. I had no idea just how much I didn't know, until he sent back his corrections. All those corrections. So many corrections.

I very quickly realized that Chris had just saved *Farmerphile*. If I had printed the first issue as it was, and sent it to Phil, I'm sure he would have killed it on the spot. He would have said, "Thanks, but no thanks, I don't think this is going to work out after all, it's me, not you..." and *Farmerphile* would have died after one issue. And I wouldn't be the co-owner of Meteor House today, which has gone on to reprint many of Phil's books and stories, and to expand his many fantastical worlds with tales written by other authors.

While publishing *Farmerphile*, I managed to surround myself with some very fine, dedicated, brilliant fans who all loved Philip José Farmer: Paul Spiteri, Win Scott Eckert, Dennis E. Power, Danny Adams, Keith Howell, Charles Berlin, and, of course, Christopher Paul Carey. But Chris was always one of the most knowledgeable on just about every topic that came up. Not only did he know Farmer's books forward and backward, he knew Farmer's inspirations, his source material if you will—Edgar Rice Burroughs, H. Rider Haggard, Arthur Conan Doyle, Jules Verne, Sir Richard Francis Burton, Joseph Campbell, et al— nearly as well as the grand master did himself.

That's why, when on my twentieth or so trip to Peoria to search through Phil's files, when I found the folder titled "Kwasin of Opar" I knew right away I wanted Chris to finish this long awaited third installment in Farmer's Ancient Opar series. But I wasn't sure if Chris would want to take on such a herculean task or not. For the story of how I sprang it on him, well, he'll tell you about that further on in this book. Chris of course did want to complete the novel, and Phil readily agreed to let him do it. Since then Chris has gone on to write other tales set in Ancient Opar and the larger empire of Khokarsa—"A Kick in the Side," "Kwasin and the Bear God," *Exiles of Kho, Hadon, King of Opar*, and *Blood of Ancient Opar*—proving Farmer's trust was well placed.

Farmerphile finished it's run with is fifteenth issue in 2009. We had several months of "retirement" from publishing when Paul, Win, and I started Meteor House and started work on our first book, *The Worlds of Philip José Farmer 1: Protean Dimensions*. Even though we couldn't talk Chris into joining us as a partner—he wants to write, not publish—he did help edit that first book and establish many of our current editorial house styles and procedures. And he is still my go to guy: I still ask him to proofread everything I write, to make me look, well, competent anyway. In fact—and I'm sure it goes without saying—I agreed to write this introduction only because Chris agreed to proofread it and polish it up.

Before you lies some of the most important and in-depth research published about Philip José Farmer over the last twenty-plus years. However, it is also very entertaining and accessible. Not only will you enjoy reading it; it will make you yearn to read the works of Farmer it dissects, and perhaps some fiction by disciple Carey as well.

Michael Croteau
Meteor House Headquarters
February, 2018

Preface

"Books should burn, not be burned.

"What they do or is done to them depends on the reader, the person who holds the book in his or her hand. Some books do indeed radiate a high heat, and blaze with a light that blinds but which, paradoxically, enables you to see as never before."

The year that I write this preface, 2018, marks the Philip José Farmer Centennial—one hundred years since the being who would come to be known as the Wizard of Peoria first appeared on the planet Earth. When Farmer, some thirty years ago, wrote the words I have quoted above, his books were already burning for me, illuminating my inner world in a way that would transform my outlook permanently. I had begun reading his fiction as a teenager, just as I was entering a three-year stretch devoted to devouring every Edgar Rice Burroughs book that I could get my hands on—books that also radiated intense heat. Farmer was like Burroughs, but he had updated the formula, and in fact often remixed it with alchemical, mind-altering substances that could leave the reader gripping the book with cold, sweaty palms well past the witching hour, eyes bloodshot and protruding like boiled eggs as they scanned every page for clues to the enciphered metastory that surely lurked behind each word. To use the metaphor of light, Burroughs' works gleamed golden and pure; Farmer's shone in a rainbow of colors, sparking with fiery embers that left behind spectral cometary trails of soul stuff as dark as the pitch black of the trackless void.

At least that's what it was like for me. Eventually I came to realize that not all readers were the same. Most readers I encountered were passive. What books "do or is done to them depends upon the reader," as the grand master said. When I talked about literature with fellow readers, the typical responses I would get (and still get) were relegated to the subjective world of Like and Dislike. That is, instead of reveling in a blinding light that revealed new modes of vision to see beyond one's experience, such readers, I soon discovered, would don lenses that filtered the light in such a way that they saw only what they already knew.

But once you've been exposed to that blazing light, it's hard to put those filtered, distorting lenses back on. And that's ultimately how this book came to be.

I began the effort to finish reading the body of Farmer's work in the late 1980s and early 1990s. In my early years of reading Farmer, I had felt there was something—an overwhelming number of somethings, actually—that I was missing. Yes, I had caught many of the Easter eggs he sprinkled throughout his work; I was well aware of those. But I sensed there was something larger present, a shadowy web interlacing the glittering and often seemingly chaotic facets of his opus.

The first corroboration that my intuition was correct came when I read Farmer's authorized Doc Savage novel *Escape from Loki* upon its release in August 1991. An account of my conclusions are found in the first two articles that appear in this collection. In these pieces, I turned the tables on Farmer, attempting to pull back the curtain that veiled his works just as he had done with the literature of pop lit authors such as Edgar Rice Burroughs and Lester Dent in his fictional biographies of Tarzan and Doc Savage, telling the "real" story behind the ostensible one. Farmer seemed tickled at my approach when I sent him one of my early articles, replying that he found it ingenious, comparing it to an essay by Rex Stout, and stating that he approved of my way of thinking. For him, it must have been a strange experience, as if things had come full circle: the creative mythographer had himself been creatively mythographed.

I first met Farmer in June 1998, at the unveiling of the Philip José Farmer Odyssey exhibition at the main branch of the Peoria Public Library. I had arrived at the library earlier that day, having driven out to Illinois from eastern Pennsylvania, and while snooping around, I ran into Maggie Nelson, who ran the library's public relations and was curating the exhibition. She brought me inside the exhibit room for a private viewing of the eclectic Farmerian artifacts she had assembled. I stared up in awe at the original painting by James Worhola that served as the cover art for Berkley Books edition of *The Book of Philip José Farmer*, which depicts Farmer against the backdrop of an alien landscape, crouching over his desk as he clatters away at his typewriter while Lord Greystoke perches on his shoulder and a spindly limbed alien picks through his trashcan. "We had a *really* hard time getting Phil to agree to part with it," Maggie told me, "even for the short period of the exhibition." We continued on around the room, my guide waiting patiently as I stopped to sift through a pile of fan letters that lay stacked on a table. When I was done, we resumed our tour through the Odyssey, but Maggie paused before a diagram of an intricately branching family tree and, pointing at it, asked me what Phil called his genealogy of fictional characters from literature so that she might caption the display. Grinning widely, I told her it was the Wold Newton family. "Oh, yes, of course!" she exclaimed. Standing there in a library that Philip José Farmer had patronized for decades, amid a bounty of sacred relics from throughout his life and career, I felt like I was a member of that extraordinary lineage myself, returned home for a family reunion.

I went back to the library that evening for the opening ceremony, and the exhibition hall swiftly filled up with a strange cast of Peorians, some of whom might have walked straight out of a Farmer story. That attractive young woman sure looked like Glinna Heithbarn from Farmer's recently released novel Peoria-based P.I. novel *Nothing Burns in Hell*, what with her trifle-too-long nose, long auburn hair, and subtly Wiccan fashion sense. The woman speaking with her might have been Ozma Fillimore Wang from *Dayworld*, minus the grasshopper body paint (at least as far as I could tell). And who could deny that the sour-faced man with a priestly bearing who was chatting with Maggie was a dead ringer for Father John Carmody from *Night of Light*? I started to feel like I had stepped through a gate into a pocket universe of Farmer's construction. Nowhere, however, did I see the Maker of Universes himself, so I hung back and took a wallflower's stance near the back of the room, which now clamored with the chattering voices and jubilant chortles of the locals, many of whom were clearly amused to discover a famous author living in their midst.

The elevator beside me rang. I turned just as the gray metallic doors slid open. And there he was, the Wizard of Peoria, holding a cane but standing with the poise and posture of an athletic, much younger man, a beautiful woman with short white hair in a pixie cut—clearly his wife Bette—at his side. Farmer did not immediately get out of the elevator, but rather stood quietly, a bemused, slightly devilish look on his face as his gaze slowly scanned over the noisy and completely oblivious gathering of attendees. No one but I had noticed the arrival of the guest of honor.

Clearly satisfied, or at least tickled, at what he saw, Phil Farmer emerged with his wife from the elevator car and caught Maggie's eye. I returned to examining the exhibit displays, but within moments Maggie was at my side and ushering me back over to Phil, introducing me as a fan of his books who had come "all the way from Pennsylvania" to meet him. Phil interjected in his deep, Gary Cooper voice, "I don't know if it'll be worth the trip." I said that it most certainly was. Then, summoning my courage, I told him I was the person who had written the article connecting *Escape from Loki* with Doc Savage's archnemesis John Sunlight (see part 2 of my article "The Green Eyes Have It—Or Are They Blue?" in this collection to understand just why I was so nervous telling him this). Phil paused, looked at me sternly, and said, "Oh, you're *that* guy." For a brief moment, my heart skipped a beat, thinking that Philip José Farmer, a giant in the world of science fiction, wanted to rake me over the coals for defiling his work with my audacious theory. But suddenly Phil was grinning like the impish trickster demon that he was and thrusting out his hand to grasp mine in a warm handshake. He'd been fooling with me, and proceeded to graciously ask me to chat with him after his talk if there was time.

Maggie went off to quiet the gatherers and gave a wonderful speech lauding the guest of honor's many literary accomplishments, while next to me in the crowd, Phil interjected wry and humorously self-deprecating comments, as well as an arsenal of puns, to those of us lucky enough to be within earshot. After Maggie's speech, we all filed into the adjoining auditorium to hear Phil's talk. He took the podium, on the lectern of which stood a plastic figure of Bugs Bunny, the character of whom Phil went on in his talk to use as an example of the trickster archetype in American culture. At the end of the talk, Phil asked for questions from the audience. When I raised my hand, he uttered an audible "Uh oh" under his breath. He must have thought I was going to bring up my controversial John Sunlight theory in front of all those people! Perhaps it was my imagination, but he seemed a little relieved when I merely asked whether there was any connection between Danny Alliger, the protagonist of his novel *Fire and the Night*, and the Alliger family that appears *Nothing Burns in Hell*. (Incidentally, Phil admitted that the Alligers from those books were one and the same family, and furthermore that Danny Alliger was a play on Dante Alighieri.)

Sadly, the night ran late due to the long line of people waiting to get their books signed, and so I wasn't able to have that chat with Phil. I was, however, able to get the books I'd brought inscribed ("To Chris Carey, who came all the way from Pennsylvania to meet me," he wrote in my copy of *Nothing Burns in Hell*) and have a wonderful conversation with Bette Farmer while she waited for her husband to finish signing. In a development even more disappointing than missing that chat after his talk, Phil asked me if I'd be in town tomorrow, so he could invite me over to his house the next day, but I told him I had work obligations and had to drive back to Pennsylvania early in the morning. Honestly, I don't know what I was thinking. It was a lost opportunity to spend more time with Phil and Bette, and to this day I regret not blowing off my job and staying that one extra day.

Fortunately, it was only the first of several occasions that I

was able to see Phil and spend time with him. And the next time I met Phil, in May 2001, he remembered who I was and said he did so because of my articles on his work, which he very much enjoyed. And that time, I did get to visit him at his home. (I also got hear more from his endless storehouse of puns, such as when I sat down on a chair in his basement den and pulled on the reading lamp's chain to no effect, only to have Phil lean over me with that by-now-familiar impish grin and say, "You've got to *screw* it to turn it on," and then watch as he turned the light bulb in the socket until the filament glowed with incandescent light. I still wonder if I was set up, if Phil held off repairing the defective lamp just so he could play this little joke on unsuspecting visitors who happened to sit in that chair.)

In the years that followed, I drew increasingly closer into Phil's orbit, coediting *Farmerphile: The Magazine of Philip José Farmer*, editing three hardcover collections of his work, attending the annual FarmerCon gatherings at the Farmers' home, being granted permission to complete the third installment of his Ancient Opar series, and flying out to Peoria on more than one occasion to celebrate Phil's birthday with him and Bette and a small group of their friends.

Joseph Campbell famously said, "Follow your bliss." Science fiction author Tobias S. Buckell once phrased it to me a different way: "Do what geeks you out." Both imperatives are true. If I hadn't followed their sentiment, I would have never ended up coauthoring *The Song of Kwasin* with a Hugo-Award-winning grand master, an honor so Brobdingnagian I still have a hard time fathoming the reality of it.

The book that you now hold tells the story of my own creative excursions into the Farmerian Monomyth as much as it seeks to make informed commentary on Farmer's rich literary works. In fact, it's often difficult for me to tell where my commentary ends and my own odyssey begins. For that reason, I have included a handful of interviews with me on my collaborations with Farmer and my own fictional works that have expanded upon his. Though I certainly can't claim I was never at a loss, the journey I experienced as I wrote the works collected herein has, in many ways, been as surreal for me as the voyages of Odysseus must have been for that ancient mariner. I often wonder how it all came to be.

But then again, the answer is obvious: "Some books…blaze with a light that blinds but which, paradoxically, enables you to see as never before." And it is by that light that I found my way down the winding corridors of Farmer's Magic Labyrinth, and wound up becoming what I'd hoped I could be ever since childhood: a professional writer.

And so this collection of my Farmerian writings is my tribute to Phil on the hundredth anniversary of his birth, my thanks for the kindness and generosity he showed me. May it serve as an example of the virtues of active reading and shed some light, however faint, on the legacy of this great Peoria-colored writer, whose works will go on burning in readers' minds for as long as there are books to read.

Christopher Paul Carey
Western Washington State
February 11, 2018

Farmer's *Escape from Loki:*
A Closer Look

*The Bronze Gazette,*Vol. 6, Issue 17, February 1996

I have been surprised at some of the reactions I have received from Doc Savage readers when I asked them what they thought of Philip José Farmer's *Escape From Loki.* While shocked at those who did not care for the novel, I was far more jolted by those who went away from it thinking they had read nothing more than a hard-boiled, fast-action pulp drama. It *is* just that, a grand adventure to stand rightfully alongside of the original 182 supersagas, *but it is also much more.*

During my first reading of *Escape from Loki* I noticed a number of curious facets in the story, not the least of which was the title. Lazy as I am, I did not follow them up immediately, but these curiosities lay dormant in my mind like tiny magic beans. On my second and third reading they sprouted, and now after my fifth reading I have a tall, stout stalk.

The title *Escape From Loki*, while seeming quite simple, does not just refer to Doc and his aides breaking out of a German prison camp. Farmer refers to Camp Loki being "named after the Old Norse evil trickster-god," but does not spoon feed the reader as to what Loki represents mythologically. The Germans in the story obviously named the camp such because it was tricky, escape-proof. Farmer named it such because Loki is the representation of adolescence in Norse mythology. Doc is escaping not just from a prison camp, but from his own immaturity. Farmer's *Escape from Loki* is a classic archetypal story of the transformation of boy into man.

If one looks at the story of the god Loki a little closer, one discovers that a more apt imagery could hardly have been chosen for the Doc Savage mythos. *The Aquarian Guide to British and Irish Mythology* states that Loki "became so troublesome that the gods caught and bound him in a cavern beneath the earth, guarded by a great serpent whose venom fell upon him," which is reminiscent of the caves in Camp Loki and the poisonous experimentations by the novel's villain, Baron von Hessel. Further, it states, "His agonized struggles caused earthquakes. At the end of the age of the gods, Heimdahl will kill him." Looking deeper into the myth, a description of Heimdahl proves most illuminating:

> Heimdahl's hearing was so sensitive that he could hear grass growing on the earth or wool growing on the backs of sheep. He could also see a distance of one hundred miles by both night or day. He lived in a castle of Himinbiore and always wore shining white armor and carried a flashing sword. He also possessed a magic horn, Gjallarhorn, which could be heard throughout all the levels of heaven, earth and the Otherworld. It will summon all the gods to battle when Ragnarok dawns.

Does this sound like a certain bronze man we have all read about, with his super-sensitive hearing and vision, as well as his metallic countenance? Ragnarok is the Norse Apocalypse, and certainly one can see Doc in this analogy sounding the horn to begin the last battle of Armageddon as he awakens the thousand and one superheroes that were to join him in the next sixty years of the popular literature of our culture.

While *Escape from Loki* is an archetypal story of adolescence transformed, Doc Savage did not have a typical adolescence. He was raised from the age of fourteen months to be an *Übermensch*, a superman. It is this factor which amplifies Farmer's novel from personal transformation into the sublime realms of world transformation.

Throughout the novel, Farmer paints a picture (or perhaps better, directs a motion picture) of Doc's *Übermensch* qualities, contrasting them with various characters. We finally get a glimpse inside his incredible mind. Doc sees things in similes. Thus when he encounters von Hessel smoking a cigar, he thinks, "If other cigars were small dirigibles, the one in his mouth was in the zeppelin class." And in viewing the beautiful Countess Idivzhopu, Doc conjures up the image of "a pendulum, succeeded by a vision of a two-stroke-cycle engine." Doc Savage is a man who experiences his thoughts in full stereo Technicolor. Could one expect any less of Nietzsche's *Übermensch*, the new-world man?

In contrast the reader is given two old-world men, the traitorous Duntreath and the evil von Hessel. To illustrate this an interesting dialogue occurs between Doc and Duntreath when Doc returns from the second banquet with the baron:

"I deal in facts, not in fantasizing," Duntreath said. "In truth, you didn't find out much of value, did you?" *(Limited view of the old-world man.)*

Maybe not to you, but certainly much to me, Savage thought. *(Deeper understanding of the new-world man.)*

Doc, as an example of the new phase of human evolution, has gained valuable psychological insight into the baron, and Duntreath, being of the old order, cannot see it. Doc has gone beyond Duntreath's black-and-white "facts" into the color of psychology.

The difference between Duntreath and von Hessel is that the baron *thinks* he is a man of the new world, while Duntreath is not even aware that the world is changing. But von Hessel is no more an *Übermensch* than the colonel, as Doc learns from his talk with the baron. Von Hessel "fears that he is too much like his father," in other words, that he has inherited the outmoded worldview of the old world.

It has been demonstrated that Doc thinks in symbols. He also acts symbolically. Farmer states that

...in times of intense danger, he tended to revert to the emotional being in him, the Old Stone Age savage who worshipped malign and benevolent forces, dark enormous things. Part of the unconscious mind took over, and the unconscious was linked to the ancient ancestral memory.

This is illustrated clearly when, shortly after mistakenly killing the innocent Captain Benedict Murdstone, Doc bites off the nose of the German train engineer. The reader will

ESCAPE FROM LOKI

Philip José Farmer

Author of *Doc Savage:*
His Apocalyptic Life

recall that in an earlier scene Farmer makes a point to describe Murdstone's very large proboscis, the tip of which has been cut off. In fact, Monk refers to him as "Schnozzola." When Doc bites off the engineer's nose, he is taken over by "the Old Stone Age savage" and cannot help physically displaying the guilt he feels over killing the innocent Murdstone.

It is interesting to note that Murdstone is an entomologist. Farmer portrays entomology as an allegory for social infiltration by parasitic or revolutionary agents in his Dayworld series and uses similar symbolism in his Hugo award-winning "The Lovers." Perhaps Murdstone wasn't what he seemed to be after all.[1]

Another of the magic beans that sprouted in my head after the first reading of *Escape from Loki* was the numerous times and the manner in which Farmer uses dogs in the novel. The key to the symbol is in a revealing dialogue between Doc and von Hessel:

"You're very cynical," Clark Savage said.

"In other words, doglike? If so, I'm the leader of the pack. Objective, clearheaded, a seer without blinders."

The Baron may be objective, but he lacks Doc's passion. Doc's encounters with dogs in *Escape from Loki* are used as a vehicle to depict Doc's confrontations with a cynical, passionless old-world outlook. In fact, the word *cynical* derives from the Greek *kynikos*, literally meaning "like a dog." Hence, just before he comes upon de Musard's chateau—a critical scene in which the seed is planted for Doc's personal decision to defeat evil-doers—Doc is attacked by scavenging dogs. When Doc is caught and sentenced to imprisonment in Camp Loki, it is by Germans using tracking dogs. He thinks,

---

1. As an aside, I have an interesting theory on Murdstone's name. Having read a great deal of Farmer's other works, I am familiar with his fondness for word-play. The prefix murd reminds me of the French exclamation "merde!" and a stone is a tough, hard rock. The name Murdstone might be interpreted as "tough shit!"—certainly a fitting vociferation from a man who was to die under such erroneous circumstances. (Follow up note: In response to another article which I wrote on *Escape from Loki*, Philip José Farmer has since informed me that the name Murdstone derives from the Murdstones of Charles Dickens' *David Copperfield*. While I was wrong in my claim that the name Murdstone was a clever Farmerism, I still believe that my interpretation is more or less correct. It refers not to Benedict Murdstone's dire fate, but rather to the strict, disciplinarian character of Edward and Jane Murdstone. However, it's a Dickensism, not a Farmerism.)

It was hard to have gone through so many dangers, suffered so many injuries, struggled so much, escaped so many times, be so close to being free of the enemy, so near his goal, and then be caught because of dogs.

Clark had always loved dogs. At this moment, he hated the entire species.

Doc encounters dogs during his first capture, and again when he gets his first look at Camp Loki. Just prior to Doc and his friends' escape from the camp, the dogs begin whining and barking as if they "sense something," and during the escape, the dogs bark once again. Further, Johnny refers to Scheisstaube "and his progeny of female dogs."

In the novel's *twenty-first* chapter (twenty-one being the traditional age of maturity throughout much of Western society), Doc and his aides do escape from Loki, but as demonstrated, Loki was much more than just a physical prison—it was a prison of the soul. Hajji Abdu el-Yezdi, Doc's Persian Sufi tutor,[2] tells Doc, "Men are like tigers, striped with character traits. You have a very broad stripe of violence. You must narrow that... If you do not, you will become as those you call evil." The "bright lightning streaks in the black clouds" that were observed as the storm rolled in before their final breakout reflect those tendencies in Doc that he has just begun to deal with—and that he conquers years later in his Fortress of Solitude.

---

2. Sir Richard Francis Burton (the real-life protagonist of Farmer's Riverworld series) wrote a curious book entitled *The Kasidah of Haji Abdu El-Yezdi*. At the time the volume was first published, Burton claimed to be merely the translator of the wise Sufi's work. However, the truth finally came out that Burton wrote it. While Haji Abdu El-Yezdi may be a fictional character in our world, we may only assume that he existed in flesh and blood in Farmer's Wold Newton universe. (Note: There are at least two other characters in *Escape from Loki* who were pulled out of popular fiction, as pointed out by Rick Lai in his book *The Bronze Age: An Alternative Doc Savage Chronology*. [Lai's wonderful and erudite examination of Doc Savage was later expanded and rereleased under the title *The Revised Complete Chronology of Bronze*, Altus Press, 2010. —CPC, 2018.] Doc's tutor in mountain climbing, yoga, and self-defense, Dekka Lan Shan, is the grandfather of a character from the 1930s pulp series Peter the Brazen. One of the recruits Renny gets to help in the escape is Abraham Cohen from Argosy's Jimmy Cordie series. Doubtless, there are more.)

The Green Eyes Have It—Or Are They Blue?
or Another Case of Identity Recased

First published online at www.pjfarmer.com in 1998, and reprinted under the title "The Blue Eyes Have It—Or Are They Green" in *The Bronze Gazette*, Vol. 11, No. 33, November 2001. The iteration of the essay presented here is lightly emended from the revised version first published in *Myths for the Modern Age: Philip José Farmer's Wold Newton Universe*, ed. Win Scott Eckert, MonkeyBrain Books, 2005. Part 2 of this article was first published under the title "Loki in the Sunlight" in *The Bronze Gazette*, Vol. 8, No. 24, June 1998.

1. The Monomyth

By no means need one use the novel *Escape from Loki* as a starting point to decode the sometimes eerie subplot of the Farmerian Monomyth. But the novel is unique in that it ties together an unusually large number of wily tentacles that lead to the mysterious beast lurking behind the scenes in much of Philip José Farmer's larger work. As Farmer himself has managed to uncover the truth behind the fiction of so many other authors' work—such as that of Edgar Rice Burroughs, Lester Dent, and Jules Verne—it is only natural that the time has come to decode the hidden messages in Farmer's own novels. This article is just a beginning, and, of course, only a few of the pieces of the Farmerian puzzle are contained herein. However, a beginning framework is offered upon which a stronger foundation may one day be built—if one keeps on one's toes. For you see, Farmer's puzzle is three-dimensional and exists on many levels, and, like his Lavalite World, is constantly shifting.

Charles Fort, the great archivist of the unexplained, once stated, "One measures a circle beginning anywhere." And so in order to begin exploration of Farmer's labyrinthine Monomyth, we find ourselves taking a second look at *Escape from Loki*, in which a young Doc Savage—the living reality of whom Farmer has demonstrated in his biography *Doc Savage: His Apocalyptic Life*—gets his first taste of adventure and likes it. I have elsewhere examined the symbolic and often shocking levels of the novel, and in the course of this research was startled to see how deep this tale really goes. But I was little prepared to dive twenty-thousand leagues into the foreboding, murky waters of an ancient worldwide conspiracy.

To understand what forces are at work in *Escape from Loki*, the reader must understand the perceptions of an Übermensch. Doc Savage, like Nietzsche's superman, does not see things as others do. He thinks (and acts) analogically. Thus, when he sees Baron von Hessel's cigar, he thinks, "If other cigars were small dirigibles, the one in his mouth was in the Zeppelin class." Or when he gazes at Countess Idivzhopu, "He was reminded of the rotary engine of his Nieuport. This image was followed by that of a pendulum, succeeded by a vision of a two-stroke-cycle engine." Without understanding the creative workings of Doc Savage's mind, we find ourselves facing a far greater task in breaking the codes of the novel, for all the signifiers are aimed at Doc.

2. Loki in the Sunlight

In order to understand who is aiming the subtle codes at Doc, and why, we must take a trip down a side tunnel of the Monomyth. Farmer wrote in his biography *Doc Savage: His Apocalyptic Life* that the only villain in the Doc Savage supersagas to meet Doc in a return engagement was the infamous John Sunlight. He appeared in two books, *Fortress of Solitude* and *The Devil Genghis*. This, as we shall see, is not exactly true. Farmer, by his comment, was seeking to draw attention to the long-fingered crook. Since Farmer's comment that Sunlight was the only one of Doc's villains to appear twice, Sunlight has reappeared in comics published by

DC Comics and Millennium Publishing, as well as in numerous speculative articles, and even Will Murray has considered donning the archenemy's mono-colored clothes in a proposed novel. The attention that Farmer has centered on Sunlight is in itself a clue that there is more than meets the eye in this strange character. In reality, as I shall demonstrate, John Sunlight appears in *three* of the published Doc Savage supersagas, not two. Strangely we find that *Fortress of Solitude* is not Doc's first encounter with the tenacious Sunlight. In the February 1996 issue of *The Bronze Gazette*, an article of mine was published on Doc's first adventure, *Escape from Loki*. In the article I attempted to get readers to delve more deeply into this subtly crafted work. Apparently, I did not succeed, because reactions were minimal, and no one made it known that I had left out the major mystery of the novel: John Sunlight makes his *first* chronological entrance in the supersagas in Farmer's *Escape from Loki*.

At first glance one might think that Sunlight must be Baron von Hessel, the evil, experimenting genius who may hold the secret of immortality. However, this is not the case. Von Hessel is not Sunlight, but he *is* a character from *Fortress of Solitude*.

Readers will remember the monocle-wearing "smooth customer" Baron Karl, fellow conspirator of Sunlight. He is described as a ruthless man who had "personally shot to death some fifty or so political enemies" in his own castle. Apparently he is a castle lover, as he approvingly looks over Sunlight's castle, comparing it to his own. Baron Karl is something of a playboy, though apparently not with the wild abandon of the Playboy Prince. He is a hand with women and wears "the best of clothes." He is an eloquent speaker, obviously intelligent and well read, as indicated by his speech to John Sunlight: "'I salute again,' he said, 'the man who has inherited the qualities of the Erinyes, the Eumenides, of Titan, and of Friar Rush, with a touch of Dracula and Frankenstein.'" He could not have been more right about Sunlight, and Baron Karl knows this, as Sunlight could not have had a better teacher—Baron Karl himself. His comparison of Sunlight to Frankenstein could not have been more apt. Sunlight, who had once been a creature of the baron

(as we shall see), now makes Baron Karl shake in fear. He is a monster out of his master's control. The previous master now treads lightly in the presence of his protégé. Also notice that Baron Karl says, "I salute again," in his praise of Sunlight. Again? When did he salute him before?

Apparently in Camp Loki during the Great War.

Baron von Hessel in *Escape from Loki* is extremely intelligent and well read. "He could quote poets, dramatists, philosophers, and scientists, both ancient and modern" and he has two doctor of philosophy degrees and a doctor of medicine degree. His features bear an aristocratic look and in the 1880s and '90s he inhabited his family's ancestral castle. On top of this, Doc observes that the baron was wearing a monocle, which at first appeared to him to be an affectation but later seemed to lend von Hessel a "superior air." Doc also observes the baron's "small belly bulge," which indicates that the baron enjoys the good things in life. He likes his women, too, as evidenced by the company he keeps with the voluptuous Countess Idivzhopu. These descriptions all might fit Baron Karl as well as Baron von Hessel.

One might think, however unlikely, that this is merely coincidence, a case of literary archetypes perhaps. But this is absolutely not so, and the proof lies in the Baron von Hessel's taste for women—for his girlfriend is none other than *Miss* John Sunlight.

Here are some descriptions of John Sunlight from *Fortress of Solitude*:

> Anyway, John Sunlight didn't look the part. Not when he didn't wish, at least. He resembled a gentle poet, with his great shock of dark hair, his remarkably high forehead, his hollow burning eyes set in a starved face. His body was very long, very thin. His fingers, particularly, were so long and thin—the longest fingers almost the length of an ordinary man's whole hand...

> John Sunlight sat on a deep chair which was covered with a rich purple velvet cloth. He wore a matching set of purple velvet pajamas and purple velvet robe, and on the forefinger of his right hand was a ring with a purple jewel.

John Sunlight had few changeable habits, but one of them was his fondness for one color one time, and perhaps a different one later. Just now he was experiencing, a yen for purple, particularly the regal shade of the color...

Now consider these descriptions of Countess Idivzhopu from *Escape from Loki*:

She wore an ankle-length white fur coat, white leather boots, and a Russian-type white fur hat...

...she gave Savage a small and exceptionally long-fingered hand in a black elbow-length glove... Her large, dark blue eyes were as dazzling as her smile...

Her narrow hips became an unusually small waist...

Her all-white gown was the most low-cut he had ever seen...

And here came Countess Idivzhopu, Lili Bugov, taking an afternoon promenade in a beautiful pink dress and wide-brimmed sky-blue hat and holding a pink parasol... she waved a pink-gloved hand...

The descriptions of the countess in *Escape from Loki* are too similar to those of Sunlight in *Fortress of Solitude* and *The Devil Genghis* to be mere coincidence, especially when the countess is juxtaposed with the Baron von Hessel, whose descriptions match exactly those given of Baron Karl. As will be demonstrated, the evidence points to the fact that Lily Bugov is John Sunlight.

The critical reader might very well point out the "sky-blue hat" which the countess is wearing while she is adorned with her pink dress, pink parasol, and pink gloves. This would seem to break Sunlight's rule of wearing only one color. There are several explanations for this inconsistency. For one, the story is occurring during the shortages and scarcities of World War I Germany. It may have been impossible for the countess to obtain all those amenities that would satisfy her fashion-sense. This explanation, however, is unlikely, as her benefactor, the baron, seems able to get any supplies he needs. It may be that the countess, who was apparently a young woman at this time, was in the process of perfecting her style. She hadn't yet quite given up wearing multiple colors. The true explanation, however, probably lies in the realism with which Farmer records the adventure. The countess is not just a caricature, and certainly there were probably times when the color of her underwear did not exactly match that of her dress.

Doc observes the servants of the countess the first time he sees her. One is Zad, "at least six feet eight inches tall... a kodiak bear of a man, a bearded behemoth." Two others are apparently her maids. Remember that Sunlight's servants were the Russian Civian, "a bestial black ox to look at," and the two sisters, Titania and Giantia, who were really not Russian, but American.

Von Hessel says that the countess "thinks she's another Catherine the Great, a Cleopatra, a Ninon de Lenclos." When he goes on to say that she is not as intelligent as they were, Doc becomes angry at the baron's ungentlemanly words, and a conversation arises about women's equality. The baron states that women have as much ability as men, both mentally and physically. He drives the screws through Doc's supposedly scientific armor by his comment that "Anybody not blinded by prejudice should be able to see that." Von Hessel finishes the topic with his opinion that women will not be treated as equals "until they wage a war for equality.... Men won't give up their power over women until they're forced to do so, and they'll fight long and hard."

Then the baron moves on to the subject of power. The countess had power in Russia, he says, but she lost most of it in the Bolshevik Revolution, with the exception of her personal servants. She is now using her beauty to try to regain her power.

We can conjecture that when the countess was maimed at the end of the novel, her drive for power became insanely amplified. She was already insane, as her bloodthirsty practices in Russia indicate, but now she sought to dominate not just peasants, but the world. Without her beauty, she was forced to meet von Hessel's challenge to become the equal of men. When we next see the countess, she has changed or disguised her sex, and ultimately wants to be mother to the entire planet. She could not achieve a man's power being a woman, so she became a man. Perhaps this was at von Hessel's suggestion. Old habits die hard, however, and when she became a man, Bugov—now rechristened John Sunlight, perhaps to symbolize that her real self was now illuminated for the world to see—still continued the odd penchant for wearing the same color. There is also the precedent set in *The Devil Genghis* that Sunlight was fond of changing his appearance: Sunlight's hair has changed from a black shock to pure white. Doc wonders if it has been dyed to match his white clothing. Sunlight certainly is an eccentric when it comes to his appearance, and in the unenlightened 1930s, any man with such odd fashion-sense might certainly be suspect of effeminacy. Remember also that he is described as having a weak appearance and the face and eyes of a poet.

Much is made in *Escape from Loki* of the countess' ability as a seductress. The baron uses her to seduce Doc and also openly discusses that she is using her charms to get back a little of the power that she has lost. Sunlight is also manipulative and seductive. He likes to use and control people rather than killing them. It is true that the countess sadistically murdered people in Russia, but by the time of *Escape from Loki* she has already changed her ways. After all, manipulation can satisfy an evil heart in ways more satisfying than outright murder.

The baron's remark about the countess' lack of intelligence does not seem to fit the character of Sunlight, until we realize that Sunlight is not really working on his own in *Fortress of Solitude*. He needs Baron Karl for his plans, and we may assume that behind the scenes Karl is coaching Sunlight. Notice that Baron Karl escapes with no punishment. Sunlight's intelligence in *Fortress of Solitude* and *The Devil Genghis* may also be reflective of much time spent with the baron, learning from him. He has taught Sunlight quite a bit since those early years in Russia and Germany. Also, the comment on the countess' low intelligence may have been merely a ruse by von Hessel to manipulate the emotions of the young Savage.

But is John Sunlight really that smart? He doesn't seem

to be. His whole plan hinges on the technology he has stolen from Doc. Without it, he's just another villain with grandiose ambitions. Baron Karl is the one smart enough to get away, and Sunlight's plans fall apart quite easily in *The Devil Genghis*. Surely, he has the seductive powers to initiate a plan, but he does not seem to have the genius to hold his scheme together.

Most likely, the countess is the baron's underling in a deeper mystery about which we have few clues to go on. While the countess and Sunlight are not what they seem to be, the baron is even more of a mystery. *Escape from Loki* reveals that the baron certainly is a "smooth customer," with his secret experiments, strange international connections, and knowledge of an alleged elixir of immortality.

There are veiled hints in the novel that the countess was probably also privy to the immortality elixir. When von Hessel questions what the countess will do when she becomes old and ugly, he abruptly changes the subject. Also, when Doc is about to interrogate the countess at the end of the novel, she is set upon and maimed by a Russian from her past before Doc can ascertain what she knows. It seems that she may have known something about the elixir and that she was working with von Hessel in the grand scheme. The truth is, if we accept that her back was broken and she was paralyzed from the waist down, as Doc learns later in his investigations, she must have known about the elixir. The elixir must have had regenerative properties that could heal her nerves, or else the baron was enough of a medical genius to cure her paralysis by some other means. Or more likely, the report of her paralyzing injury was faked. Remember that Doc got his report on the baron and the countess a long time later. The fake paralysis was probably the first step that Lily Bugov took to start a new identity as John Sunlight. This is why it is stated in *Fortress of Solitude* that Sunlight is not Russian. Bugov was a Russian, but when she became Sunlight, he became unique in the world, a nation unto himself. After all, one of Sunlight's big ambitions was to do away with nationalities.

Here I must mention Win Eckert's theory espoused in his fascinating article "The Malevolent Moriartys, or, Who's

Going to Take Over the World When I'm Gone?" In response to an earlier draft of my article uncovering the mystery behind John Sunlight's true identity, Eckert proposes that Sunlight may be the progeny of a union between Doc Savage and Lily Bugov. I did consider this possibility when writing my original article, and alluded to this in correspondence with Mr. Farmer when I remarked:

> In *Loki*, there is a scene in which the countess gives Doc "a small and exceptionally long-fingered hand in an elbow-length glove." However, in *Fortress of Solitude* it states about John Sunlight that "His fingers, particularly, were so long and thin—the longest fingers being almost the length of an ordinary man's whole hand." I find it hard to reconcile the small hand of the countess in *Loki* with Sunlight's hand in *Fortress*, which seems to be freakishly large.

Such a discrepancy would certainly be cleared up by Win Eckert's assertion that John Sunlight is the son of the countess. I have dismissed this idea based on certain other evidence, some of which turns up in various facets of the Farmerian Monomyth.

For instance, if Farmer has hinted that John Sunlight was indeed once a woman, there is precedence for this concept in his other work. In his science fiction novel *Dayworld*, the character Wyatt Bumppo Repp, a "great TV writer-director-producer of Westerns and historical dramas" has a predilection for writing storylines involving role-changing. In the novel, Repp is currently writing a treatment for a movie called *Dillinger Didn't Die* in which Dillinger escapes from the F.B.I. "by magically turning into a woman." One character chides Repp, asking,

> "...why didn't you drag Robin Hood in? Though I suppose that he would have turned out to be Maid Marian!"

As *Escape from Loki* was written just after Farmer completed his three-volume Dayworld series, and as each of the split personalities of the protagonist of Dayworld seem to be aspects of Farmer's own complex personality, it can be seen that Farmer, as Repp, has laid down an ultimate foreshadowing of his next work.

In addition, much of Farmer's other work has involved the recurring theme of the consequences for society when it loses the female element (see *Night of Light* and *Hadon of Ancient Opar*). Lily Bugov is compared to Haggard's Ayesha, which is a quintessential example of Jung's concept of the anima. In fact, Doc Savage expert Will Murray, in his article "The Genesis of John Sunlight," depicts John Sunlight as if he were Doc's anima. Sunlight is the antithesis of Doc, a mirror-self: strong, but weak-looking compared to Doc's powerful physique, pale-hued to Doc's deep bronze skin, sunken eyes to Doc's mesmerizing gold-flecked orbs. Both the countess *and* John Sunlight seem to be expressions Doc Savage's anima.

Furthermore, there is the question of Sunlight's age were he conceived in 1918 by Doc and the countess. This would make Sunlight perhaps twenty years old at the time of the events in *Fortress of Solitude*. If Sunlight is not Bugov, but rather a relative, it would be more believable that he would be a sibling or cousin, not a son. The clues left by Farmer, however, indicate that the countess and Sunlight are one and the same.

It is interesting to note that Sunlight surrounded himself with Titania and Giantia, women whom Dent describes as "such amazons." He states in *Fortress of Solitude* that "all their lives men had been scared of them." Dent also says that they had never been afraid of any other man except Sunlight. Perhaps this is because Sunlight wasn't a man. Then Dent makes a curious statement: "But they [Titania and Giantia] did not *worry* about Sunlight" (the italics are Dent's). What does he mean by this? First Dent states that the sisters are afraid of Sunlight, then he states that they do not worry about him. Dent must be indicating that they do not worry about Sunlight in a sexual sense. Even though they fear the terrible power he wields, they do not fear that he will make sexual advances toward them—because he is a woman. In addition, the presence of the two muscular women with Sunlight seems to fulfill Baron von Hessel's statement that women also have the potential to match the physical ability of men. Ham would vouch for this—because of Titania, the dapper lawyer's dashing smile is now missing a front tooth. The baron's

DOC SAVAGE
His Apocalyptic Life
Philip José Farmer

prophetic statement is also borne out in the apparent physical strength of the weak-looking Sunlight.

Intimations that Sunlight is a woman can be seen in the fact that Doc was so intimidated by Sunlight. Doc, as we all know, cannot read women and they constantly pose a threat to his ability to solve a case. If Doc has encountered Sunlight before, as the countess, at some point he must surely have recognized him for what he was. At this point, all of Doc's defenses must have shattered. Not only had a woman made away with his one of a kind death dealing devices, but it was the very woman with whom he had had his first intimate encounter. "The Eternal Feminine," Doc reflects after sleeping with the countess, "was incomprehensible and unpredictable. More the latter than the former." How unpredictable he could not have guessed.

The final clue that the baron and the countess will return in the following supersagas is the big one at the end. Farmer writes, "But Clark Savage was not certain that he would not hear from the baron again. Nor from the countess. Both had reason to hate him." What a way to end a novel if it wasn't true!

Doc Savage readers had long been craving a return of John Sunlight. Like the devious creature that he is assumed to be, Sunlight has managed to slip himself in for his last bow—right under the reader's nose.

Let us conclude this discussion of John Sunlight by pondering a line from *Fortress of Solitude*:

"No one knew what he was, exactly."

3. The Slippery Baron

The Baron von Hessel is a mysterious character. As I have just demonstrated, the baron appears in Lester Dent's Doc Savage pulp novel *Fortress of Solitude* as the murderous Baron Karl. One thing is for certain, and that is that von Hessel presented himself to Doc in the role of the Norse All-father god Odin to Doc's Siegfried.

Odin is the cynical god who gave up his left eye for a look at the future. Similarly, von Hessel wears a monocle over his left eye which at first "had seemed foolish, an affectation" but which later "seemed to give him a superior air." He also knows the future, predicting the Second World War in which Germany would again rise to power, foreseeing the victories of the women's rights movement, as well as the problems of overpopulation. At the crucial first banquet scene during which the baron is manipulating Doc, he plays Wagner's *Siegfried's Funeral March*, a very dramatic score which must have played on Doc's creative mind. Further, when in his anger Doc topples the massive iron tub, a soldier remarks, "Er ist ein Siegfried." One cannot but speculate that this entire scene, as well as several others, were prearranged by the baron to manipulate the emotions of the youthful Doc Savage. Though inexperienced, Doc wonders if this is indeed the case.

The playing of Wagner's classic opera of Norse myth also echoes the actions of the enigmatic Baron von Hessel. In *The Ring of the Nibelungen*, the All-father god Wotan (a.k.a. Odin, Woden, etc.) appears disguised as an old man before the hero Siegfried. (Incidentally the Old Norse word for "old man" is "Karl," thus confirming my speculation that the Baron von Hessel is one and the same as Baron Karl from *Fortress of Solitude*; another Karl will be shown to play a crucial role in Doc Savage's life by the end of this article.) Wotan proceeds to taunt Siegfried's youthful inexperience. Eventually, Siegfried penetrates Wotan's disguise and recognizes him as the murderer of his father. Wotan and Siegfried struggle, with the result that Siegfried breaks Wotan's greatest weapon, his spear *Runestaff*, in two. Wotan then disappears into the shadows. This is the perfect echoing of the events as they occur in *Escape from Loki*. Von Hessel repeatedly taunts Doc's youthful inexperience. The baron drops countless clues (as we shall see) as to his own and Doc's origins, which we can only assume Doc eventually decodes. I will make a bold statement here, for which I shall momentarily present the evidence, that von Hessel is responsible, at least by association, for the death of Clark Savage, Sr., Doc's father. Doc then breaks von Hessel's greatest weapon, Countess Idivzhopu, in two by causing the train wreck which breaks her back at the end of the novel. Finally, the slippery baron disappears into the shadows.

So the question remains: What is the baron's game? Here we need to perform some three-dimensional thinking. We see that the baron has been sending Doc a strange symbolic message by placing himself in the role of the god Wotan and Doc in the role of the hero Siegfried. Might there not be other clues, not so obvious, which the ingenious baron has managed to send to Doc without his knowing it?

Observe the name von Hessel. "Hessel" in Old Norse means "hazel." Besides being a type of shrub or tree, the word hazel is most often used to describe eye color, namely "a light brown to strong yellowish brown." "Strong yellowish brown" certainly calls forth a comparison to Doc's eyes, which "tawny and gold-speckled in a bright light, looked dark." Farmer certainly makes a point of the gold-flecked and yellow eyes of the ancestors of Doc Savage in Addendum 2 of *Tarzan Alive: A Definitive Biography of Lord Greystoke*. It is by tracing the genetic trait of eye color that Farmer pieces together many of the gaps in the Wold Newton family genealogy. We can only surmise that, by assuming a pseudonym meaning "hazel," the Baron von Hessel was subtly indicating something about his ancestry to the bronze man.

A further mystery is presented in *Escape from Loki* regarding eye color, and this one is blatant. Doc, however, seems to miss the clue entirely. Later, I will explain why the usually ever-vigilant Doc is apparently so befuddled. What he misses is the dramatic change in the color of von Hessel's eyes. When Doc gets his first close-up look at the baron during the first banquet scene, he observes that his eyes are "large, *green*, and seemed to shine with an inner light" (the italics are mine). Later, in the second banquet scene, when Doc slips several pieces of chocolate into his pocket, he reflects, "Von Hessel had observed this—those *blue* eyes seemed to miss nothing—but he only smiled with one side of his mouth" (again, italics mine). Certainly Farmer, who pays such scrutinizing attention to eye color, would not make such an error. What, then, is the meaning of this drastic shift in eye color, from *green* to *blue*?

Again, the answer seems to be that von Hessel is indicating to Doc something about his ancestry. Von Hessel is smiling not at

Doc's theft of chocolate, but at the trick he is pulling on him. He must know that Doc, with his photographic memory, will someday realize the symbolic message that has been sent to him and that he will decode its true significance. Utilizing clues that are provided in Farmer's biographies of Tarzan and Doc Savage, we may piece together the message that Doc probably decoded many years ago.

Only one of Doc Savage's ancestors is known to have the same color-shifting eyes as the baron's. This was Wolf Larsen, Doc's maternal grandfather and the Nietzschean rogue captain who appears in Jack London's novel *The Sea-Wolf*. The narrator of this adventure, Van Weyden, describes Larsen as follows:

> The eyes themselves were of that baffling protean gray which is never twice the same; which runs through many shades and colorings like inter-shot silk in twilight; which is gray, dark and light, and greenish-gray, and sometimes the clear azure of the deep sea.

If there is any doubt that von Hessel is referring Doc to his tough, mysterious, philosophizing grandfather, reflect on this. Wolf Larsen is referred to by his crew as "Old Man," the pseudonym of Wotan when he confronts Siegfried. Further, when Van Weyden first boards the *Sea Wolf*, he is told, "The cap'n is Wolf Larsen, or so men call him. I never heard his *other name*" (again, the italics are mine). The name Wolf Larsen, like von Hessel, is most certainly a pseudonym. The true identity of the captain of the *Sea Wolf* may be traced by another clue dropped by the slippery Baron von Hessel.

In the final climactic scene in *Escape from Loki*, in which von Hessel tempts Doc with immortality, he tells Doc, "You were *twenty thousand leagues* off the mark when you surmised that I was trying to create a disease which would be even worse than the black death of the medieval ages" (italics mine). While not the final clue given to Doc, this is perhaps the most important, for it indicates a connection between von Hessel and Jules Verne's classic tale *Twenty Thousand Leagues Under the Sea*. Farmer, in his *The Other Log of Phileas Fogg* and Addendum 1 from *Doc Savage: His Apocalyptic Life*, has recorded some of the missing details behind Verne's story, including his conclusion that

44

Captain Nemo is really Professor Moriarty, the archenemy of Sherlock Holmes. Another look at Nemo provides some more surprising conclusions.

Captain Nemo, like von Hessel and Wolf Larsen, is a man of mystery. Even his name (also a pseudonym) literally means "Nothing." When Professor Arronaxe and Ned Land are taken on board the *Nautilus*, Nemo tells them, "for you I shall merely be Captain Nemo," indicating that this is not his real name. And like von Hessel and Larsen, he lures in a young man of above-average intelligence, taunting and seducing him. While von Hessel toyed with Doc, Wolf Larsen did the same to Humphery Van Weyden, and so Nemo did to Professor Arronaxe. Indeed, one cannot help but compare the banquet scene in *Twenty Thousand Leagues*, in which Nemo entices Professor Arronaxe[3] with an overabundance of exotic sea food, with the first banquet scene in *Escape from Loki*, in which von Hessel makes Doc quiver in anticipation of an unbeatable table spread (with Mozart's *Jupiter Symphony* sounding in the background, nonetheless!). Nemo is also a cynic like von Hessel and Larsen. He sees humankind "fighting, destroying one another and indulging in their other earthly horrors" while "they can still exercise their iniquitous rights." Nemo, Larsen, and von Hessel also all smoke large cigars. In fact, Nemo compares his submarine to a giant cigar.

Like Farmer and Professor H. W. Starr, I can hardly conclude that Nemo is really the Indian Prince Dakar, as Nemo claims in Verne's *The Mysterious Island*. In fact, the one shred of evidence put before Professor Arronaxe while on board the *Nautilus* points to the probability that Nemo is German. Regarding a handwritten note from Nemo, Arronaxe observes, "The handwriting was clear and neat, but somewhat ornate and Germanic in style."

Nemo's physical description is equally revealing. Arronaxe writes:

> One strange detail, his eyes, which were rather far apart, had an almost ninety-degree range of vision. This ability—I was later able to verify—was backed by

3. Verne spelled this "Aronnax," but I have retained Farmer's spelling from *Doc Savage: His Apocalyptic Life*.

eyesight even better than Ned Land's. When this man fixed his look upon some object, he would frown and squint in such a way as to limit his range of vision; and then he would look. And what a look! How he could magnify objects made smaller by distance! How he could penetrate to your very soul!"

This is reminiscent of Baron von Hessel's monocle, which was like "a microscope through which von Hessel studied the smaller creatures of the world." *The Other Log of Phileas Fogg* reveals that Nemo, an agent of a secret extraterrestrial society, is utilizing a piece of alien technology to change his eye color. This is how Farmer explains how Nemo had black eyes while Moriarty had gray eyes, even though they were one and the same person. Von Hessel is apparently using a similar, perhaps perfected, means to change his eye color. That the baron's eyes "seemed to shine with an inner light" may be an indication of the artificial optical device that he uses. Remember also that Van Weyden described Wolf Larsen's eyes as being "wide apart as the true artist's are wide," just as Nemo's are described as being "rather far apart." Those still in doubt about the similarities of Nemo and Wolf Larsen can recall that both men suffer from nervous disorders resulting in severe headaches. While Farmer in his *Other Log* attributes Nemo's fits to suppression of trauma via extraterrestrial mind control techniques, the true reason for the malady may lie in the unanticipated effects of the elixir.

With von Hessel's subtle and not so subtle references to Wolf Larsen and Nemo, the pieces of a bizarre puzzle begin to fall into place. We see a remarkable resemblance among all three men, von Hessel, Larsen, and Nemo, as well as Moriarty and Baron Karl. If we look at the characters' lives chronologically, we see that they all neatly follow one another. First comes Nemo in the 1860s, then Moriarty in the early to mid-1890s, then Larsen in the late 1890s, followed by von Hessel in 1918 and Baron Karl in the 1930s. The inference, until now shrouded in utter obscurity, becomes obvious. We are dealing with one man, who, aided by an age-slowing elixir, is living down through the ages, repeatedly changing his identity, but not his character.

THE BRONZE Gazette

The Unofficial Magazine for the Fan of Bronze

November 2001   Vol 11/Issue 33 $6.00

FAVROTE

4. The Doubtful Heritage

Here we must follow another wily tentacle that leads from *Escape from Loki* to Farmer's pastiche of Tarzan and Doc Savage, *A Feast Unknown*. In this novel we discover that a secret society known as the Nine has been manipulating and molding human society since prehistoric times. The Nine possesses an age-slowing elixir, which is used as leverage to keep its members in check. One of the leading members of the Nine is XauXaz, who Lord Grandrith (Farmer's Tarzan character) and Doc Caliban (Farmer's Doc Savage character) discover is none other than the real-life basis for Wotan, the Norse All-father god. XauXaz has secretly been planting his genes throughout Grandrith's and Caliban's lineages, and in fact was really their grandfather. Grandrith and Caliban also find out that they are really brothers. Their father, John Cloamby, was an agent of the Nine. Due to mysterious side effects of the elixir, Cloamby went on a violent rampage while in England and is the man history knows as Jack the Ripper. Cloamby raped Grandrith's mother, who later bore her child on the shores of Africa. Cloamby changed his name to Caliban and moved to America, where he raised his second son to be a bronze superhero devoted to righting wrong and punishing evildoers. In *A Feast Unknown* and its sequels, *The Lord of the Trees* and *The Mad Goblin*, Caliban and Grandrith learn that they were both created as experiments by the Nine. The stranding of Grandrith's mother and uncle on the shores of equatorial Africa and his subsequent adoption by a species of semi-human anthropoids was prearranged by the Nine. Similarly, Doc Caliban's father was manipulated by the Nine into creating a scientific superman.

In *The Mad Goblin*, Doc Caliban believes that his father raised him to combat the Nine. However, before his father could reveal this to him, the Nine contacted Caliban and initiated him into the society without his father's knowledge. Then his father had been killed by the Nine because he was suspected of treason. Doc Caliban hunted down and killed his father's murderers without knowing that they were agents of the Nine.

This story would be consistent with what is told in Lester Dent's *The Man of Bronze*. Doc Savage's father, just before he is killed, sends a letter to his son which is only partially complete due to sabotage by Savage, Sr.'s killers. Doc's father tells him in his letter that he is passing to his son a "doubtful heritage." He writes:

It may be a heritage of woe. It may also be a heritage of destruction if you attempt to capitalize on it. On the other hand it may enable you to do many things for those who are not so fortunate as yourself, and will, in a way, be a boon for you in carrying on your work of doing good for all.

The reader is left thinking that this letter refers to a valley of gold which Doc Savage will inherit from his father. This is not what Doc's father is really referring to, however, and he states as much in his letter when he says, "You will find that I have nothing much to leave you in the way of tangible wealth." Certainly a valley of gold would be considered tangible wealth! Therefore, we must conclude that Doc's father was leaving him something other than a source of wealth. We may assume that Savage, Sr., was going to finally inform Doc about the Nine (certainly a heritage of woe) and that he was going to tell his son about his own experiments with the age-slowing elixir. If Doc would decide to capitalize on the elixir, he would certainly be destroyed by the Nine, who wish to keep the elixir a secret. On the other hand, if Doc could live forever, or at least a long, long time, he could do much good for the world. Of course, the same could be said of an inheritance of gold, but does Doc Savage really need to worry about resources? A man of his genius could easily find a way to make millions, billions even. Certainly he is already well on his way to this before the events of *The Man of Bronze*. A man who can rent the top floor of the Empire State Building in the midst of the Great Depression is not doing too badly for himself.

With this information as a background, we can begin to reconstruct the events leading up to Doc Savage's birth, and their connection with Nemo/Moriarty/Larsen/von Hessel/Karl. We know from Farmer's biography of Doc Savage that

Savage, Sr., Hubert Robertson, and Ned Land were present at Doc's birth on the schooner *Orion* off the coast of Andros Island. We also know that Doc's mother is Arronaxe Larsen, who is Ned Land's granddaughter and Wolf Larsen's daughter. [In his insightful article "The Good Ship Orion," John L. Vellutini dismisses Farmer's statement that Arronaxe Land is Doc's mother. He can see no reason to accept her as Doc's mother other than Farmer's unsupported statement. I think, however, that the present article explains Farmer's reasoning. As for those, like Vellutini, who note that Wolf Larsen appears to die at the end of *The Sea-Wolf*, recall Maud Brewster's words when his body is found: "But he still lives." Similarly, there is evidence that Professor Moriarty survived his terrible plunge from Reichenbach Falls when we remember Sherlock Holmes' contention that "I give you my word I seemed to hear Moriarty's voice screaming at me out of the abyss."]

In all probability, events occurred as follows: Doc's father had long ago become involved with a secret society, which Farmer calls the Nine, a shadowy group that controls human society and possesses an age-slowing elixir. He attempted to distill the elixir himself, but was unfruitful because of unanticipated side effects which made him prone to violence. Having come to be at odds with the Nine, he raised his son to fight them but never had the chance to inform Doc of his mission. Savage, Sr., enlisted the help of Ned Land in his designs against the Nine. Ned Land was at odds with the Nine for several reasons. For one, Wolf Larsen, a.k.a. XauXaz, etc., had married his daughter and then left her destitute. Two, Ned Land also knew about the Nine from his experiences on board the *Nautilus*. He knew that Nemo was the same man as Wolf Larsen. That Nemo—whom he had grown to hate with a passion while on board the *Nautilus*— had married his daughter was the ultimate blow to Land. That his great-grandson would be raised to defeat Nemo must have given Land a great feeling of satisfaction. The three men had gathered on the *Orion* to discuss their plan of attack against the Nine. Farmer states that Doc's birth was not registered in the ship's log because he "had good reason to leave it unrecorded." We now know why: he wished to leave no clue that the Nine could trace. Something went wrong, however, when Doc was born on that stormy night off Andros Island. The *Orion* was driven onto a reef. Farmer speculates that Doc's mother was drowned. Savage, Sr., must have worried that his well-thought-out plans were going to come to a quick end. But his son survived the mysterious demise of the *Orion* and would later take on his "doubtful heritage."

We know from *Escape from Loki* that Doc's father *did* know about von Hessel. Doc once overheard his father speak of the baron "to some cronies." These cronies may have been Ned Land and Hubert Robertson. Savage, Sr., mentions his informants, who were apparently keeping tabs on von Hessel.

But who, ultimately, is von Hessel? Having demonstrated that the baron is changing identities down through the ages, what did he mean when he told Doc that he was conceived in an illegitimate liaison between a Danish lady and the Crown Prince Frederick and that he, von Hessel, was really half-brother to the Kaiser Wilhelm? If we compare von Hessel's supposed lineage with Doc Caliban's lineage in *A Feast Unknown*, we see remarkable similarities. The same genealogical relationships are presented in both cases, but with different names filled in the blanks. Again, von Hessel was sending a coded message to Doc. This time it was a blueprint for his own true lineage, which differs considerably from the lineage he had been told by his father. So while von Hessel states that he is half-brother to the Kaiser, he is sending a coded message that Doc Savage is really half-brother to Tarzan. Like von Hessel, Tarzan's father isn't who he thinks he is. Farmer, in *A Feast Unknown*, goes into great detail to show that Grandrith's (read Tarzan's) father-in-name did not have intercourse with Tarzan's mother. We can guess that, like Grandrith's (Tarzan's) grandfather, his father-in-name was also sterile. This would match what von Hessel says about his own father-in-name's sterility.

MYTHS for the Modern Age

PHILIP JOSÉ FARMER'S

★ WOLD NEWTON UNIVERSE ★

Edited by Win Scott Eckert

5. The God of a Thousand Names

A final note on von Hessel's name provides some more shocking conclusions. According to the *New Dictionary of American Family Names*, Hessel—in addition to meaning "hazel"—indicates "One who came from Hessle..., villages in both the East and West Ridings of Yorkshire." A pivotal event in the Farmerian Monomyth occurs in this area of England. I am referring to the crash of the Wold Newton meteorite, in the East Riding of Yorkshire, which irradiated and mutated the genes of Doc Savage's and Tarzan's ancestors. In connection with this, Farmer, in *Tarzan Alive*, states that the Greystokes can trace their ancestry back to "the great god Woden in Denmark of the third century A.D." He also says, "The founders of the Greystoke line were secret worshippers of Woden long before their neighbors had converted to Christianity." Then Farmer curiously adds, "Perhaps the great god of the North is not dead but is in hiding. It pleased the Wild Huntsman to direct the falling star of Wold Newton near the two coaches. Thus, in a manner of speaking, he fathered the children of the occupants. The mutated and recessive genes would be reinforced, kept from being lost, by frequent marriages among the descendants of the irradiated parents." This, he says, created at least fourteen near-superhumans.

So we find that von Hessel, by his name, is indicating to Doc not that he is *like* Wotan but that he *is* Wotan, and that he is responsible for the mutated genes in Doc's lineage. Von Hessel caused the Wold Newton meteorite to fall where it did, thus irradiating Doc's ancestors. Remember von Hessel, under the identity of Professor Moriarty, was the author of the acclaimed *Dynamics of an Asteroid*.

6. The Golden Elixir

In *Escape from Loki*, Doc recalls that von Hessel also once made quite a stir in scientific circles with "His monograph on the mutations of the bacteria *Treponema pallidum* after bombardment by Roentgen rays while suspended in diluted *Cannabis sativa*." Von Hessel, of course, must have been working on experiments involving the elixir. Translated into everyday language, what does von Hessel's monograph mean? *Treponema pallidum* is the bacteria that causes syphilis. Roentgen rays are X-rays. *Cannabis sativa* is marijuana. Therefore, the subject of von Hessel's monograph, in layperson's terms, is about the bacteria that causes syphilis after bombardment by X-rays while suspended in diluted marijuana. This provides us with a clue as to what the elixir is and how it is administered.

Von Hessel is a man who loves cigars, and his cigars are "of the zeppelin class." It would only be fitting that he is literally displaying the elixir under his, and everyone else's, nose. The reverse pun on Freud must have appealed to the baron as well. The chemical composition of the elixir must involve marijuana, as indicated by his early experiments. What a better way to disguise the powerful aroma of *Cannabis sativa* than to hide it under the even more potent odor of cigar smoke? There are indications in *A Feast Unknown* that the elixir may be administered through smoke. When Lord Grandrith and Doc Caliban are in the caves of the Nine, they are certain that they are being administered the elixir. However, they do not know how this is done or what form the elixir takes. Doc Caliban suspects it is in the mead-tasting drink which all initiates are given, but Lord Grandrith is not so sure. Farmer mentions "nine giant torches of wood and pitch projecting from moveable stone pillars." It is possible that the elixir lies within smoke from these torches. Observe Baron von Hessel's curious behavior in the first banquet scene. As he taunts Doc about the countess and thoughts of escape, he laughs and throws "his half-smoked cigar into a corner." "An orderly hastened to pick it up," writes Farmer. "Instead of placing it in a waste container, he stubbed it out and placed it in his jacket pocket." The reader is left thinking that the orderly is just hoarding the leftovers of the wasteful baron. But might we not conclude that the orderly was acting under von Hessel's directions to retrieve and save any of his discarded precious elixir-bearing cigars?

In *A Feast Unknown*, Caliban and Grandrith find out that the elixir to which they have been exposed is interacting with their genetic makeups to create violent side effects. This greatly affects their sex life, allowing them pleasure only when they erupt in violence. The elixir seems to be intimately connected with the sexual act. This makes sense historically, as traditions interested in developing an immortality elixir, such as Taoist alchemy, place a great emphasis on the transformation of generative or sexual energy into vital energy, or *chi*, in the distillation of the elixir. In fact, Taoist alchemists use the term "Golden Elixir" to describe their immortality potion. In this tradition, generative energy, which is produced in relation with the sexual center, is blended with other energies in the body to produce the elixir. This makes one wonder about the baron's designs to get Doc to sleep with his mistress, Countess Idivzhopu. Doc has strong suspicions that the baron wanted him to have sex with the countess, but he cannot fathom the reason. Perhaps von Hessel needed Doc and the countess to have sex in order to distill the elixir. This would explain why, the day after Doc's intimacy with Lili Bugov, the baron smiles widely at Doc as he strolls by with the countess, even though the baron knows that Doc has slept with his mistress. Doc's mutated genes may also be a factor in the re-creation of the age-slowing formula.

There are parallels between the baron's manipulation of Doc in other books by Farmer. *Fire and the Night* is seemingly a mainstream novel about the problems of black–white relations among even the well-educated and liberal. However, a strong case may be made that it is actually thinly cloaked science fiction, dealing with Farmer's recurrent themes of immortality and secret societies. A character in the story, Vashti Virgil, bears an identical resemblance to the Egyptian queen Nefertiti, wife of the pharaoh Ikhnaton. This in itself could be coincidence, but other strange events occur in the novel. Danny Alliger, the protagonist of the story, has visions of a "Lady in White." Later in the story Alliger encounters Mr. Virgil, Vashti's husband, whose father had been involved in an interracial rape, referred to as "The Case of the Lady in White." This indicates that Alliger has had a genuine premonition. At the end of the novel, Alliger is lured to Vashti's house, where the two have an intimate encounter.

When they kiss, sparks fly between their lips. Eventually Alliger discovers that his encounter with Vashti has been prearranged, a set up to fulfill the psychological needs of Mr. Virgil, who desires Alliger's "whiteness" to rub off on his wife so that he can sleep with the "Lady in White." When Alliger leaves Vashti's house, he runs into Mr. Virgil, who reaches out with a finger and shocks Alliger with a static charge. But the story may not be just a psychological study of interracial issues. There are references to initiation into a secret society in a boyhood story that Mr. Virgil relates to Alliger. We can speculate that the Virgils were members of a secret society that dates back to ancient Egyptian times. Alliger, in his strange intimate encounter with the Virgils, may have been undergoing some sort of ancient initiation ritual akin to that of which Lord Grandrith and Doc Caliban partake in *A Feast Unknown*. Or Mr. Virgil may have been using Alliger to distill the elixir, just as von Hessel did to Doc. Certainly the novel ends with Alliger as baffled as Doc. (The Alliger family, by the way, appears more recently in Farmer's hardboiled, Peoria-based detective novel *Nothing Burns in Hell*.)

There are also a great many similarities between Farmer's elixir and the elixir depicted in Sir Arthur Conan Doyle's Holmes story "The Adventure of the Creeping Man." This story, in which a man injects himself with monkey hormones to increase his vitality and youthfulness, also bears a striking resemblance to the events of Robert Louis Stevenson's *The Strange Case of Dr. Jekyll and Mr. Hyde*. In both of these stories, as well as in Farmer's Grandrith/Caliban novels, the elixir brings on violent reactions in its subjects. If the baron is exposing Doc to the elixir in *Escape from Loki*, we may better understand Doc's recurrent emotional outbreaks in the novel.

7. A Most Mysterious Game of Bridge

In *Escape from Loki*, Doc Savage is baffled by more than just the baron and his mistress. He also cannot fathom the details behind the events leading to the deaths of Duntreath, Cauchon, and Murdstone. The sequence of events is certainly somewhat confusing. Doc Savage assigns Johnny Littlejohn the task of keeping tabs on Murdstone, the entomologist, who, due to his slight accent, Doc suspects is a German spy. Just before the scene in which the three men die, Doc asks Johnny where Murdstone is. "In the colonel's room," replies Johnny, "playing bridge with him, Major Wells, and Deauville." However, when Renny Renwick, assigned to follow Cauchon, announces that Cauchon, Murdstone, and Duntreath are locked in Duntreath's burning office, Major Wells and Deauville seem to have vanished. They are never mentioned again. Doc rushes in and stabs the pain-blinded Murdstone, who then croaks out a number of fragmentary sentences. These few words leave Doc thinking that Duntreath was really a German agent and that he has mistakenly given Murdstone a fatal wound.

But some of Murdstone's final utterances do not make sense. He seems to indicate that Cauchon had spied on Doc and his followers and reported their plans for escape from Camp Loki. But he also seems to indicate that Duntreath, the supposed traitor, had been fighting with Cauchon. Why would Cauchon and Duntreath, who are supposedly both German agents, be coming to blows with one another? Doc questions Murdstone if it is Cauchon or Duntreath who is the German agent. In fragments, Murdstone replies:

"The colonel...a plant. Cauchon...must've...colonel stabbed him...I...we struggled. Lamp fell, broke...fire... stabbed me...shot me...killed...colonel...couldn't see, thought he might still be alive...attacked...shot, stabbed, got me. Or somebody else?"

We assume that Murdstone means to say that Colonel Duntreath was a plant, a German spy. But we still do not know who Cauchon was and what he was doing. He is definitely not innocent, as when Doc asks Murdstone about Cauchon, he replies, "Went to...reported...you...others." How can we come to terms with these facts in the light of Murdstone's final testimony?

First of all, we must look at what these men had in common. All of them, Duntreath, Murdstone, and Cauchon, were in the habit of playing bridge together in Colonel Duntreath's office. Doc observes that Murdstone had been getting on an intimate footing with Duntreath by playing bridge with him and two other cronies. These latter must be Deauville, who is Duntreath's assistant, and Major Wells, about whom we know nothing. Doc also observes that Cauchon, who is a Belgian infantry captain, was in the habit of playing bridge with them when a regular was absent. Those who know anything about the history of card games might recall that bridge evolved out of the once popular game of whist.

Here we must pause and consider where the game of whist appears in winding tunnels of the Farmerian Monomyth. In *The Other Log of Phileas Fogg*, the card game plays a pivotal role among agents of an extraterrestrial secret society. Members of this society use the individual cards and their varying combinations to communicate esoteric information among one another. In this way, Fogg knows that he should proceed as ordered on his mad rush around the globe. Whist also appears in Doyle's "The Empty House" in a game involving the notorious Colonel Moran, Moriarty's cohort, who also appears in *Other Log*.

Now things begin to take shape. It is reasonably safe to assume that there is more than meets the eye in Duntreath's game of bridge. Unquestionably the men were using the game to send signals to one another. That Murdstone was involved probably means that Doc's original suspicions that the entomologist was not innocent were correct. If there are two opposing secret societies involved, as in *Other Log*, we might guess that Murdstone belonged to one and Duntreath to the other. But we should not be so hasty. When Murdstone, in his final testimony, refers to the "colonel," he may be referring to von Hessel, who is the Baron *Colonel* von Hessel. If so, it may be the *Baron Colonel* who is a plant, not Colonel Duntreath. In fact, it is possible that the baron made a brief appearance at Duntreath's game of bridge. Recall that the train steams up and halts on Doc's side of the enclosure right before Duntreath's office bursts into flames. Doc thinks, "The train was standing by. For whom? Why?" Maybe it was waiting for the baron, who had one last errand to perform before he left camp. That the baron *was* on the train we discover later. When he boarded it, we do not know.

Benedict Murdstone is still one big question mark. Farmer has connected Murdstone to the family of the same name who appear in Charles Dickens' *David Copperfield*. We may guess that he is the offspring of either sibling, Edward or Jane Murdstone. He does bear the family proboscis. Further, we must wonder about his relation to Countess Mary Anne Liza Murdstone-Malcon, who appears in Farmer's "The Adventure of the Three Madmen." Her stage name, Liza Borden, is strikingly reminiscent of "Lily Bugov." That Murdstone-Malcon appears in the story juxtaposed with the von Hessel-like Von Bork (who is also one-eyed, like Odin) is equally curious.

Earlier in *Escape from Loki*, Murdstone tells the suspicious Doc that he was never in Germany except on one summer holiday but later contradicts this by stating, as he is dying, that he was "born Bremen...ten years old...raised Berk..." This discrepancy is difficult to fathom.

8. A Worm Unknown to Science

Sherlockians must have been baffled and amused by a certain aspect of what is perhaps the most important scene in *Escape from Loki*. In this scene, Doc enters the abandoned chateau of Baron de Musard. He soon locates a secret chamber bearing all the gruesome accoutrements of a Satanic ritual. This scene is important for two reasons. One, it gives Doc a taste of true evil, which later inspires his journey to do good and punish evildoers. Secondly, what Doc encounters in this room of horrors is the biggest clue of all in unraveling the tangled skein that is his dubious legacy.

To explain this statement, I shall cite two passages. The first comes from this crucial scene in *Escape from Loki*:

> Savage leaned over the stone basin to see better what was inside it. Old dried bloodstains splotched its cavity. The bones of an infant, perhaps six months old, lay in the center. Beside them was a large sharp knife.
>
> Savage was horrified.

What horrified him even more, while also mystifying him, was a long whitish worm moving slowly over the spine bones.

He thought that he had a thorough grounding in the invertebrate phyla. But he could not classify this creature. It was, as far as he was aware, a worm unknown to science.

The second passage, which must be read in conjunction with the above quotation, comes from one of Doyle's classic Sherlock Holmes stories, in which Dr. Watson recounts three cases left unsolved by the Great Detective. This is from "The Problem of Thor Bridge":

A third case worthy of note is that of Isadora Persano, the well-known journalist and duellist, who was found stark staring mad with a match box in front of him which contained a remarkable worm said to be unknown to science.

It is too bad that the great Sherlockian scholar William S. Baring-Gould did not live to read Doc Savage's first adventure. Imagine the look on his face when he compared the above two passages! In any event, Farmerian scholars must have been equally stunned, for there is a third story that not only mentions the "worm unknown to science" but that revolves entirely around it.

This third story is Farmer's "The Problem of the Sore Bridge—Among Others," a companion to Doyle's "Thor Bridge" in that it solves the three mysterious cases which so perplexed Holmes. This is Harry "Bunny" Manders' account of how he and his fellow gentleman burglar, A. J. Raffles, race one step ahead of Holmes to solve the cases of the disappearance of James Phillimore, the disappearance of the cutter *Alicia*, and the strange, unknown worm.

In the story, placed in 1895, Manders and Raffles discover that James Phillimore is in reality a shape-shifting extraterrestrial who manages to disappear from his house by turning into a chair. He has come to earth to lay his offspring, which begin their incubation in a crystalline state resembling star sapphires, later transforming into hideous worms with a dozen needle-pointed tentacles and tiny pale-blue eyes. This is the species of worm that drives Isadora Persano "stark staring mad" and undoubtedly precisely the same kind of creature that Doc Savage encounters in de Musard's chateau. Doc does not mention the tentacles, but his descriptions are vague. Either Farmer just failed to mention the tentacles in Doc's encounter or the worm was in a pre-tentacle transitory state between crystal and worm. Later Manders and Raffles come across the parent creature in its apparently true form, which resembles an enlarged version of Isadora Persano's tentacled worm. It has the ability to split itself into smaller entities which still have the ability to shape-shift.

The conjunction of these three stories, one edited by Doyle and two by Farmer, is quite shocking and absolutely beyond coincidence. But even more ominous comes the realization that the entities that Doc, Manders, and Raffles encountered appear in several more recorded accounts. We may recall from Manders' account that the Phillimore creature arrived from the heavens in a ship that plunged into the English Channel off the Straits of Dover. The ship was most likely a submersible vessel not unlike Nemo's *Nautilus*, which Farmer, in *Other Log*, reveals was really built with extraterrestrial technology. With this in mind, recall one of the most memorable scenes in *Twenty Thousand Leagues Under the Sea*, in which the *Nautilus* is attacked by a giant tentacled kraken. Nemo himself takes axe in hand to battle this fearsome creature. Who can but doubt that Nemo's giant squid is a larger version of the shape-shifting entity witnessed by Manders?

What is more, there are *two more* stories in which Doc Savage encounters the mysterious worm being. By this time, however, he has begun to understand the nature of the threat that challenges him. In John W. Campbell's classic 1938 story "Who Goes There?", which was the basis for the films *The Thing from Another World* (1951) and *The Thing* (1982), Doc Savage makes a disguised appearance as the giant bronzed scientist McReady. Doc, as McReady, heads a team of scientists who discover a shape-shifting extraterrestrial that has been hibernating at the

South Pole until it was disturbed. The creature appears at the end of the story in its original form: as a writhing, tentacled monster, identical with the one run across by Manders and Raffles. Doc must have been following some lead to the Antarctic continent that connected the monster he encounters there with the whitish worm he saw when he was sixteen. With just a little more digging we can trace what clue this probably was.

Farmer, in his biography of Doc Savage, mentions a curious item. He states that Johnny Littlejohn, Doc's geologist aide, was the narrator of H. P. Lovecraft's tale of terror *At the Mountains of Madness*. The story, set in 1929, chronicles the ill-fated expedition sent by the Miskatonic University to conduct geological tests in Antarctica. The team accidentally awakens a group of "Old Ones" (note this is the same phrase used to describe the extraterrestrials in Farmer's *Other Log*), who are none other than tentacled extraterrestrial entities. Here we wonder if it was really the lost continent of Atlantis that Nemo shows Professor Arronaxe or really "the frightful stone city of R'lyeh." Whatever the case, the Old Ones were also the creators of shape-shifting being known as shoggoths, who sometime seem to appear as giant rubbery spheroids. There is also mention of "a land race of beings shaped like octopi and probably corresponding to the pre-human spawn of Cthulhu." [Though Mr. Vellutini was wrong in his dismissal of Arronaxe Larsen as the mother of Doc Savage, he was dead-on in connecting Doc with the Cthulhu Mythos. Some more details of this are provided in the introduction to Farmer's fragmentary Doc Caliban novel *The Monster on Hold*.] This tale, recounted by Johnny to Doc, most certainly provided Doc with enough clues to connect his unknown whitish worm with the beings the Miskatonic expedition found in Antarctica. It is revealing that one member of the team was named Larsen. Could this have been a code left in Johnny's manuscript by Lovecraft? If so, it probably indicates that our slippery baron was tagging along with the expedition. Or perhaps it was a code that Doc's father, who had married a Larsen, accompanied Johnny in disguise. There is also a character named Lake in Johnny's account. *Other Log* reveals that agents of the secret society of

Philip José Farmer

TARZAN ALIVE

A Definitive Biography of Lord Greystoke

immortals bear names which have certain coded meanings, such as Fogg or Head. (We may wonder about the name "Farmer," if we dare...) Lake may have been an agent of the Nine, sent to Antarctica to awaken the Old Ones or perhaps Cthulhu himself. Farmer's *The Monster on Hold* indicates that the Nine awakened a Cthulhu-like entity, called Shrassk, in order to destroy renegade agents. The clues, whatever they are, were there for Doc to see. Thus we find Doc investigating the entities at the South Pole in the 1938 story "Who Goes There?"

Doc, however, did not solve the riddle of his doubtful heritage on the Antarctic continent. Perhaps he never did. But he does come closer than before in his last recorded adventure, *Up from Earth's Center*. It is fitting that Doc's first adventure, *Escape from Loki*, begins with the phrase "Spiders, men, and Mother Nature make trapdoors," for his last adventure begins with a man making "a crude thatched trapdoor which he could close against the black things of the night." This is surely Farmer's indication that these two stories are intimately connected.

To illustrate how they are connected, we bring forth the last Karl of this article, Dr. Karl Linningen. Strangely, Dent quickly drops the name Linningen, referring to the man as simply "Dr. Karl." Karl, as has been shown, is another name for Wotan, the Norse All-father god. It literally means "Old Man," which was one of Wolf Larsen's names. Therefore, we may immediately suspect that there is something peculiar about Dr. Karl. Just as H. W. Starr contends that Nemo/Moriarty was really only an amateur sailor, so Dent portrays Dr. Karl. He constantly seems to be toying with Doc, prodding him on. When he meets Doc, he takes out a cigar, the tobacco wrapper of which he notices is broken, and remarks to Doc without looking up, "You seem to know me by sight." Doc counters by saying, "Why shouldn't I know you?" Doc at this point probably realizes that the game is afoot, that he is dealing with the same forces that he encountered in 1918 when he was sixteen. But Doc is much more experienced now, much more adept at reading the signs. Thus he knows that the doctor has signaled him with the broken tobacco wrapper. The cigar has been tampered with. It is a sign that the elixir is at hand, and the elixir, working in conjunction with Doc's mutated genes, often produces undesirable results. It is no wonder that the bronze man's usually impregnable calm poise is broken and that he screams aloud at the novel's end.

Dr. Karl dogs along with Doc on his most bizarre adventure, constantly asking his opinion of what is going on in the strange affair. It is almost as if he is mocking him, or testing Doc to see how much of the puzzle he has pieced together. The possible devil, Mr. Wail, apparently has the ability to appear and disappear at will. This very much resembles the shape-shifting Phillimore's ability, and we can guess that Wail is also a shape-shifter. Wail even admits that he is only temporarily in human form. Doc becomes very alarmed at the strange developments in the case and gives an impassioned speech to his aides that this may be the real thing, their toughest case ever. He prods them with more force than he ever has to keep on the lookout for anything unusual. Right after this, Doc and his aides are drugged, although Doc cannot understand how—he was looking for it, but still missed it. Doc then proceeds to follow Wail into the New England caverns that Wail claims lead to Hell. Doc and Monk test for gas as they descend the caves, but neither of these two experts in chemistry finds anything unusual. Then all Hell does break loose. Doc is attacked by shapeless boulder creatures, like Lovecraft's rubbery spheroids. Doc and his crew are chased by these beings, whose "clicking and hissing, a sound that was rage and hunger and bestiality" must truly have been what Lovecraft and Poe attempted to depict by the utterance "Tekeli-li! Tekeli-li!" Finally, Doc's defenses break, and, as he is attacked by a tentacled being, he screams, "probably the first shriek of unadulterated terror that he had given in his lifetime."

Up from Earth's Center ends with no explanation except the one provided by Dr. Karl that the caves had been filled with hallucinogenic gas. No mention is made of the fact that Doc and Monk, two of the world's greatest chemists, had tested for gas and found none. Doc is in great doubt as his final adventure closes, and little wonder. As warm sunlight melts the snow on the roof of the lodge where the story ends, Doc stares into space and frowns as icicles form on the eaves. There is beyond contention something supernatural at work.

And so we finally see that the Farmerian Monomyth is a complex pattern of meaningful, though subtle, hints. While Farmer is Jungian in the use of his symbols, he is also Levi-Straussian in that many of his symbols make sense only when considered structurally within a larger framework of myths. Truly it is with a sense of the eerie that one reads a description of the city of the Old Ones as portrayed by H. P. Lovecraft in *At the Mountains of Madness*. It shows better than anything what is at play in the work of a certain Peorian:

> Naturally, no one set of carvings which we encountered told more than a fraction of any connected story; nor did we even begin to come upon the various stages of that story in their proper order. Some of the vast rooms were independent units as far as their designs were concerned, whilst in other cases a continuous chronicle would be carried through a series of rooms and corridors. The best of the maps and diagrams were on the walls of a frightful abyss below even the ancient ground level—a cavern...which had almost undoubtedly been an educational centre of some sort. There were many provoking repetitions of the same material in different rooms and buildings; since certain chapters of experience, and certain summaries or phases of racial history, had evidently been favorites with different decorators or dwellers. Sometimes, though, variant versions of the same theme proved useful in settling debatable points and filling in gaps.

The Farmerian Monomyth certainly is a *mono*-myth: its intricate labyrinth tells many stories, but the maze as a whole—winding as it does through dark depths, occasionally opening upon awe-inspiring, glittering vistas—tells The Story, a single Grand Adventure. Anyone who doubts this should consider the fact that Kickaha, the protagonist of Farmer's World of

Tiers series, has Phileas Fogg for a great grandfather,[4] while remembering Red Orc's insistence that Kickaha was half-Lord. There is always more to The Story than meets the eye...

Bibliography

Campbell, John W. "Who Goes There?" in *Science Fiction: The Science Fiction Research Association Anthology*. HarperCollins: New York, 1988.

Carey, Christopher Paul. "Farmer's *Escape from Loki*: A Closer Look" in *The Bronze Gazette*, Vol. 6, No. 17. Green Eagle Publications: Modesto, February 1996.

————. Letter to Philip José Farmer, dated May 9, 1997. *The Official Philip José Farmer Web Page*, ed. Michael Croteau, http://pjfarmer.com/fan/chrisl1.htm/.

————. "Loki in the Sunlight" in *The Bronze Gazette*, Vol. 8, Issue 24. Green Eagle Publications: Modesto, June 1998.

Dent, Lester (Kenneth Robeson). *Fortress of Solitude*. Bantam: New York, 1968.

————. *The Devil Genghis*. Bantam: New York, 1974.

————. *The Man of Bronze*. Bantam: New York, 1964.

————. *Up from Earth's Center* in *Doc Savage Omnibus #13*. Bantam: New York, 1990.

Dickens, Charles. *David Copperfield*. Signet: New York, 1962.

Doyle, Sir Arthur Conan. "The Adventure of the Empty House," "The Adventure of the Creeping Man," and "The Problem of Thor Bridge" in *The Complete Sherlock Holmes*. Doubleday: New York, 1988.

Eckert, Win Scott. "The Malevolent Moriartys, or, Who's Going to Take Over the World When I'm Gone?" *An Expansion of Philip José Farmer's Wold Newton Family*, Win Scott Eckert, ed., http://www.pjfarmer.com/woldnewton/Articles3.htm#Moriarty/. Revised as "Who's Going to

---

4. There is an incongruity in Farmer's writings regarding Kickaha's relationship to Phileas Fogg. Chapter VIII in *The Lavalite World* reads, "Philea Jane's parents were of the English landed gentry, though his [Kickaha's] great-grandfather had married a Parsi woman." This is apparently a reference to Phileas Fogg, who married the Parsi Aouda Jejeebhoy in 1872. Thus, Farmer seems to be stating that Kickaha's great-grandfather is Phileas Fogg. However, according to the information in *Doc Savage: His Apocalyptic Life*, Phileas Fogg is Kickaha's granduncle, not his great-grandfather. I had the opportunity to clear up this discrepancy in a conversation with Mr. Farmer, in which he stated that in the time between writing the biography and *The Lavalite World* he had forgotten the exact lineage. The correct relationship is as described in *Doc Savage: Apocalyptic Life*.

Take Over the World When I'm Gone? A Look at the Genealogies of the Wold Newton Family Supervillains and Their Nemeses" in *Myths for the Modern Age: Philip José Farmer's Wold Newton Universe*, ed. Win Scott Eckert. MonkeyBrain Books: Austin, 2005.

Farmer, Philip José. "The Adventure of the Three Madmen" in *The Grand Adventure*. Berkley, 1984.

———. *Dayworld*. J. P. Putnam's Sons: New York, 1985.

———. *Doc Savage: His Apocalyptic Life*. Bantam: New York, 1975.

———. *Escape from Loki: Doc Savage's First Adventure*. Bantam: New York, 1991.

———. *A Feast Unknown*. Playboy Paperbacks: New York, 1981.

———. *Fire and the Night*. Regency: Evanston, 1962.

———. *Hadon of Ancient Opar*. DAW Books: New York, 1974.

———. *The Lavalite World*. Ace Books: New York, 1977.

———. Letter to Christopher Paul Carey, dated June 17, 1997. *The Official Philip José Farmer Web Page*, ed. Michael Croteau, http://www.pjfarmer.com/fan/chrisl2.htm/.

———. *Lord of the Trees / The Mad Goblin*. Ace: New York, 1980.

———. *The Monster on Hold* in *Program to the 1983 World Fantasy Convention*. Weird Tales: Oak Forest, 1983.

———. *Night of Light*. Berkley Medallion: New York, 1966.

———. *Nothing Burns in Hell*. Forge: New York, 1998.

———. *The Other Log of Phileas Fogg*. Tor: New York, 1982.

———. "The Problem of the Sore Bridge—Among Others" in *Riverworld and Other Stories*. Berkley: New York, 1981.

———. *Tarzan Alive*. Playboy Paperbacks: New York, 1981.

Levi-Strauss, Claude. *Structural Anthropology*. Basic Books: New York, 1963.

London, Jack. *The Sea-Wolf*. Signet: New York, 1962.

Lovecraft, H. P. *At the Mountains of Madness* in *The Annotated H. P. Lovecraft*. Dell: New York, 1997.

Murray, Will. "The Genesis of John Sunlight, Parts 1 & 2" in *The Monarch of Armageddon*. Millennium Publications, 1991.

Orchard, Andy. *Cassell Dictionary of Norse Myth and Legend*. Cassell: London, 1997.

Poe, Edgar Allen. "The Narrative of Arthur Gordon Pym of Nantucket" in *The Tell-Tale Heart and Other Stories*. Bantam: New York, 1982.

Reaney, P. H. *The Origin of English Surnames*. Barnes & Noble: New York, 1957.

Smith, Elsdon C. *New Dictionary of American Family Names*. Harper & Row: New York, 1973.

Stevenson, Robert Louis. *The Strange Case of Dr. Jekyll and Mr. Hyde*. Washington Square Press: New York, 1995.

Vellutini, John L. "The Good Ship Orion" in *The Bronze Gazette*, Vol. 5, No. 14. Green Eagle Publications: Modesto, February 1995.

Verne, Jules. *The Mysterious Island*. Signet: New York, 1986.

————. *Twenty Thousand Leagues Under the Sea*. Bantam: New York, 1981.

A Meteor Over Pangea

First published online at *An Expansion of Philip José Farmer's Wold Newton Universe*, 2004

Douglas Preston and Lincoln Child, authors of the bestselling novels *Relic* and *The Cabinet of Curiosities* (among others), have themselves remarked on the interconnections between characters in their various works (see "The Preston-Child Pangea or, A Cyclopedia of the Cross-Correlations in the Preston-Child Universe.") However, perhaps even they are not aware of the connections, potentially quite important, to Wold Newton studies.

While it is my belief that Agent Pendergast certainly exhibits many traits to indicate that he may well bear the mutated genes of the Wold Newton lineage, it is Eli Glinn from *The Ice Limit* who brings the Preston-Child Universe into the larger Wold Newton Universe. As the president of Effective Engineering Solutions, Inc., a company that specializes in solving unsolvable problems, Glinn is a man obsessed with calculations and probabilities. The company, under his direction, has an unbelievable success rate of one hundred percent (until the events of *The Ice Limit*, that is). One reason for the perfect track record is Glinn's philosophy of "double overage," the belief that all obstacles may be overcome by accounting for twice the assessed difficulty for any problem. Another reason is Glinn's clockwork character.

A description of Glinn proves most revealing:

> The man looked, at first glance, as inscrutable as the Sphinx. There was nothing distinctive about him, nothing that gave anything away. Even his gray eyes were veiled, cautious, and still. Everything about him looked

ordinary: ordinary height, ordinary build, good-looking but not handsome, well-dressed but not dapper. His only unusual feature... was the way he moved. His shoes made no sound on the floor, his clothes did not rustle on his person, his limbs moved lightly and easily through the air. He glided through the room like a deer through a forest.

By now the perceptive Wold Newton scholar will already begin to notice the resemblances between Eli Glinn and his ancestor Phileas Fogg. Like Fogg, everything about Glinn, every action that he performs, is calculated. In fact, even some of Glinn's proverbs (such as "There's no such thing as an unpredictable person") sound as if they might have been uttered by Fogg himself. Glinn's eyes also exhibit the familial gray, the same color as Phileas's (as uncovered by Philip José Farmer in his *The Other Log of Phileas Fogg*). Glinn, however, is of average height, as opposed to the tall Phileas. This dismisses the likelihood that Glinn is Phileas Fogg under an assumed identity (the possibility of which does come to mind when remembering Farmer's contention that Fogg was likely still alive somewhere in England during the 1970s). Surely Glinn must have been aware of his ancestor's famous dash around the world. Perhaps he had even read his story as told by Verne or Farmer. Or, if Fogg still lives, perhaps he heard the story firsthand.

Having established Eli Glinn's probable relation to the Wold Newton family, another curious facet from *The Ice Limit* must be explored that makes Glinn's genealogical roots more certain. The novel recounts the efforts of several individuals to recover what is believed to be an extra-solar meteorite. Glinn's company is hired by billionaire Palmer Lloyd to complete the task. While onboard the *Rolvaag*, a sophisticated tanker modified to retrieve the meteorite, Glinn addresses the crew in an attempt to alleviate their concerns over the dangerous mission. One man, who goes by the name of Lewis, raises objections:

"I don't like it," he said in a broad Yorkshire accent.
He had a mass of red hair and an unruly beard.

UQ1048

No. 48   95c

THE OTHER LOG OF PHILEAS FOGG

PHILIP JOSÉ FARMER

The interstellar drama behind Jules Verne's
AROUND THE WORLD IN EIGHTY DAYS is revealed
at last in this startling new novel by the
Hugo-winning author of TARZAN ALIVE.

Glinn attempts to quiet the man's concerns that the Chilean government has legal rights to the meteorite and may cause trouble for the *Rolvaag* and its crew. He states:

"This is not Chilean cultural patrimony. It could have fallen anywhere—even in Yorkshire."

That a probable ancestor of Phileas Fogg is to be found discussing the hypothetical falling of a meteorite in Yorkshire is too much to be a coincidence. This is certainly a reference to the Wold Cottage meteorite and an indication that Glinn is aware of his roots in the Wold Newton family. But what is his game? Why would Glinn make this subtle genealogical reference to a common sailor?

Perhaps the sailor was not common after all. We know little about him, and he does not appear again in the novel. The only clue to his identity lies in his "mass of red hair" and "broad Yorkshire accent." Yet by these attributes, combined with Glinn's subtle reference, we may guess (though it is far from certain) that this sailor may also have Wold Newton ancestry.[5]

Given that Glinn and his company would accept a job only if they could be guaranteed success, one wonders what motives prompted the usually cautious Glinn to attempt retrieval of the Chilean meteorite. Perhaps Glinn anticipated Dr. Samuel McFarlane's later theory that this meteorite was an example of cosmic panspermia, a seeding of our planet with alien life— but how could he have known this? If he were aware of the Eridanean-Capellean conflict related in Farmer's *Other Log*, it is possible he may have had inside knowledge that the Chilean meteorite was not merely a giant rock from space. I have elsewhere demonstrated that Clark Savage, Jr., stumbles onto an ancient conspiracy involving aliens who bear a striking resemblance to creatures from Lovecraft's Cthulhu Mythos. Further, Savage,

---

5. Could this red-haired man be the wily Red Orc, the secret Lord of Earth from Farmer's World of Tiers series? It must be remembered that Phileas Fogg is Kickaha's granduncle, and that Red Orc suggests that Kickaha is half-Lord. This connects the Eridanean-Capellean conflict with the World of Tiers. Certainly Red Orc would have knowledge of the ancient alien conspiracy surrounding many members of the Wold Newton family. He would not hesitate to investigate a meteorite like the one found in Chile.

under the disguised name McReady, investigates another alien-bearing meteorite in John W. Campbell's "Who Goes There?" It is likely that Glinn, an ancestor of Phileas Fogg, is doing the same many years later in *The Ice Limit*.

Unfortunately, we may never know the truth about the Chilean meteorite, as the world has not heard from the Lloyd expedition since it embarked on its mission destroy it.[6] But meteorites and the Wold Newton family seem to be inextricably bound together. That Fogg's ancestor, Eli Glinn, is mixed up in the affair of *The Ice Limit* tells us that the mysterious conspiracy still proceeds in our day.[7]

Bibliography

Carey, Paul Christopher. "The Blue Eyes Have It—Or Are They Green? or Another Case of Identity Recased" in The Bronze Gazette, Vol. 11, No. 33. Green Eagle Publications: Modesto, November 2001. Revised as "The Green Eyes Have It—Or Are They Blue? or Another Case of Identity Recased" in Myths for the Modern Age: Philip José Farmer's Wold Newton Universe. MonkeyBrain Books: Austin, 2005.

Farmer, Philip José. *Tarzan Alive*. Doubleday: New York, 1972.

———. *Doc Savage: His Apocalyptic Life*. Doubleday: New York, 1973.

———. *The Other Log of Phileas Fogg*. DAW Books: New York, 1973.

Preston, Douglas and Child, Lincoln. *The Ice Limit*. Warner: New York, 2000.

———. *The Ice Limit* (expanded ebook edition). iPublish.com, 2000.

———. "The Preston-Child Pangea or, A Cyclopedia of the Cross-Correlations in the Preston-Child Universe." *The Official Website of Douglas Preston and Lincoln Child*, https://www.prestonchild.com/faq/pangea/PANGEA;art55,88/.

Verne, Jules. *Around the World in Eighty Days*. Oxford University Press: Oxford, 1995.

---

6. Reference to this second Lloyd expedition is made only in the epilogue to the expanded ebook version of *The Ice Limit*.

7. Since this article was written, Eli Glinn has appeared several times as a character in Douglas Preston and Lincoln Child's Gideon Crew series, including in *Beyond the Ice Limit*, a sequel to *The Ice Limit*. I have fallen behind in my reading and have not had the pleasure of delving into any of these later works featuring Eli Glinn, and so I do not know what havoc they may have dealt to this article's thesis; such are the perils of engaging in the creative mythography of an ongoing fiction series. This article was written in good fun, with complete deference to the authority Preston and Child hold over their own highly entertaining literary creations. —CPC, 2018

The Innocent Dilemma:
Reflections on "The Unnaturals"

Farmerphile: The Magazine of Philip José Farmer,
No. 2, October 2005

"It is such an uncomfortable feeling to know one is a fool." The words of the Scarecrow in L. Frank Baum's *The Wonderful Wizard of Oz* are a perfect summation of the human condition. We, as humans, stand somewhere between our festering proclivity to fulfill the impulses of greed and lust and our desire to seek out creative, peaceful solutions to our problems. How do we reconcile such disparate parts of our nature? Such is the dilemma that Philip José Farmer addresses in "The Unnaturals."

Innocent, Farmer's Scarecrow, is truly the living personification of his name at the story's opening. This surely is not coincidence. Farmer has chosen his protagonist carefully. Thrusting a wholly guiltless, child-like character into an ethical quandary is certainly the most effective way to explore how humanity might come to understand a tough issue. The true artist knows how to remove the baggage of millennia and present his or her question in the clearest of terms. Farmer achieves this superbly by giving us an insightful glimpse into Innocent's creation.

In "Extracts from the Memoirs of Lord Greystoke" (included in *Mother Was a Lovely Beast*, Chilton, 1974) and *The Dark Heart of Time* (Del Rey, 1999), Farmer writes of how Tarzan, in the innocence of his youth, believed that the movement of trees, leaves, and grass caused the motion of the wind. In the same vein, Innocent, in the story at hand, believes that the pressure of the light from the sun pushes the wind and that crows pull in the dawn or push it ahead with the flutter of their wings. This is the idea of mythical thought (or "bricoleur") versus the paradigms of science as expressed by the French social anthropologist Claude Lévi-Strauss in his classic work, *The Savage Mind* (University of Chicago Press, 1966). Whereas science begins with structure and extrapolates events, mythical thought begins with events and forms a structure. Farmer, well-versed in the fields of anthropology and mythology, understands this concept well.

What then is the ethical dilemma which the innocent Innocent and his fellow band The Unnaturals face in this story? We may see it in the plans of Anonymous Legion, general and "head of G.O.D., the Good Old Days party." Legion is a greed-filled warmonger. Reflective of the Biblical passage ("My name is Legion," Mark 5:9), Legion is possessed; in this case, possessed with the idea of doing away with all humans and replicating a nation of mindless scarecrows, a nation that would be easily cared for or, in other words, manipulated.

Innocent and his companions fight and ultimately subdue Legion, but the price for Innocent is the very trait that is his namesake. Innocent knows that unless he kills Legion, as Stan prods him to do, then Legion will very likely kill many more people. But to kill to prevent killing is something that Innocent cannot bear. Therefore he puts off the issue and jails Legion until he, Innocent, can return with brains enough to do the right thing. "'There's nothing like refusing to face an ethical issue,'" says Innocent, adding, "'I must be getting more human by the minute.'"

Innocent's dilemma is probably much older than human history, but it is clearly reflected in the events which occurred at the time Farmer wrote this story: 1973, in the midst of the trying times of the Vietnam War and Watergate. Public opinion about the war began to shift considerably after the infamous Tet Offensive and General Westmoreland's call for yet more troops to join in the conflict. "'That man would kill Twinkletoes and every human in the world to get a perfect world,'" says Innocent in "The Unnaturals." Certainly this statement summed up how many in America felt about Westmoreland, and their leaders in general, at this point in history. This is further reinforced when Stan says, "'He'll kill more people before somebody does your

0-425-05641-4 • $5.95 • IN CANADA $6.95 • BERKLEY SCIENCE FICTION

BESTSELLING AUTHOR OF THE RIVERWORLD NOVELS

PHILIP JOSÉ FARMER

A BARNSTORMER IN OZ

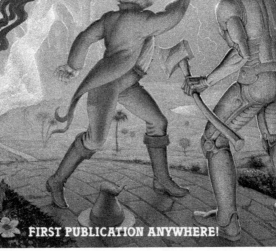

FIRST PUBLICATION ANYWHERE!

job for you... Maybe Twinkletoes. Many little girls and boys, you can count on that.'" Farmer's attitude toward the conflict in Vietnam is a matter of public record, as his name—along with seventy nine others, many of whom are well-known science fiction and fantasy authors—was listed in an advertisement opposing the war in the June 1968 issue of *Galaxy* magazine.

It may be that the xenophobic paranoia of President Nixon can be glimpsed in the rant of Punchkin's mayor after Innocent performs "Who Blew My Blue Hugh?"—a protest song decrying the incessant lies of politicians. "'Spies! Criminals! Revolutionaries! Foreigners! Nonhumans!'" the mayor screams. The Watergate scandal broke in June 1972 and was reaching a fever-pitch when Farmer wrote "The Unnaturals" in 1973.

One can, of course, never be certain as to the precise allegorical meaning of an author's work; but nevertheless, the parallels are there to be made, and history has shown that the dilemma faced by Innocent has been cycling sorrowfully throughout the ages.

So how *do* we solve the problem of resisting violence and tyranny without resorting to violence and tyranny ourselves? What does Farmer, through Innocent, have to say about this?

The answer lies in Innocent's not-so-innocent, though cautiously hopeful final verse: we must look for new colors and trust that human creativity—through artists who write such imaginatively thoughtful stories as "The Unnaturals"—will help to raise the level of human, and humane, understanding.

On *Hadon of Ancient Opar*

Farmerphile: The Magazine of Philip José Farmer,
No. 3, January 2006

"...Opar, that hidden city of 'gold, and silver, ivory, and apes, and peacocks...'"

Opar has become almost an archetype in literature, and it is certainly a cornerstone of fictional lost civilizations, along with Haggard's Zu-Vendis and Kôr and Hilton's Shangri-la. Opar is, of course, the creation of Edgar Rice Burroughs, first used as a setting in his *The Return of Tarzan* (1913) and later depicted in *Tarzan and the Jewels of Opar* (1916), *Tarzan and the Golden Lion* (1922), and *Tarzan the Invincible* (1930). ERB was unquestionably influenced by Haggard and obviously meant to echo the Biblical Ophir in his lost African city inhabited by cruel half-anthropoidal priests and stunningly beautiful priestesses. In the same way that ERB's Opar was inspired by past and contemporary lost race literature, Farmer's *ancient* Opar is a unique and original work based on and extrapolated from numerous sources. These sources are too rich to go into detail here (that subject will be broached in a future article, tentatively titled "The Archaeology of Khokarsa"), but suffice it to say that Farmer has his bases covered and that the two novels that make up the Ancient Opar "series" are as inventive and deep as they are a worthy tribute to ERB, the Master of Adventure.

The rich level of cultural and descriptive detail in both *Hadon of Ancient Opar* (1974) and its sequel *Flight to Opar* (1976) make them prime examples of fantastic world building. Set twelve thousand years ago against the backdrop of a civil war between

UW1241 $1.50

In Tarzan's Africa – 12,000 years ago!

HADON OF ANCIENT OPAR

PHILIP JOSÉ FARMER

the priests and the priestesses in the Empire of Khokarsa, the books reveal a complex pantheon of gods and goddesses. First and foremost is Kho, known also as the Mother Goddess, the White Goddess, and the Mother of All. She is the central deity of the Khokarsan people. Carefully balanced against Kho is her son Resu, the Flaming God, the god of the sun, the rain, and war. While Resu has been declared the equal of his mother, most Khokarsans still regard Resu as secondary to Kho. At the time *Hadon of Ancient Opar* begins, the priests of Resu have been locked in a delicate struggle for supremacy against the priestesses of Kho for over eight hundred years.

Many other intriguing deities, both lesser and greater, intimately influence everyday life in Khokarsa. There is Adeneth, goddess of sexual passion; Besbesbes, goddess of bees and mead; Bukhla, the goddess of war before she was usurped by Resu; Kasukwa, the river godling; Khuklaqo, the Shapeless Shaper; Khukly, the heron goddess; Lahla, "Kho's fairest daughter," goddess of the moon and patroness of music and poetry; Piqabes, "the green-eyed daughter of Kho," goddess of the sea; the dread Sisisken, "grim ruler of the shadow world"; and Tesemines, goddess of the night. But perhaps none of these Khokarsan deities is as intriguing (especially to ERB enthusiasts) as Sahhindar, the Gray-Eyed God, also the Archer God and the god of plants, of bronze, and of Time. Legend has it that he was doomed to wander in exile at the edge of the world after he stole Time from his mother Kho. A note in the "Chronology of Khokarsa" at the end of *Hadon of Ancient Opar* indicates that Sahhindar is undoubtedly the time traveling character Gribardsun from Farmer's own novel *Time's Last Gift* (I'm hoping Paul Spiteri will do the honors of writing up the Bibliophile for this latter, one of his all-time favorite Farmer novels). Gribardsun, as most Farmer readers are aware, bears a striking resemblance to ERB's famous jungle lord, and his appearance in the Ancient Opar books has brought about much lively discussion in the field of literary archaeology.

Many other aspects of Khokarsan society are revealed in the novels. For example, the reader learns that the empire is held together with totemic glue. Hadon is a member of the Fish-Eagle Totem, while other characters belong to the Ant Totem, the Leopard Totem, or the Pig Totem. These totems are local organizations with widely varied customs. All Khokarsans, however, witness a nine year cycle, represented by "a fish-eagle, a hippopotamus, a green parrot, the hero Gahete, a sea-otter, a horned fish, a honeybee, a millet plant, and the hero Wenqath." Bards are considered to be universally sacred, as are the oracles who inhabit the temples of Kho. And while the queen and high priestess is considered the most wise and powerful, it is the king who has direct control over the military.

The Empire of Khokarsa is vast, spanning the two inland seas of ancient Africa (it cannot truly be called *prehistoric* Africa, as Khokarsa has written history, which has survived to the present day in the form of the golden tablets witnessed by Tarzan in Opar). There are thirty queendoms in the Empire, each ruled by its own high priestess. These cities bear outlandish names such as Dythbeth, Miklemres, Qethruth, Sakawuru, and Wentisuh. Some of the cities along the inland seas, such as Kethna, border on the rebellious. Then there is the pirate stronghold of Mikawuru, which is outright defiant. Thus exists a complex system of both dependent and independent trade, as well as a bountiful variety of localized customs. Beyond the coasts, in regions seldom visited by the Khokarsans, lie the Wild Lands, filled with savage beasts and peoples.

It is against the exotic background described above that *Hadon of Ancient Opar* begins. Hadon, the son of a disgraced *numatenu* (or honored swordsman), sets off in a galley from his home city of Opar, bound for the island of Khokarsa, located thousands of miles away on the north shore of one of ancient Africa's inland seas. There he is to compete in the Great Games, the winner of which will marry the queen and be declared king of the mighty Empire.

Hadon, though noble blood runs in his veins, is the common man. It is only through his own resources and resiliency that he may hope to rise above the misfortunes of his family and become something greater. Together with his good-natured friend Taro and his squat and powerfully muscled nemesis Hewako, Hadon competes in athletic contests and bloodthirsty battles against the Empire's bravest heroes. After competing in racing, the high jump, the high dive, boxing, wrestling, and tightrope walking over ravenous crocodiles, Hadon faces off with wild gorillas, bulls, and leopards. The barbaric spectacle in the Coliseum of the Great Games rivals any of the gory sport in Caligula's Rome.

As Hadon sees his friends and fellow contestants die, he hears whispers that all is not well in the Empire and slowly begins to wake up to the fact that the world is a more complex place than he could have imagined. *Hadon of Ancient Opar* is as much a tale of maturing youth as Farmer's depiction of the sixteen year old Doc Savage in *Escape from Loki*. But Hadon learns quickly. He has not forgotten that it was plotting and politics that crippled his father and forced him to serve as a lowly sweeper of floors in the temple of Kho. The rumblings of King Minruth's ambition to place Resu over Kho disturb the young hero. Still, Hadon's youthful exuberance urges him on. After all, what nineteen year old wouldn't want to be king of an empire and husband to a beautiful queen?

But soon Hadon finds out that winning isn't everything. Minruth has other plans for the hero from Opar. Instead of claiming the crown of victory, Hadon is furious to learn that he must instead clear one more hurdle and lead an expedition to the Wild Lands to retrieve a group of wanderers said to be under the protection of Sahhindar, the Gray-Eyed Archer God. Only then may he be proclaimed king. Thus Hadon finds that what he believed to be the end of his adventures is really only the beginning.

Hadon of Ancient Opar is an epic in the true sense of the word. It is the beginning of the Hero's Journey, the Campbellian mythological archetype. Our hero leaves his home, full of hope and testosterone, ready to conquer the world. When this exuberance begins to wear off, he does not want to accept the call to adventure; but the oracle has decreed it. Begrudgingly, Hadon accepts the task and crosses the threshold into the dangerous realm of the unknown. In the Wild Lands he tests himself against savage enemies and finds his allies in the fair Lalila, her daughter Abeth, the manling Paga, the bard Kebiwabes, the guide Hinokly, and, most unlikely of all, his giant cousin Kwasin, exiled ravager of a priestess of Kho.

Only when Hadon returns from the Wild Lands does he begin to face his real ordeal. Though he might wish to be free of it, Hadon does not turn away from his Hero's Journey. He has been tried by fire in the wilderness and has found love. Now he will do anything, face anyone—even a god—to protect his prize.

I will not try to fool you: *Hadon of Ancient Opar* is not a standalone novel. Anyone who reads the last sentence of the book will not only *have* to track down the sequel but will leap flying from the chair to find out where to obtain a copy. I promise you, it is worth the effort.

Through the Seventh Gate:
Pursuing Farmer's Sources in Savageology

Farmerphile: The Magazine of Philip José Farmer,
No. 6, October 2006

Everyone knows that long ago, on a fateful day in 1970 in a Chicago motel room, Philip José Farmer met Tarzan of the Apes. Farmer's interview of Lord Greystoke is a matter of public record. But did Farmer, the Grandmaster of Science Fiction, ever meet Doc Savage, the Bronze Hero of Technopolis and Exotica?

Never does Farmer mention this in either of his biographies, *Doc Savage: His Apocalyptic Life* (Doubleday, 1973; rpt. Meteor House and Altus Press, 2013) or *Tarzan Alive* (Doubleday, 1972; rpt. Bison Books, 2006), or in any of his many books, short stories, articles, or interviews from his half-a-century-spanning career. Farmer *does* reveal he learned and deduced some of the Savage family history during his genealogical researches into Lord Greystoke's lineage, connecting James Wilder from Sir Arthur Conan Doyle's "Adventure of the Priory School" with Lester Dent's Clark Savage, Sr. (or as Farmer names him, James Clarke Wildman). And yet how to account for the abundance of "new" information presented above and beyond the Doyle connection in Farmer's Doc Savage works—information not revealed to Dent or any of the other "Kenneth Robesons" in the biographical supersagas of the Man of Bronze?[8] To believe that Farmer made it all up is, of course, absurd.

Yes, we could suppose it is possible that Farmer received the exclusive information he presents in *Doc Savage: His Apocalyptic*

---

8. Although an alternate genealogy has been provided for Doc Savage in the new series of novels by Will Murray, the present article only concerns itself with James Clarke Wildman, Jr., the real-life basis for the fictional character.

Life, Escape from Loki (Bantam Books, 1991), and *Tarzan Alive* from a meeting with Clark Savage, Jr. himself, or perhaps one of Doc's aides or even his knockout cousin, Pat. It is true that in 1973 Farmer interviewed Patricia Clarke Lupin Wildman, James Clarke Wildman, Jr.'s daughter,[9] but there is reason to believe that he also received his information from another source.

First let us look at the "new" or "exclusive" information Farmer presents regarding Doc Savage, and from there attempt to elucidate his source or sources. In *Tarzan Alive*, Farmer reveals that Lord Greystoke sent a number of Kavuru elixir pills to his cousin for analysis. Savage then synthesized the formula, and that is why Doc and his aides have not aged since 1933. We may guess this story came to Farmer via "Lord Greystoke." But when? The information about the Kavuru pills and Doc's involvement with them does not appear in Farmer's interview with Greystoke on September 1, 1970. In that interview, Farmer was allowed to look at photostats from the diary of Greystoke's father, but was told that he must not take the photostats with him. Presumably those were the only documents Farmer observed during the interview, so when did our intrepid biographer learn about Doc's synthesis of the Kavuru pills? What other contact did Farmer have with Lord Greystoke?

Presumably a fair amount. For example, in Chapter Four of *Tarzan Alive*, Farmer has intimate knowledge of the report, archived in the British files, that details Lieutenant Paul d'Arnot's first encounter with Tarzan in West Africa. From this we see that Farmer's sources are extensive, and since no other known Tarzanic scholar has been able to locate the British files on Tarzan, the conclusion is that Farmer got the files directly from Lord Greystoke himself. There are numerous other instances of exclusive data re Lord Greystoke in *Tarzan Alive* that indicate Farmer must have had much more extensive contact with the ape-man, at least in terms of an exchange of documents, correspondence or phone conversations, than just his 1970 interview, but to list these would go beyond the scope of this

9. See "A Chronology of Events Pertinent to *The Evil in Pemberley House*" by Win Scott Eckert in *The Evil in Pemberley House Limited Edition Chapbook*, Philip José Farmer and Win Scott Eckert (Subterranean Press, 2009).

article. We do know for certain that after the 1970 interview Greystoke agreed to mail "portions of his memoirs" to Farmer (see *Mother Was a Lovely Beast*, Chilton, 1974), one extract of which has been reprinted in the new Bison Books edition of *Tarzan Alive*.

The point remains that some of Farmer's sources on Doc Savage came directly via Lord Greystoke. But may we assume that all of it did? I do not believe so.

In *Tarzan Alive*, we next learn from Farmer that Doc's mother was Arronaxe Larsen, and that "[t]here is little doubt that Arronaxe's father was Wolf Larsen" from Jack London's *The Sea Wolf*. This information seems to have come from Farmer's research into the Wold Newton family utilizing Burke's *Peerage*, as well as the comparative study of eye color in literary characters. However, certain evidence supports the conclusion that those sources may have been only Farmer's cover, or, at most, merely his secondary sources.

Farmer himself, I believe, alludes to his main source for his exclusive information on the life Clark Savage, Jr. in *Doc Savage: His Apocalyptic Life*. In fact, he states the source outright, though he does not claim to have had access to it. Lester Dent, Doc's first biographer, was also privy to this source, though if he had full access to it, he did not divulge much of its contents in the Doc supersagas.

Farmer's source for most of his exclusive information on Doc Savage is, I believe, the same top-secret intelligence files that Dent references in the Doc Savage supersaga *The Golden Man* (Street & Smith, April 1941). In this story, a mysterious "golden man" appears from the sea who can predict future events and knows many things from the past that he cannot possibly know, including Doc's origins. The golden man says that he knows Doc was "born on the tiny schooner *Orion* in the shallow cove at the north end of Andros Island." Doc is shocked, as he is the only living person who should know this information about his past. The golden man also knows that Baron Orrest Karl Lestzky is dying in Vienna that night. Lestzky is the only other person alive at the time who really understands the intricacies of Doc's brain operating technique to cure criminals. At the end of the adventure, Doc discovers the golden man is really Paul Hest, an intelligence agent of an unnamed country (presumably Germany) who had temporarily suffered from amnesia.

How may we surmise that Farmer himself has seen this intelligence file on Doc? Because of a name Hest cites from the files: *Baron* Orrest *Karl* Lestzky (italics mine). As I have illustrated elsewhere (see my "The Green Eyes Have It—Or Are They Blue?" in *Myths for the Modern Age: Philip José Farmer's Wold Newton Universe*, MonkeyBrain Books, 2005), the character Baron Colonel von Hessel from Farmer's Doc Savage novel *Escape from Loki* is an analogue for the character Baron Karl, the so-called Playboy Prince from the original Doc Savage supersaga *Fortress of Solitude* (Street & Smith, October 1938).[10] Baron von Hessel, like Baron Orrest Karl Lestzky, is a surgeon with exceptional skills who knows Doc. The two barons are, I propose, one man. Hest calls Lestzky Doc's "friend," but surely this is a facetious remark. They are more like nemeses. Doc certainly would have been keeping tabs on Lestzky, the man who, as Baron Karl, worked in such close quarters with Doc's other grand nemesis, John Sunlight. This is why Doc is moved by news of Lestzky's death—not because they are friends, but because Doc has been following the baron's career very closely since he first matched wits with him in Camp Loki in 1918. Those still in doubt need only reference *Escape from Loki* to see that von Hessel was privy to secret intelligence files on Doc and his family. "'Our Intelligence has a dossier on you and Doctor Clark Savage, Senior,'" von Hessel states. "'Quite a lengthy one.'" Again, Doc is astounded.[11]

Now we begin to understand how extensive the German intelligence files truly were, and because Farmer cites the files

---

10. The two supersagas featuring Doc's nemesis John Sunlight, *The Fortress of Solitude* and *The Devil Genghis*, have been reprinted in a convenient double-novel edition (Nostalgia Ventures, 2006).

11. Rick Lai, in his excellent work *The Bronze Age: An Alternative Doc Savage Chronology* (Fading Shadows, 1992; reprinted and expanded as *The Revised Complete Chronology of Bronze*, Altus Press, 2012), points out the intelligence dossier mentioned in *Escape from Loki* must be the same as that referred to in *The Golden Man*; I am sure other dedicated Doc Savage readers caught the reference as well.

Keep Your Mouth Shut

farmerphile

Issue No. 6
October 2006

and *Up from the Bottomless Pit* - Part 6

in both *Escape from Loki* and *Doc Savage: His Apocalyptic Life*, it becomes clear that this is where he garnered much his exclusive information on Doc. It is no wonder Farmer chose to write about Doc's adventure in Germany during the Great War: the Germans' files on Doc would have certainly concentrated on those years.

However it was that Farmer managed to get extensive access to the dossier, there can be little doubt this is where he corroborated the research he had sussed out of Burke's *Peerage* on the Savage/Wildman genealogy. There, in the top-secret German files, he learned that Hubert Robertson and Ned Land were aboard the *Orion* when it sank less than a year after Doc's birth. He confirmed that Doc's mother's name was Arronaxe, and that her father was the blue-green eyed master of the *Sea Wolf*. And in those files, he read about the slippery Baron von Hessel, a man of many names, who would one day again duel with Doc. Further, perhaps something in the files led Farmer to another source, the aforementioned Patricia Wildman, who then related to Farmer the events of *The Evil in Pemberley House* (Subterranean Press, 2009). Or it may be that Patricia provided Farmer with the German files. We do not know.

How I would love to have a look at those files—what more might we learn about the history of the Man of Bronze! But something tells me, Farmer had a good reason for disguising their contents as fiction. Some things are better left to the imagination.

The Grand Master of Peoria

Published online at *The Zone*, November 2006

Casual sex with alien species is so common these days that it is hard to open a science fiction novel or turn on the television without being exposed to it. China Miéville offhandedly describes the intimate relations between an insectoid khepri and his humanoid protagonist in *Perdido Street Station*. A character on *Star Trek: Voyager* returns to his ship after contracting an extraterrestrial STD and the ship's doctor unceremoniously treats and chides his careless patient. Is anyone today even mildly shocked by these examples?

Now travel back in time to the early 1950s. A young new writer, struggling to support his family by working overtime in a steel mill, submits his first piece of science fiction to *Astounding*. John W. Campbell doesn't want it. The writer sends the story to H. L. Gold at *Galaxy*, but the manuscript is again returned. The story is just too mature for a genre marketed toward adolescent males: "there is no sex in science fiction." Disgruntled, the writer resigns to try one last time and submits the story to Sam Mines at *Startling Stories*. This time comes a different response. Mines, sensing he has a winner, albeit a controversial one, buys the story and publishes it in his August 1952 issue. The story is "The Lovers" and the unknown author bears the strangely exotic sounding name of Philip José Farmer. The response from readers is electric. "Letters poured into *Startling Stories* praising the story," says Michael Croteau, webmaster of *The Official Philip José Farmer Home Page*, who has extensively researched the history of Farmer's groundbreaking novella. "Several commented on how good the story was for a first-time author," Croteau continues, "while others speculated that the story must have been written by an established pro who used a pseudonym because of the story's subject matter."

"The Lovers" tells the tale of Hal Yarrow, an Earthman sent on assignment to the planet Ozagen, who finds himself daring to rebel against his own planet's religious fundamentalism by engaging in intimate contact with an alien. The story is tame by today's standards, but the mix of Farmer's raw talent, his ingenious description of photokinetic reproduction, and subject matter that was risqué for its day led to an ecstatic reaction among science fiction readers, who suddenly found their misbegotten genre gaining some maturity. "So many letters came in [to *Startling Stories*] over the next several months," says Croteau, "that six months or so after the story appeared, people started writing letters about the letters." In fact, letters about Farmer's story continued to be printed consistently in the magazine for the next two years. Many came from readers who had missed the August issue in which the novella appeared and desperately wanted to get their hands on a copy so they could join in the excitement. It was not surprising that in the year following the publication of "The Lovers," Farmer won the Hugo Award for "most promising new talent." "Science fiction never had any sexual relationships in it," says the now eighty-eight-year-old Farmer. "I felt that that was a part of life and so should be a part of SF." History has proved Farmer unquestionably right.

But like his character Hal Yarrow in "The Lovers," Farmer is a *joat*, an acronym for "jack-of-all-trades." More specifically he is a literary joat. Not content with resting on the laurels of his pioneering story, Farmer continued to write speculative fiction over the next half a century, covering just about every topic under the sun with a compelling combination of realism and the fantastic that is his trademark.

After his initial success, Farmer went on to publish a number of SF stories, including "Sail On, Sail On," which Farmer says is his most often reprinted short story, and "Moth and Rust," a sequel of sorts to *The Lovers*. But ironically Farmer's promising career threatened to stall in 1953 when he entered the Shasta

Science-Fiction Novel Contest. Farmer wrote a 150,000-word novel, *Owe for the Flesh*, and won the contest; but after he went to pick up his prize, he discovered that Shasta had used the prize money to invest in a hair-brained scheme that had gone sour. Farmer was left penniless and, with his new novel hanging in limbo, he was forced to quit writing full time and take up a job as a dairy laborer. Farmer, however, endured, and years later the novel he had submitted to the Shasta contest became the basis for his Hugo Award-winning novel *To Your Scattered Bodies Go*, the first volume of the Riverworld series. Certainly one of the grandest undertakings of his legacy, if not in the entirety of science fiction, Riverworld seemed the perfect vehicle for Farmer's fertile mind. In this new creation, every person who has ever walked the face of the Earth is resurrected on an alien world and left to fend for her- or himself. The Riverworld series spanned five volumes, and was followed by two anthologies including stories by authors other than Farmer, and more recently a Sci-Fi Channel movie, *Riverworld*.

In the late 1960s, Farmer began writing pastiches of his favorite pop lit characters, and in the early 1970s, he wrote two "fictional biographies," *Tarzan Alive: The Definitive Biography of Lord Greystoke* and *Doc Savage: His Apocalyptic Life*. Using a premise almost as staggeringly expansive as that of Riverworld, he elaborated what he called the Wold Newton family, a genetic lineage of characters from popular literature whose ancestors were exposed to a radioactive meteorite. Farmer's presentation of the Wold Newton genealogy is erudite, complex, and straight-faced, and the subtlety of his sly, tongue-in-cheek wit simultaneously reveals the genius of both master scholar and trickster.

Farmer's fictional genealogy has continued to inspire several genre authors. In the mid-1970s, Farmer granted permission for J.T. Edson to make extensive use of the Wold Newton genealogy in his Bunduki series, as well as in his Western novels. Horror author Kim Newman, while not using Farmer's genealogy per se, remains heavily influenced by Farmer's frequent borrowing of characters from literature. Spider Robinson continues to use Farmer's character Ralph von Wau Wau, a super-intelligent talking dog cited in one of the Wold Newton "biographies," in his notoriously pun-filled Callahan series. And those familiar with Alan Moore's comic book series *The League of Extraordinary Gentlemen* may experience a feeling of déjà vu when encountering many of the pulp adventure characters discussed by Farmer in his Wold Newton works. This is not a coincidence, as Moore himself has cited Farmer as an influence. Farmer admits he did not see the movie based on Moore's comic. "I understand," he says, "that it was too cartoonish."

Much as devotees of Sir Arthur Conan Doyle's Sherlock Holmes canon have carried on pseudo-academic studies of their favorite character, enthusiasts of the Wold Newton family have continued and expanded upon Farmer's faux genealogical concept. In 1997, Win Scott Eckert put up the first website devoted exclusively to what he calls the Wold Newton Universe, which goes beyond Farmer's Wold Newton family to encompass an even wider array of fictional characters. "I think the overarching draw of the concept," says Eckert, "is the ability to blend characters in new and interesting ways, and to see the characters against the backdrop of a larger universe." Eckert is the editor of *Myths For The Modern Age: Philip José Farmer's Wold Newton Universe* (MonkeyBrain Books, 2005), a first-of-its-kind anthology themed exclusively around the Wold Newton Universe. While nine selections in this new collection are by Farmer, the bulk of Eckert's anthology is composed of essays by other scholars, writers, and pop-culture historians paying tribute to Farmer's postmodern literary conceit.

Farmer himself, inspired by the pantheon of fictional characters he encountered during his youth, has fulfilled his childhood ambition to write novels in the universes of Oz (*A Barnstormer in Oz*, 1982), Doc Savage (*Escape From Loki*, 1991), and Tarzan (*The Dark Heart of Time*, 1999). He achieved another aim in 2001, when—in recognition of his lasting contributions to the field of science fiction—he was awarded the Grand Master Award, the highest honor granted by the Science Fiction Writers of America. In the same year he was also awarded a

A
N
C

TODAY'S SCIENCE FICTION—TOMORROW'S FACT ·   AUG. 25c

STARTLING *stories*

A THRILLING PUBLICATION

featuring **THE LOVERS** *a novel by Philip José Farmer*
and **THE HOUR OF THE MORTALS**
a novelet by Kendell Foster Crossen

World Fantasy Award for a lifetime of achievement. With the satisfaction of having realized these goals, little new has been published by Farmer until now, when it seems a Farmerian renaissance may be in the making.

One of the new publications is *Farmerphile: The Magazine of Philip José Farmer*, launched in summer 2005 by Michael Croteau, after finding a treasure trove of never before published gems in the grand master's basement. "Having had the privilege of reading all these unpublished stories," says Croteau, "my first thought was, how can we make these available to Phil's fans? Publishing a magazine completely by and about Philip José Farmer is something I have wanted to do for years, so this seemed the perfect time to finally start it." *Farmerphile* is a print digest available through Farmer's official website and promises at least ten issues bearing new content by Farmer, including the serialization of his "lost" novel, *Up from the Bottomless Pit*, a suspense thriller about the ultimate disaster in the oil industry.

Also hitting the shelves is *Pearls from Peoria* (Subterranean Press, 2006), a mammoth hardcover collection that editor Paul Spiteri says is "a culmination of over two years' work to collect, edit, and illustrate the rarer pieces in the Philip José Farmer canon." Among the unpublished gems in the book is Farmer's previously unreleased screen treatment for a sequel to George Pal's 1976 *Doc Savage: Man of Bronze* feature film, as well as a host of brilliant but little known short stories, such as "The Terminalization of J. G. Ballard," "A Princess of Terra," and "The Doge Whose Barque Was Worse Than His Bight."

And if that isn't enough, two additional collections reprinting vintage Farmer have found their way into print. Fittingly, *The Best of Philip José Farmer* (Subterranean Press, 2006) includes the original novella version of Farmer's classic "The Lovers," while *Strange Relations* (Baen Books, 2006) features the expanded novel.

Thus it seems that Farmer's opus has come full circle. The grand master, who has oft used immortality as a theme in his works, has attained his own kind of literary immortality. Over half a century after he shocked the science fiction world and urged it to mature, Farmer's legacy continues in the hearty reprinting of his works and by his marked influence on writers, both past and present. "Robert Heinlein once wrote and thanked me for breaking taboos," Farmer says, recalling a bygone age. "He said it helped him in a book he was doing. I don't recall if that was *Stranger in a Strange Land* or not, but he did dedicate that book to me." Asked what he thinks is his single most lasting impact on science fiction, Farmer doesn't hesitate: "Giving younger writers the courage to come forward with new ideas as I did with 'The Lovers.'"

Philip José Farmer on the Road to the Emerald City

Introduction to *Up from the Bottomless Pit and Other Stories* by Philip José Farmer, ed. Christopher Paul Carey, Subterranean Press, 2007

Philip José Farmer's words glitter in the dreamer's mind like Dorothy's magic shoes in the brilliant sunlight of Oz; they teleport us to lands fantastic and never before imagined. With a vision so uniquely creative that it may only be called Farmerian, Phil has fathered a pluriverse of outlandishly entrancing ideas. He gave science fiction its first mature taste of alien sex; he mixed Freud with zoology; he sent a space-faring atheist priest on a mission that would unwittingly hasten the birth of God's evil twin; he resurrected everyone who ever lived along the banks of a 10,000,000-mile river; he made his heroic alter ego break through the walls of our universe with a song; he excavated the ancient motherland of Tarzan's Opar, barnstormed over Oz, and popped synthesized elixir pills with Doc Savage; and each day of the week he woke up a new man, ready to challenge the system that sought to bind his free-soaring spirit.

Like Odin, the All-Father god of the Norse peoples, Phil's glimmering eye watches keenly over all of his multifaceted creations (an analogy which may not be too much of a stretch for a man who proudly acknowledges descent from Thorfinn the Skull-Splitter, Ivar the Boneless, and Sigurd Snake-in-the-Eye). But also like the God of Many Names, the Grand Master of Peoria has peered with his all-seeing eye into the dark side of human nature, as well as the light, and the stories in this volume— collected here for the first time—bear witness to this fact.

Though Phil wears well the mantle of Maker of Universes, of

worlds fantastic and sublime, an unerring sense of realism pervades all of his work. This execution of realism, held in suspension with the unbelievable, is in fact what makes his created worlds stand apart from those of his world-building peers. Of course, every writer of speculative fiction attempts to balance the real with the unreal; but among the field's many successes, few achieve their goal with such an ardent meticulousness as does Phil. Phil's ideas, no matter how weird or unorthodox, are backed by rock-solid reasoning. Sometimes that reasoning may lie shrouded in the dark well of the human soul—but rest assured that Phil has crawled down the well-shaft with a portable laboratory in hand and thoroughly analyzed the gurgling ectoplasmic goo at the bottom. He knows well his characters' motivations, and the laws of the worlds in which they live, even if they do not.

Most of the stories in this collection are set in our own world, which—as Phil's touch always lends a sense of the compelling—I hesitate to call mundane. Here we get a unique glimpse of what might have been: Philip José Farmer as a writer of mainstream literature. Though Phil was nurtured at a young age on the works of Sir Arthur Conan Doyle, H. Rider Haggard, and Edgar Rice Burroughs, his childhood years were also spent poring over the pages of Cervantes, Milton, Swift, and Homer. Phil has described how his youthful love of pop lit receded as he further explored classic literature as an adult. He went on to earn a Bachelor's degree in English Literature in 1950, and, while still attending school and afterward, submitted his stories to such mainstream publications as *Good Housekeeping* and *The Saturday Evening Post*. Heralding what looked to be a promising career writing literary fiction, the prestigious *Post* agreed to purchase his story "O'Brien and Obrenov," if only Phil would excise the drunk scene; but Phil, never one to bend willingly to censorship, stuck to his literary guns and the sale went to *Adventure* in 1946.

The path to a career in mainstream fiction would end here for Phil. His next sale would not be until 1952 with his groundbreaking science fiction novella "The Lovers." From this point on Phil would rekindle his interest in the fantasy literature

Up from the Bottomless Pit

and Other Stories

PHILIP JOSÉ FARMER

of his youth, while raising high the bar for his newly chosen genre, science fiction.

And yet the present collection—which includes seven short stories that are unarguably mainstream, and a speculative novel which, after the horrifying events of September 11, 2001 and Hurricane Katrina, no longer seems so hard to imagine—is not merely a footnote in the career of a much lauded science fiction giant. In this collection, even in the four selections that may be labeled science fiction or fantasy and the three nonfiction pieces, we see Phil employing his secret weapon: his sense of unerring realism, albeit more often than not fused with his trademark wit.

Reading through the early stories included here, a veil is lifted that reveals with stark clarity what puts the Farmer in Farmerian. It is not enough to say that Phil has a boundless imagination and that he is adept at world building. Remember Phil's Odin-like eye, with which he scrutinizes human nature, and indeed everything old and new under the sun and beyond. While the scholar of a later day might debate whether the prose reads a tad less smoothly in "The Essence of the Poison" than it will eleven years later in "The Lovers," it remains clear that in each of the stories at hand Phil's vision cuts deep into the soul-stuff.

But there is also plenty here to satisfy the many lovers of Phil's science fictional works. *Up from the Bottomless Pit*, while set in our world, is fantastic in scale; and though such an oil industry catastrophe has yet to occur (and hopefully never will), it is with uncanny Vernean foresight that Phil describes how humanity responds, or in many cases fails, in the face of wide-scale disaster. "The Rebels Unthawed"—a television treatment first written in 1966 for *Star Trek* but reworked here into an original piece (with a special introduction by *Star Trek* and Farmerian scholar Win Scott Eckert)—will certainly intrigue any student of science fiction history. That the surreal, politically charged "The Unnaturals" and compellingly prophetic "The Frames" have languished for so many years in a filing cabinet in Phil's basement is—as a certain Peorian writer might say—a crime of Brobdingnagian proportions; these two stories present a welcome time capsule from the 1970s, a period when Phil was arguably at the height of his literary powers.

First published serially in the limited-run small press digest *Farmerphile: The Magazine of Philip José Farmer* (2005–2007), the novel, stories, and speeches that follow this introduction have never previously appeared in book form. Special thanks from both Phil and myself must go to Michael Croteau, Paul Spiteri, Win Scott Eckert, and Bill Schafer, all of whom worked heroically to put this volume together. And yet that these works survived to be recognized and published so many years after they were written remains more than anything a testament to Phil's own fierce determination. Do not forget this is the man who once proclaimed, "If we were not given immortal souls, then we must create our own." Phil, when faced with insurmountable odds, is not one to knuckle under. And with the publication of this volume he, along with all lovers of his work, will no doubt take great satisfaction at watching these glittering gems...perhaps made from the same magical substance as Dorothy's slippers?... as they dematerialize from some neglected pocket universe and reappear in our own.

The Archaeology of Khokarsa:
Sources in Farmer's Ancient Oparian Motherland

Farmerphile: The Magazine of Philip José Farmer,
No. 9, July 2007
Winner of 2008 Farmerphile Award for Best Article

"'Good stranger,' I continued, 'I am ill and lost.
Direct me, I beseech you, to Carcosa.'" —*Bierce*

When Philip José Farmer's *Hadon of Ancient Opar* and *Flight to Opar* hit the bookshelves in the mid-1970s, faithful initiates of the Burroughsian tradition no doubt winked at one another conspiratorially when they brought the books home and read of Hadon navigating the tunnels under Opar, climbing a narrow flight of spiral steps, and emerging on the top of an enormous boulder. They knew that this was the same path Tarzan of the Apes had trodden in *The Return of Tarzan* (1913), and that the ape-man would one day stand upon that same giant boulder (although by Tarzan's day the rock had weathered into a kopje). Similarly, readers of H. Rider Haggard no doubt smiled at the names Lalila, Paga, and Wi (characters drawn from Haggard's 1927 novel *Allan and the Ice Gods*), and how they must have chuckled when, on multiple occasions, Farmer uses the adjective "haggard" to describe beauteous though fatigued Lalila! In crafting his ancient Khokarsa—the prehistoric empire that spawned Tarzan's Opar—Farmer drew on many more sources than just these examples. The present article seeks to examine such less well-known sources or those hitherto unknown altogether.

In terms of developing theme in his series about life and death in ancient Africa, one of Farmer's strongest influences was Jessie L. Weston's classic examination of Arthurian legend, *From*

Ritual to Romance (1920). A precursor to the work of Joseph Campbell, Weston's book takes a cross-cultural approach to determine a myth's essential meaning, and in one chapter the author discusses a particular theme common to both the tales of King Arthur and ancient Indian *Rig-Veda* hymns. Weston calls this theme "The Freeing of the Waters," in which the fate of the land is tied to the actions of the people who inhabit it, and above all, the deeds of its hero. "Tradition relates," writes Weston, "that the seven great rivers of India had been imprisoned by the evil giant, Vrita, or Ahi, whom Indra slew, thereby releasing the streams from their captivity." Anyone who has seen the movie *Indiana Jones and the Temple of Doom* will immediately recognize this theme, whereby the hero completes his mission and miraculously drought and famine are replaced by blessed rain and an abundance of crops.

Those who have read *The Return of Tarzan* may recall La's recounting of Opar's history to the ape-man, in which she states that more than ten thousand years ago a "great calamity" occurred to her city's distant motherland. This is the impending sense of doom which hovers constantly over Farmer's Khokarsan civilization. At any moment the reader expects La's great calamity to rattle apart the island of Khokarsa, and indeed many tremors and convulsions of the earth do occur throughout the series. Each quake is seen as "Kho's wrath" upon the inhabitants of Khokarsa, who have sought to place the impudent sungod Resu above the righteous mother goddess. Similarly, when the pile city of Reba burns to its embers in *Flight to Opar*, it is the wickedness of the people who are to blame. Just as in Weston's thesis, the fate of the lands is determined by the actions of its inhabitants. Farmer goes further to amplify this theme by having his characters possess accurate and repeated premonitions of doom, which occur in visions, dreams, or feelings of general foreboding.

Since Farmer's series ended prematurely, the reader ultimately never gets to witness the great calamity and how the hero's actions might have influenced or diffused the impending disaster. However, because it is known that the city of Opar survives in the time of Tarzan, the reader does have an understanding that Hadon, in some sense, must have succeeded in his task. His people have endured the cataclysmic eruptions that sank the motherland, although in due course the Oparians must have faced great hardships. Eventually, the survivors will be forced to intermingle with the native paranthropoids, and the high priestess of Opar will forsake Kho and become Resu's high vicar. Still, the reader knows that Hadon's bloodline survives over ten thousand years into the future through Tarzan's La, a prediction made by the oracle at Kloepeth in *Flight to Opar*. Following Weston's theme, this was due to the successful completion of Hadon's task in bringing his daughter to be born in Opar.

"The Freeing of the Waters" theme is also inversely illustrated in Plato's story of Atlantis, and one can only imagine that Farmer had this in mind as he wrote *Hadon* and *Flight*. In the *Critias*, Plato writes of the once righteous and semidivine inhabitants of Atlantis:

> So long as these principles and their divine nature remained unimpaired the prosperity which we have ascribed to them continued to grow. But when the divine element in them became weakened by frequent admixture with mortal stock, and their human traits became predominant, they ceased to be able to carry their prosperity with moderation. (*Timaeus and Critias*, trans. Desmond Lee, Penguin, 1981)

Though Burroughs does not state that Opar is a lost colony of Atlantis in *The Return of Tarzan*, he does make the claim in *Tarzan and the Golden Lion* (1923). However, ERB scholars such as John Harwood and Frank Brueckel, with whom Farmer consulted during the creation of his Khokarsa, argue that Burroughs' "Atlantis" was not located on the Atlantic Ocean but rather on a great inland sea that existed in Africa circa ten thousand years ago (*Heritage of the Flaming God*, eds. Alan Hanson and Michael Winger, Waziri Publications, 1999). Farmer also covers this ground in his *Tarzan Alive: A Definitive Biography of Lord Greystoke* (1972), though by the time he wrote his Ancient Opar series he had pushed the date back to twelve thousand years ago. It seems likely that Farmer's decision to emphasize Weston's thesis was at least partially an attempt to explain Burroughs' conflation of the legendary Atlantis with Opar's ancient motherland. Interestingly, Pierre Benoit, a French author following the Burroughs and Haggard traditions, also placed Atlantis in inland Africa in his 1919 novel *L'Atlantide*.

Just as Plato relates in the *Critias* that the Atlanteans were once gods who had lost their divinity and fallen victim to their more mortal vices, so Farmer portrays his Khokarsans. Hadon's giant cousin Kwasin is said to be "like a hero of old," emphasizing that the glory days of the Khokarsans have long since passed and the empire has begun to weaken; and though Kwasin bears some of the attributes of a god, his character, like many in the land, is deeply flawed by greed, lust, and overbearing ego. The fate of Kwasin, who is last seen swinging his mighty axe in a battle with Minruth's soldiers, is never learned, but unless he manages to miraculously redeem himself his destiny will doubtless follow that of Plato's Atlanteans and be very bleak indeed.

Early in his plans for his series, Farmer decided he would have two heroes appearing alternately throughout the books: Hadon of Opar and his cousin Kwasin of Dythbeth. Now that it has come to light that Farmer based his main theme on Weston's thesis in *From Ritual to Romance*, this makes perfect sense. Hadon, succeeding in his quests by his exhibitions of honesty, loyalty, and integrity, would succeed in "freeing the waters." By his valiant actions of heroism, he would save his home queendom of Opar from utter destruction in La's great calamity. Conversely, Kwasin, by his very vanity, rage, and undisciplined nature, might have unwittingly contributed to the total catastrophe that was surely to have befallen Khokarsa at the series' conclusion. After all, he is a native of the island of Khokarsa.

When conceiving the series, Farmer originally intended that Hadon would "slay the dragon" that stalked the jungles along Ancient Opar's southern inland sea. Again, this was to echo Weston's "Freeing of the Waters" theme, although this time very literally as Hadon freed the Kemuwopar of a terrorizing monster based on the ancient Babylonian creature known as the *sirrush*. Farmer had been inspired by a chapter he had read in Willy Ley's book *Exotic Zoology* (Viking Press, 1959). Ley claimed that the dragon-like beast depicted on the Gate of Ishtar at Babylon was based on a living animal, reported to have been seen in modern times in central Africa. The idea of the *sirrush* also appears in the deuterocanonical Biblical parable Bel and the Dragon, in which the Babylonians are seen to worship one of the beasts as their deity before Daniel decrees it a false god and poisons it. Not the first modern author to entertain writing a story based on the *sirrush* legend, Farmer was preceded by L. Sprague de Camp's *The Dragon of the Ishtar Gate* (Lancer, 1968). The *sirrush* in that story is also said to exist in Africa (and one may only conjecture that de Camp had also read Willy Ley's book), although the creature in the end turns out to be a hoax. Farmer's story of the *sirrush* would certainly have featured a living creature and much heroic adventure, but for whatever reason he abandoned the storyline, though not the idea. The *sirrush* still appears, albeit offstage, in the form of the diorite and basalt statues of the *r''ok'og'a* that Hadon encounters as he arrives at the city of Khokarsa in *Hadon of Ancient Opar*.

If Farmer had proceeded as originally planned, Hadon's quest to slay the dragon would have echoed very closely the quest of Jason and his Argonauts to retrieve the Golden Fleece. In that myth, Jason sets out to retrieve the Fleece, which is guarded by a dragon, so that he may be placed on the throne of Iolcus in Thessaly. Similarly it may be imagined that Hadon, in this early conception of the story, would have been sent out by Minruth to slay the dragon that hunted along the shores of the great inland seas. While this plot point never occurs in Farmer's published book, the idea of a quest that would put Hadon on the throne of Khokarsa survives in the form of his mission to retrieve Lalila, Abeth, and Pag from the Wild Lands, and in its way that plot point remains a tribute to the ancient Greek myth of Jason and the Argonauts.

Throughout the two Ancient Opar novels, allusions to the myths of various cultures abound. For instance, the frequent

The Rebels Unthawed

farmerphile

Issue No. 9
July 2007

IN THIS ISSUE!
- Robert R. Barrett
- Christopher Paul Carey
- Paul Spiteri
- Win Scott Eckert
- Dennis E. Power
- Danny Adams
- Charles Berlin
- Shannon Robicheaux
- Keith Howell
- Chuck Loridans

And previously
unpublished works by
Philip José Farmer

and *Up from the Bottomless Pit* - Part 9

plagues which sweep across the empire are inspired by the Ten Plagues of Egypt as described in the book of Exodus. Much of Farmer's Khokarsan religion comes directly from Robert Graves' *The White Goddess* (1948), which proposed a common origin for the majority of European goddess figures as well as their ousting by the worshipers of a monotheistic god. And Farmer's descriptions of the oracle of Kho come straight out of Euripides' *Ion* and other ancient accounts of the Greek Oracle of Delphi, in which an old hag sits within a temple upon a three-legged stool, breathes in intoxicating gas that rises from a crack in the floor, and utters vague prophecies that will shake the foundations of the empire.

Many of the characters in the novels also stem from ancient, and sometimes modern, myth. Kwasin, while originally to be called Khonan by Farmer as a play on Robert E. Howard's barbarian hero Conan, was in the end based on the enormously strong Greek hero Heracles (or the Roman Hercules) and the Sumerian hero Gilgamesh. Further, Kwasin's (and Hadon's) travels through the Wild Lands echo the wanderings of Greek Odysseus, and the name of the series' antihero is derived from Kwasind, Hiawatha's Indian strongman friend from Longfellow's *The Song of Hiawatha* (1855). In his "The Purple Distance" (*Pearls from Peoria*, Subterranean Press, 2006), Farmer cites many similarities between the characters Hiawatha and Tarzan of the Apes, so it is not surprising the author decided a character based on Kwasind would feel at home in a series sparked by a lost city discovered by the lord of the jungle.

By using Haggard's Laleela (Lalila) as a character, Farmer may have meant to draw reference to the Akkadian mother goddess A-a (which perhaps Farmer took as a derivation of "Lalila," i.e., "Lalila" > "aa"), whose name meant "night," hence alluding to the meaning of Lalila's own name, "moon of change." This also may have been Farmer's subtle cue that Lalila was a predecessor to Haggard's Ayesha, as another spelling of A-a is Aya (i.e. Aya > Ayesha). It should be noted that A-a was the consort of the Akkadian sungod Shamash, thus reinforcing Farmer's own Khokarsan dichotomy of Kho and Resu.

As alluded to at the start of this article, Lalila and Paga feature prominently in Haggard's *Allan and the Ice Gods*, which serves as a sort of prelude to *Hadon of Ancient Opar*. While much attention has been given to the Burroughs connections in Farmer's Ancient Opar novels, the available literature on the books' Haggardian elements is scattered and sparse. This is unfortunate, as one of the important subplots of the book and more than one significant theme stem directly from Haggard. The important subplot is the Ax of Victory, which Paga crafted from meteoritic iron for the hero Wi in *Allan and the Ice Gods*. Haggard went to great lengths to recount the history of the ax in his novels, from its creation by Pag in *Ice Gods*, to its inheritance by the great Zulu warrior Umslopogaas when he became leader of the "People of the Ax" in *Nada the Lily* (1892), to the fateful role of the ax during the battle against the giant Rezu in *She and Allan* (1921), and finally ending with the ax's destruction by Umslopogaas in the climactic scene of the classic adventure *Allan Quatermain* (1887). Farmer had once planned to write as many as twelve books in the Ancient Opar series, including the story of how Hadon's son Kohr eventually acquired the ax and brought it with him when he founded the city of Kôr, which appears as a lost city in Haggard's novels (see David Pringle's interview with Farmer in *Vector* #81, June 1977). By bringing the ax within his own series, Farmer managed to fill in the missing story of the legendary weapon; but more than that, its inclusion may have brought new retrospective meaning to Haggard's work.

In his article "Astar of Opar: The Secret Origin of Sumuru" (*The Wold Newton Universe* website, http://www.pjfarmer. com/woldnewton/Astar.pdf/), pulp expert and creative mythographer Rick Lai points out that the giant Rezu from *She and Allan* bears a striking resemblance to Farmer's character Kwasin. Even more curious is the fact that Rezu's Achilles' heel is Umslopogaas' Ax of Victory and that Rezu seems to be a near immortal. The present article does not seek to employ the methods of creative mythography, but any reader of Farmer who has read *She and Allan* is left wondering if perhaps Kwasin somehow survived the great calamity of Khokarsa and partook of an longevity treatment similar to that of Tarzan or Ayesha.[12] Or Rezu may be a descendant of Kwasin, perchance through one of the many children he spawned while roaming the Wild Lands. In any case, if it is Kwasin himself, by the time of *She and Allan* he has for some unknown reason turned against his upbringing and forsaken the mother goddess in favor of the sungod.

Of course, the name Rezu itself appears in Farmer's Khokarsa as "Resu" the sungod. This provides an interesting insight into the author's "reverse engineering" world building. By tying in Haggard's ancient cultures with his own, Farmer ingeniously creates a faux history that justifies Burroughs' lost race cultures (and also "explains" some cultural survivals in real life cultures, such as sun worship in ancient Egypt). Just as Brueckel and Harwood proposed that the lost cities discovered by Tarzan were the remnants of a single motherland culture (Central African Atlantis, i.e., Farmer's Khokarsa), Farmer goes further to illustrate that Haggard's lost cities are also post-deluge remnants of that same ancient motherland. What is ingenious here is that Farmer picked up on a little observed thread flowing through both Burroughs' and Haggard's lost races: the similarity of their matriarchal-based religious structures. Here we see Farmer not just writing simple pastiche but rather innovating within tradition on a quite sophisticated level. The matriarchal element repeats itself frequently in Haggard's fiction, from the tales of Ayesha, to the Zu-Vendis of *Allan Quatermain*, and on to *The Ivory Child* (1916), in which the "Oracle of the Child" (the "Child" being a sacred idol in the story) is always a woman with a half-moon birthmark—thus correlating with Farmer's Khokarsan oracles, who are always female and have religious ties to the moon. In this latter novel, the religious matriarchy is balanced against a male ruling class headed by a king who is addressed as Simba, meaning "lion." (Interestingly, Farmer originally planned to use a word meaning "great lion" to

---

12. As concerns Rezu, such a treatment is mentioned in *She and Allan*, although it seems to have occurred much later than 12,000 years ago.

represent the King of Khokarsa, though he later dropped this idea.) Perceiving the strange mix of matriarchy and patriarchy throughout the lost races of Burroughs and Haggard, Farmer decided to incorporate Haggard's work into his own and in this way caught the spark of a grand tradition.

Because Haggard explained the correlation between some of his lost cities and ancient Egypt, Farmer's merging of Haggard's lost races into his own served to flesh out the entire historical landscape of fictional Africa in a way that was anthropologically and almost uncannily sound. In Farmer's creative fusion of Burroughs, Haggard, Brueckel, and Harwood, the destruction of Khokarsa in the great calamity gave birth to numerous lost cities across the African continent in which the struggle between the mother goddess and the sungod existed in a diverse spectrum. In some of the cities, either the priests or the priestesses continued to rule. In others, like Tarzan's Opar, a compromise had been reached in which the priestesses presided over religious functions while worshiping the sungod. In yet other lost cities, like Ayesha's Kôr, the battle between the priests and the priestesses still raged twelve thousand years after the fall of Khokarsa.

If one were to superimpose the "Map of Ancient Africa" from *Hadon of Ancient Opar* overtop the map of post-great calamity migrations devised by Brueckel and Harwood for their essay "Heritage of the Flaming God," a tiny glimmer of the depth and scope of Farmer's collaborative world building emerges. One sees that the survivors from Wentisuh migrated to the southeast and founded the city of the Kavuru (doubtless also related to Farmer's Kawuru) from Burroughs' *Tarzan's Quest* (1936), and to the south to found Xuja from *Tarzan the Untamed* (1920). The survivors of Siwudawa migrated to the southeast and founded Cathne and Athne from *Tarzan and the City of Gold* (1933), while the former inhabitants of Miklemres migrated to the southwest and those of Bawaku migrated to the southeast and founded Tuen-Baka from *Tarzan and the Forbidden City* (1938). Without reference to Brueckel and Harwood, Farmer located Haggard's Kôr in the back regions of Portuguese South East Africa based on descriptions of Allan Quatermain's journey in *She and Allan*.

But the lost cities of Burroughs and Haggard were not Farmer's only inspirations for his ancient African civilization. The name Khokarsa itself derives from Ambrose Bierce's classic tale of mysticism and horror "An Inhabitant of Carcosa" (1886). In Bierce's story, a medium channels a spirit that drifts back in time to a forlorn age and witnesses the ruins of dead civilization. That civilization, in Farmer's view, is ancient Khokarsa, the ancient motherland of Tarzan's Opar. The passage of time, or perhaps a faulty transmission by the medium, has undoubtedly inverted the syllables of "Car-co-sa" into Farmer's "Kho-kar-sa"; and the monoliths erected to the dead heroes of the Great Games in *Hadon of Ancient Opar* may indeed be meant to be Bierce's "number of weather-worn stones" that were "broken, covered with moss and half sunken into the earth" and were "obviously the headstones of graves."

In conclusion, a survey of the sources drawn upon in the creation of the Ancient Opar novels indicates that Farmer was working within a tradition that stemmed from both classical antiquity and modern literature. The degree to which he fused the two, in conjunction with a deep understanding of history and anthropology, signifies a major achievement in literary world building that places Farmer as a legitimate heir to the lost race tradition of Burroughs and Haggard.

The Magic Filing Cabinet
and the Missing Page

Farmerphile: The Magazine of Philip José Farmer,
No. 11, January 2008

Sometimes the Great Whangdoodle appears just when you need Him. What follows is the story of how two Farmerian mysteries came to be solved.

I was in Peoria, Illinois for FarmerCon II, happy to be back among the living after having undergone surgery earlier in the year, and overjoyed to be in the presence of my favorite living writer. In fact, I was near ecstatic because I was editing a new collection, *Venus on the Half-Shell and Others*, by The Wonderful Wizard of Peoria himself. The book's contents had already been selected, the text of Philip José Farmer's scintillating fictional-author stories had all been scanned and converted to electronic format, I had read and re-read the stories, and now I was preparing to write the introduction and story headers.

I already had some idea of what I was going to write, *Venus* and the fictional-author stories being some of my favorites among Phil's work, but I figured I might pick the brain of Grand Master and his lovely wife Bette while I was visiting for the convention. Most of all I wanted to tie up the loose ends of the two mysteries alluded to above.

The first mystery is broader than the second, and its answer is, I believe, of great interest to science fiction history. It concerns a long-running hoax perpetrated by Phil that you can read about in much more detail in the introduction to the new collection (no, that's not a mystery; I did manage to complete the introduction). Suffice it to say that word of mouth, and a couple of brief mentions in printed but unsourced articles,

Popular Culture

Joe Gores
WRITING FOR TV

Cordwainer Bird

Barry Malzberg

King Kong · Sherlock Holmes · Raymond Chandler
Pro Wrestling · The Beatles Tapes · Punk Rockers

had it that Phil was going to edit an anthology of fictional-author stories by other writers. But was this just hearsay? Or had perhaps someone mistaken something said by Phil when he had spoken elsewhere about publishing his own fictional-author stories? And even if it were true, who were the authors Phil was considering to solicit for the anthology? Philip K. Dick was an author who came up in one of the unsourced articles, but was this true? And who else would have been included, and did Phil actually contact any of them? No one seemed to know.

There stood the first mystery.

The second mystery had to do with "The Impotency of Bad Karma," a story selected for the lettered edition of the book, one which even many hardcore Farmer fans have had a hard time tracking down. In fact, despite having scoured eBay for many a year, I had only ever seen a photocopy of its original publication in the extremely limited-run preview issue of *Popular Culture*, which Mike Croteau had obtained from the defunct magazine's publisher, Brad Lang. Problem was, the photocopies Mike had obtained ended with the words, "They did send his blood pressure up, though in a healthy manner." Anyone who has read the more readily available rewritten story "The Last Rise of Nick Adams" will know this is not where that version of the story ends, and that in fact these words end just before the story's climax (pun very certainly intended). Was this a printing error in *Popular Culture* or was there a missing page? I shot off emails to the top Farmerian experts, but even uber-Farmer-collector Rick Beaulieu, and the kind and knowledgeable webmaster of the exhaustive *Philip José Farmer International Bibliography*, Zacharias Nuninga, hadn't a clue. In fact—and this says something about the tight-knit though global community of Farmer collectors—these two gentleman had the very same photocopied version as Mike and I. To further the mystery, Mr. Lang had told Mike, upon graciously sending him the photocopies several years prior, that the story had definitely ended with that line. Further, it could not have been a typographical error, or Phil would have certainly let Mr. Lang, who had copyedited the story himself, know about it.

But how could the story end there, with…well…literally no climax?

And there, mystery number two.

FarmerCon, it would seem, is the perfect place to tackle the nebulous questions of metafiction. In truth, at the first FarmerCon I was able to meet and converse with the very real Eric Clifton from Phil's *The Lavalite World* and *More Than Fire*, as well as Hans Kordtz from *Escape from Loki*. I kid you not. So I fully believed I might have a good chance of solving both mysteries while I was in Peoria in August 2007. With such a gathering of Farmerphiles (the fans, I mean, not magazines) I held high hopes that someone among them would have some answers for me. This did not turn out to be the case. And yet, before I even had the chance to sit down with Phil and Bette on the day following the convention, Mike Croteau called me aside and showed me what he had found in The Magic Filing Cabinet.

Let me back up. For those who don't know, The Magic Filing Cabinet is The Wizard of Peoria's secret weapon, kept in a well-hidden subterranean chamber and sealed tight from unwanted intruders by magical enchantment. Inside The Cabinet, the intrepid Farmerian explorer will find a treasure trove of mojo-laden folders bearing age-yellowed parchments upon which are written the secrets of the pluriverse. From it comes much of the wealth that is published in *Farmerphile*, as well as rare gems in the form of partial manuscripts and outlines like *The City Beyond Play*.

And so on that summer day Mike (who possesses a secret key bequeathed him by The Wizard) opened The Magic Filing Cabinet and showed me a folder that bore the mind-blowing title "FICTIONAL-AUTHOR PERMISSIONS." After getting permission from The Wizard to look through the folder myself, it was indeed as if my mind had exploded in a supernova of splendor. In the folder were all the answers to the first mystery, and much more. The Great Whangdoodle had cawed, and the illuminations thus revealed may now be read in the introduction

to *Venus on the Half-Shell and Others.* I'll give you a hint so you don't want to banish me to some hellfire pocket universe of Red Orc's devising: In addition to all the answers poised above about Phil's proposed fictional-author anthology, the introduction also includes a list and description of several hitherto unknown fictional-author stories Phil either had begun writing and never finished, or ones he planned to write but never did. And in case you're still considering that not-so-nice pocket universe for me, here's a bonus tidbit that didn't make the cut for the intro: Did you know Phil once planned to write a biography of Oz, and that he received permission from L. Frank Baum's estate to do so? You do now.

As to the mystery of the missing page, Phil took a look at the photocopies I brought of the story and told me that to his knowledge there was indeed an absent portion of text. That mystery was not solved in Peoria, but rather about a week or so later when I managed to finally track down Brad Lang, the editor of *Popular Culture.* I presented the conundrum to him again and lo and behold the missing page magically appeared: it had been in that issue of *Popular Culture* all along, but before now, for some unfathomable reason, it had previously eluded Brad! Seems there was still a bit of magic floating about that must have stuck to my clothes and luggage from when I had visited Peoria. Or was that a distant cawing I heard?

Oh, by the way, there is a third mystery: that of how the very real Tom Wode Bellman, who appears in fictionalized form in Phil's "The Light-Hog Incident," came to write the foreword to *Venus on the Half-Shell and Others.* But that, I am afraid, is a story I will have to leave to Mr. Bellman.

How Much Free Will Does a Pumpkin Have?
Philip José Farmer and Sufism

Farmerphile: The Magazine of Philip José Farmer,
No. 12, April 2008

"Drunk without wine; sated without food; distraught; foodless and sleepless; a king beneath a humble cloak; a treasure within a ruin; not of air and earth; not of fire and water; a sea without bounds. He has a hundred moons and skies and suns. He is wise through universal truth—not a scholar from a book."

The quote is from Mawlānā Jalāl-ad-Dīn Muhammad Rūmī, better known to English speakers as simply Rumi, the great Sufi poet and mystic. The quote itself, taken from Idries Shah's *The Sufis* (Anchor Books, 1964), is said to be Rumi's definition of a Sufi, and I cite it here as a point of reference, in particular for the last line: "He is wise through universal truth—not a scholar from a book." I do this to point out a curiosity, a seeming contradiction. That is that Philip José Farmer, known far and wide for both his many fantastical novels and stories and his ravenous appetite for reading, would choose to include the subject of Sufism in a significant number of his writings. Farmer is an omnivore when it comes to knowledge, and it would not be an exaggeration to say that he has read more widely in a broader array of subjects than the vast majority of his peers in the science fiction writing world. Why then Sufism, a mystical discipline that in its very definition decries book learning? One might believe the question to be a straw dog, but consider that at least seven characters in Farmer's fiction are Sufis, with several other characters, including one based on himself, either serving as disciples to Sufi masters or flirting with the idea of becoming disciples. Clearly something in Sufi doctrine appealed to Farmer, but what?

Farmer's initial interest in Sufism probably emerged from his enthusiasm for the life and works of Sir Richard Francis Burton. In the essay "The Source of the River" (*Pearls from Peoria*, 2006), Farmer states that he conceived the idea of the Riverworld from reading John Kendrick Bangs' *A Houseboat on the River Styx* during the same period in which he read Burton's the *Kasîdah*. Farmer calls the Kasîdah "my second spark of inspiration."

The *Kasîdah*, or *A Lay of the Higher Law* was first published in a private edition in 1880 and was attributed not to Burton but to Haji Abdu El-Yezdi, a fictional Sufi personality created by Burton. In a move reminiscent of Farmer's own fictional-author trickery, Burton himself annotated the book under the initials F.B., which stood for Frank Baker, one of Burton's old pseudonyms (see Fawn M. Brodie's *The Devil Drives: A Life of Sir Richard Burton*, W. W. Norton & Co, 1967). Farmer would later go on to use Hajji Abdu El-Yezdi as one of his own characters, most notably in *Escape from Loki*, in which the Haj is revealed to be one of Doc Savage's many expert tutors. Farmer must have liked the symmetry of the Man of Bronze having been mentored by a Sufi, as the title of Lester Dent's last Doc Savage novel, *Up from Earth's Center*, is taken directly from Omar Khayyam's famous poem, the *Rubaiyat*, which is said not be the celebration of hedonistic wine drinking that Fitzgerald's translation makes it out to be but rather a Sufi parable for divine intoxication. Interestingly, Haji Abdu El-Yezdi also appears as the main character in Farmer's unpublished and incomplete Lovecraftian fictional-author story "The Feaster from the Stars." Even more interestingly, a certain Frank Baker also appears in the story.

But it is in the Riverworld series where Farmer explores his interest in Sufism in the greatest detail. Riverworld itself is a Brobdingnagian Sufi-themed allegory for life on Earth. Everyone who had ever lived awakens on the banks of a 10,000,000-mile-long river. For a brief interval, humanity is electrified by the question of why it has been resurrected. But before long the old habits, prejudices, and greeds set in. Then come wars, slavery, and the struggle for survival. Just as on Earth, the human inhabitants

PHILIP JOSÉ FARMER
THE UNREASONING MASK

of the Riverworld quickly become distracted from the Real. Like the great Sufis storytellers, Farmer is fond of encoding many layers of meaning within his tales.

In placing Burton as the series' main protagonist, Farmer not only seeks to draw an allusion to Burton's role as a great explorer of the world, but also as a great explorer of the soul. Burton himself is a self-described master Sufi, indoctrinated into the mystical order during his travels throughout the Middle East. But by the time he is resurrected on Riverworld, Burton has lost the true faith. In a lengthy monologue in *The Magic Labyrinth*, Burton remarks that his observations of the Sufis, who proclaimed themselves to be God, led him to conclude that "extreme mysticism was closely allied with madness." Then he exclaims,

"Great God! I will penetrate His heart, to the heart of the Mystery of the mysteries. I am a living sword, but I have been attacking with my edge, not with my point. The point is the most deadly, not the edge. I will be from now on the point.

"Yet if I am to find my way through the magic labyrinth, I must have a thread to follow to the great beast that lives in its heart…why didn't I think of this before?—I am the labyrinth."

Then, in a complete reversal of his criticism of the Sufis, Burton says, "…though I was deeply learned, I never understood that wisdom had little to do with knowledge and literature and nothing to do with learning." In the end Burton cannot escape the fact that the Sufis' wisdom is in truth his own. In fact, in describing his own self-truth, he almost verbatim quotes Rumi's definition: "He is wise through universal truth—not a scholar from a book."

But Burton is not the only Sufi to appear in the Riverworld series. The Japanese Piscator is one of two dueling Sufi masters in *The Dark Design*. Piscator serves mainly as a foil for Jill Gulbirra's internal conflicts, placing himself in the role of mentor. Although Jill is too independent to realize she needs a mentor, Piscator is her guide nonetheless, plucking her from the waters as if she were one of the fish with which he is so obsessed.

The second of the dueling Sufi masters in *The Dark Design* is

Nur ed-Din el-Musafir. Nur is Peter Jairus Frigate's mentor, and because Frigate is Farmer's mirror self, the interactions between the two characters are particularly revealing as to Farmer's inclination to return so often to Sufi themes and characters in his work. Though Frigate is critical of organized religion, he is keen enough to see a difference in Nur's teachings, at least at first. Despite having been an obsessive reader (like Farmer) during his earthly existence, Frigate realizes that Nur's wisdom comes from a place deeper than personality. And like Farmer, Frigate believes in free will. He states, "God might not exist, but free will did. True, it was a limited force, repressed or influenced by environmental conditioning, chemicals, brain injuries, neural diseases, lobotomy. But a human being was not just a protein robot. No robot could change its mind, decide on its own to reprogram itself, lift itself by its mental bootstraps."

Frigate, fearing rejection, hesitates to ask Nur to take him on as a disciple. Nur, though he tells Frigate he has potentiality, says he is not ready. This may illustrate Farmer's own struggle between rational doubt (intellect) and the desire to enact his free will (spirit). And here we begin to see an explanation for Farmer's interest in a mystical doctrine that decries the primacy of the intellect. Throughout Farmer's writings, the question of free will—and the belief that free will does indeed exist, at least in a qualified sense—rises again and again. Whether it be Simon Wagstaff's comic search for meaning in *Venus on the Half-Shell* or Kickaha's wild and whooping optimism in the face of adversity in the World of Tiers novels, so often the Farmerian protagonist falls back on the idea that will is stronger than either nature or nurture—if, that is, will is enacted. As Farmer states in the introduction to *The Grand Adventure*, "We do have free will, but we don't use it very often."

Frigate does go on to become Nur's disciple, but by the time of the last book in the series, *Gods of Riverworld*, he resigns from Nur's tutelage. He does this so that he does not have to suffer the humiliation of being "flunked" by his master. Frigate's irrational fear of failure and rejection is his chief psychological imperfection, a flaw which Nur warned him about early on.

Though Frigate is intellectually aware that his fear is irrational and an impediment to his growth as a human being, he cannot overcome it. His mental bootstraps are just too tight, and in the end he joins Burton to play devil's advocate with the man they both know is right. "Burton and Frigate felt uncomfortable," Farmer writes in *Gods of Riverworld*. "They usually did when they talked to Nur about serious subjects."

But the exploration of Sufi themes in the Riverworld series does not end on that sour note. In "Coda," a story which is in fact the literary coda of the entire series—and also the coda of Farmer's short fiction period, since it is the last short story he wrote and had published before his retirement—Farmer again introduces a Sufi master and disciple. This time it is Rabi'a el-Adawia, a female Sufi saint who lived 717–801 A.D., teaching the most unlikely of followers: the "pataphysician" Alfred Jarry, previously known on the Riverworld by his fictional personality Doctor Faustroll (see Farmer's "Crossing the Dark River" in *Tales of Riverworld*, 1992 and "Up the Bright River" in *Quest to Riverworld*, 1993). Jarry, like Farmer and Frigate, has throughout his life questioned the world about him only to respond to his own questions with playful humor and a sharp wit. In a way, all three men—Farmer, Frigate, and Jarry—play the role of Doctor Faustroll. But also like Faustroll, who in the story has again becomes Alfred Jarry, something in them recognizes the immaturity of such a response. In "Coda," Jarry finds a mysterious Artifact near the source of the River. The Artifact becomes his obsession, despite the fact that Rabi'a warns him the object is a distraction to the Path. Here again Farmer is playing out the same struggle between intellect and spirit that faced the character Frigate. But in the moment of truth, Jarry responds differently than Frigate. Jarry has not only seen his weaknesses, but he has conquered them. He knows beyond intellect who he is and that knowledge—that wisdom—allows him to enact a rare moment of free will. There could be no more fitting conclusion for the Riverworld series, in which Farmer's characters not only struggle to find answers, but also struggle to live The Answer. I would argue that "Coda" is not only one of Farmer's most psychologically autobiographical stories; it is also one of his best.

In an unlikely turn, Farmer combines his interest in Sufism with his fascination with feral human literature in "Hayy ibn Yazqam by Aby ibn Tufayl: An Arabic Mowgli" (*Farmerphile*, No. 4, April 2006; *Up from the Bottomless Pit and Other Stories*, Subterranean Press, 2007), a paper presented in 1990 before the International Conference on the Fantastic in the Arts. In his study, Farmer concludes that Hayy ibn Yazqam, the hero of this "Sufi didactic story," is quite a different sort of feral man than Tarzan or Mowgli, stating that he "untiringly pursues a quest for the Creator, the One, the Truth, the Ineffable, the Way." While Tarzan does ingeniously extrapolate his own mythology in "The God of Tarzan" in *Jungles Tales of Tarzan*, the ape-man's journey through life is ultimately not a quest for meaning. Tarzan knows who he is and is content; he is an ineffable part of Nature, and that understanding is in itself his theology.

Farmer's interest in Sufism may also be seen in *The Unreasoning Mask*, in which a strange green robed man appears to Captain Ramstan of the alaraf drive starship al-Buraq. Ramstan, an agnostic Muslim, suspects that the green robed man is none other than al-Khidr, a mysterious Sufi prophet who is said to show up at times of great importance. The name of Ramstan's ship, al-Buraq, literally means "the lightning" in Arabic, which would seem to describe the ship's ability to instantaneously travel between two points; but al-Buraq is also the name of the winged ass which the Koran says carried Muhammad to heaven and back, and the name is certainly also meant to be indicative of Ramstan's journeys throughout the Pluriverse.

Al-Khidr also appears as a character in Farmer's "St. Francis Kisses His Ass Goodbye," a tale in which St. Francis of Assisi falls victim to a time travel experiment from the future and is unwittingly transported to the twentieth century. Many Islamic and Biblical scholars believe al-Khidr to be analogous to the prophet Elijah, who is known in eastern European folklore as being responsible for bad weather, and indeed it is during a thunder-cracking tempest that St. Francis is plucked from the

PHILIP·JOSÉ·FARMER

THE·GRAND
ADVENTURE

BERKLEY SCIENCE FICTION · 0-425-07211-8 · ($8.95 CANADA) · $7.95 U.S.

thirteenth century and deposited in the future. It is here where al-Khidr, calling himself "Kidder," appears to the shocked friar, helping him make his way to the scientists whose experiment will end in a worldwide disaster if St. Francis is not sent back to his past with the exact matter-mass which he brought with him to the future. In the end St. Francis is left wondering if the vision of the six winged, crucified seraph which he experiences years later in his own timeframe might not somehow have been connected with his trip to the future. The reader might also ponder two other questions: Were St. Francis' stigmata the result of scientists from the future returning to take back some extra mass he had carried with him to the past? And when St. Francis encountered al-Khidr, did he in reality encounter himself? That is, did St. Francis encounter an advanced future version of himself who, because of his faith and labors, has gone on to a higher plane of existence and become a cosmic individual with the important task of managing world-scale crises? One should note that Farmer did not pair up St. Francis and al-Khidr arbitrarily. Idries Shah, in his *The Sufis*, makes a powerful argument that St. Francis of Assisi had knowledge of Sufi doctrine, and that he based much of his own teaching upon it.

In closing I feel obliged to point out that St. Francis of Assisi is also a hero of Tom Corbie, the protagonist of Farmer's Peoria-based P.I. mystery novel *Nothing Burns in Hell*. When disturbed by the loud noise of his neighbors, Corbie states,

"I thought of vengeance vile and violent. Yet, I was trying to climb a high peak of spiritual development. Though I wasn't a Catholic, my hero and role model was St. Francis of Assisi. But it seemed to me I was a pumpkin trying to change into a gilded coach in a place where midnight never came. How much free will does a pumpkin have?"

Here Farmer returns to old ground, the question of free will. It is a subject that, as I have tried to illustrate in this essay, is inextricably tied up with Farmer's interest and flirtations with the subject of Sufism. But Farmer is not interested in the question academically. He knows it is a question that belongs to the realm of essence, of soul, not transient personality. And because of this often self-doubting recognition, Farmer reveals not only that he possesses a humility that might be worthy of St. Francis himself, but also that he might bear a mystical pearl of wisdom which he most likely doesn't even know he has.

An Inhabitant of Khokarsa

Farmerphile: The Magazine of Philip José Farmer,
No. 13, July 2008

Farmerphile: The idea of a third novel set in the Khokarsa cycle will be sure to thrill fans of Philip José Farmer everywhere. Explain to us a bit about how the partial manuscript and outline were uncovered and how you came to complete one of Phil's long lost novels.

Christopher Paul Carey: In July 2005, Mike Croteau and Win Eckert took a trip to Phil and Bette Farmer's Peoria home to look for previously unpublished material by Phil to reprint in *Farmerphile*. This was the same trip during which Mike and Win came back with the partial manuscript and outline for Phil's *The Evil in Pemberley House*, in addition to a number of other lost treasures that have since been published in *Farmerphile*. At the time I was the senior editor for *Farmerphile*, so Mike immediately sent me a list of all the items he and Win had uncovered. I was very excited to read the email that described what they had come back with, but then my jaw must have dropped nearly to the floor and squeaked on its hinges when I eyeballed the last item in the list, which Mike, tired from his turn-around trip from Georgia to Illinois and back, seemed to have mentioned almost as an afterthought: "Kwasin of Opar. Not sure what to do with this. Need to read it and see if it is compelling enough to either put in *Farmerphile* or sell photocopies" [for Phil on *The Official Philip José Farmer Home Page*]. I thought, Compelling enough?! With trembling fingers, I typed back a reply to Mike asking him to send me photocopies as soon as possible. I received them a few days later just as I was heading out to an author reading at the Science Fiction Museum in Seattle. I brought the copies along with me to the reading and, having arrived at the museum early, read the entire outline while I sat in the theater. That evening I barely listened to a word of the speaker, who was quite famous and well-regarded, and to whom, in other circumstances, I would have paid attention quite intently. But I was off in another world of "gold, and silver, ivory, and apes, and peacocks." The outline of *Kwasin of Opar* galloped forward at the pace of a Barsoomian thoat, and I could practically see Phil's enthusiasm for the adventure leaping from every page. Here at last was the story of what happened on the island of Khokarsa after Hadon flew with Lalila and their companions to Opar—the whole bloody war with King Minruth in its entirety! I knew then and there that the story had to be told, so I drafted a proposal and sent it to Phil. He replied with a very enthusiastic note granting permission for me to complete the book. I know that as late as 1999 Phil was still very seriously considering wrapping up the series novels in one final book, so I think the idea of at long last having the trilogy completed must have excited him. As per Phil's wishes *The Song of Kwasin* will be the last book in the series proper. While Phil's notes give some indication of events that would have occurred after the third book, any further adventures that might conceivably be written would be considered part of a separate cycle.

F: Why was the original name of the book changed from *Kwasin of Opar* to *The Song of Kwasin*?

CPC: Phil was never satisfied with the original title, which was suggested by *Science Fiction Review* editor Richard E. Geis in response to a letter Phil had sent in to that magazine. Phil was at a loss as what to call the novel, since none of the action took place in the city of Opar but was rather set on the island of Khokarsa. Further, Kwasin is actually a native of the city Dythbeth, not Opar. Regardless, Donald Wollheim, who was then publishing the series, insisted that "Opar" be somewhere in the title. In frustration, Phil at first joked that he would call the book *Far from Opar* or *Nowhere Near Opar.* His notes reveal that before he'd fully outlined the story he was considering calling it *The Siege of Opar*, but then, perhaps realizing that there would be no attack on Opar in the book, he crossed out the latter title and wrote "KWASIN RAZES HELL." That certainly would have been a very appropriate title! In any case, when the book was finally resurrected, Wollheim's restriction no longer applied. Phil and Bette and I sat down and decided that *The Song of Kwasin* made a fitting title for a number of reasons. First, the title indicates that the book is a slight departure from the first two books in that it concentrates on Kwasin's epic struggle against Minruth rather than Hadon of Opar's adventures. Second, the title calls up the great ballads of the Khokarsan bards. In the Khokarsan language, the title of the book would be the *Pwamwotkwasin*, the Song of the Hero Kwasin. And finally, the title is a play on "The Song of Hiawatha," the poem that inspired Phil to create the character of Kwasin in the first place. In Longfellow's poem, the character Kwasind is Hiawatha's giant strongman friend. For all those reasons we knew we had the right title.

F: We all know that Phil had a lifelong wish to write "official" books about his favorite childhood characters: Tarzan, Doc Savage, and the Wizard of Oz. Was getting to write this book anything like that for you?

CPC: Absolutely, more than you can probably imagine. Before I ever read Philip José Farmer I was the hugest fan of Edgar Rice Burroughs. Between the ages of twelve and fifteen I devoured each and every novel then published that Burroughs ever penned. But more than that, it was on a brisk, perfectly blue-skied March afternoon in rural Pennsylvania that I lay in my room and read my first ERB book, *A Princess of Mars.* That was when the crazy notion that I wanted to be a writer seized my astral body like some soul-leeching alien and never let go. Of course back then I wanted to write a story in ERB's worlds, and in fact I did. I remember when I was in ninth grade lit class I was told to write an ending to Frank Stockton's short story "The Lady or the Tiger?" Very consciously I made the decision to treat the assignment as an authentic Burroughs pastiche, although it turned out more like ERB's grimmest novel *I Am A Barbarian* than his more frequent the-hero-saves-the-princess stories. I had the lady choose for her lover the door with the tiger standing behind it. Then she ran back to her chambers and thrust a dagger into her breast. All told in ERB's entrancingly romantic, melodramatic style, of course, or as close as I could approximate. I must have hit the mark at least somewhat because the teacher chose it as the best ending of the batch and read it aloud before the class—fortunately without attributing it to me, or I would have been very embarrassed.

I encountered PJF at the same time I was reading ERB, and in fact I read him because of my love for ERB. Like many of Phil's readers, I was blown away to find a copy of *Tarzan Alive*, claiming that Tarzan was a real person, on the bookstore shelves. I picked up that, the two Hadon books, and *The Maker of Universes* first. At first I set aside the Tarzan-related material and didn't read it because I wanted to finish the original Tarzan novels first (I was probably up to book 8 or 9 in the series by then), so I read the first World of Tiers book. That immediately sold me on Farmer's writing and I dived into *Hadon of Ancient Opar* and *Tarzan Alive*. Phil has said that a number of Burroughs readers were unable to get into the Hadon novels because they were told with more realism than the romance of ERB's Tarzan novels. Let me tell you it was never that way with me. I couldn't get enough of it. Phil's expansive take on the Burroughs universe matched Burroughs' own take in my mind. Burroughs himself rather intricately connected most of his own books, much in the same way that Phil utilized the Wold Newton family to connect his own work to that of many other authors. Even before I read Phil, I was actively working to connect various subtle details of one Burroughs novel with another, so when I encountered *Tarzan Alive* and the Wold Newton-related stories, they fit like a well-worn fedora. I've never heard anyone ask Phil this, but I've often wondered how ERB's own attempts to make a coherently connected world out of his own stories may have set the spark that erupted in Phil's mind as the Wold Newton supernova.

Anyway, I'm trying to give you some small understanding of what it means to me to complete a novel begun and outlined by one of my favorite writers (can you say "understatement"?) that was inspired by the writer who inspired me to write. All I can say is it's a bizarre universe, and that Joseph Campbell was right about following one's bliss and all that.

F: What was your source material for this book? We know you had the beginning of the novel that Phil wrote, and his outline of the remainder, but did he have any other notes referring to his research? Did you do any other research outside of Phil's materials?

CPC: I was at Phil's house in July 2006 for FarmerCon I when Mike Croteau emerged from having once again delved into what we've begun calling The Magic Filing Cabinet. At the time, I had already obtained permission to complete *The Song of Kwasin*, and Mike remembered from the time he had originally found the *Kwasin* manuscript and outline that he had seen another folder in the files labeled "The Road to Opar." So while the house party was going on merrily about us, Mike quietly slipped me that folder, along with several other thick folders. It was a treasure trove! The folders included Phil's original outlines to *Hadon of Ancient Opar* and *Flight to Opar*, in multiple draft forms, some handwritten that varied wildly from the printed books, and others typed that aligned pretty closely with the published novels. But more importantly, the folders contained Phil's extensive notes on the world building of the Khokarsan civilization and culture. Everything I needed to know to make *The Song of Kwasin* an authentically Farmerian novel in its details. Perhaps the most significant folder was labeled "Khokarsan Language." Later that evening I was sitting in the lobby of the hotel where a lot of us were staying and I showed the finds to science fiction author Mary Turzillo, who wrote a wonderful book on Phil's writings. She remarked to me that the detail of Phil's Khokarsan notes was literally Tolkienesque, and she couldn't have been more right. I was even able to transcribe from Phil's nearly illegible handwriting (sorry Phil!) an entire

UW1238

No. 197 $1.50

In Tarzan's Africa – 12,000 years ago!

FLIGHT TO OPAR

PHILIP JOSÉ FARMER

essay on the Khokarsan language that will hopefully be included as an addendum to the new novel. Phil's notes also included an extensive and invaluable list of the Khokarsan syllabary, which allowed me to create authentic Khokarsan words and names when Phil's otherwise detailed outline didn't provide them. And Phil's original pencil-drawn maps of ancient Khokarsa were also recovered and provided to the artist Charles Berlin for new renderings. "The Road to Opar," by the way, turned out to be an alternate title for *Flight to Opar*.

But besides the world building, the new notes Mike uncovered also included descriptions of many of the themes, behind-the-scenes plotlines, and plans for *Kwasin* and the future series. He also cited books like Jessie L. Weston's *From Ritual to Romance* and Willy Ley's *Exotic Zoology* which I referenced while I was preparing to write the novel. Further, there are mentions in the notes of certain details from Haggard's Allan Quatermain novels that astute readers will pick up in *The Song of Kwasin*.

So the newly discovered notes were my most important source materials besides the original novels and Phil's outline. Of course, I also went back and reread the Tarzan novels that featured Opar, more for inspiration than anything else, since *The Song of Kwasin* is set on the island of Khokarsa and the world building and storyline are completely Phil's. And I went back and reread my Haggard so I could retrace the history of the ax in Kwasin's possession. In an interview many years ago Phil expressed the idea that a future book in the series ultimately would explain why the ax which the character Pag crafts in *Allan and the Ice-Gods* looks so different from the one Umslopogaas later goes on to wield in *Nada the Lily*, *She and Allan*, and *Allan Quatermain*. Do we find out the answer in *The Song of Kwasin*? You'll have to read the book!

In any case, I spent a year and a half doing research, reading *Hadon* and *Flight* over and over, compiling a detailed glossary, working out and reconciling the exact amount of time that passed between events in the first two books and collating them with the events in *Kwasin*, transcribing and digesting Phil's notes, pouring through books on African prehistory, Greek oracles, the construction of the Great Pyramid, warfare in the ancient world, as well as the monograph that inspired Phil to write the series, Brueckel and Harwood's "Heritage of the Flaming God," before I even started writing. Research for me is the fun part. It's also seductive. At some point you have to stop, knuckle down, and just write.

F: Having had the privilege of reading the complete manuscript, it really "reads" or "feels" like *Hadon* and *Flight*. Was this something you did on purpose, and did you have to work very hard at it?

CPC: Can you see me wiping the sweat from my brow? Thank you kindly, that's high praise indeed. To answer your question, a little of both I think. While I intentionally tried to emulate Phil's phraseology, and studied his style actively, at the same time I've been reading Phil for so long that I'm sure there's some PJF in my natural style as well. I did have to deprogram a lot of modern stylistic conventions from my writing in order to maintain Phil's voice. For instance, recent schools of writing favor a very deep viewpoint, so that every word that appears on the page has to be something that would be in the mind of the character one is writing about. And yet Phil uses the word "half-Neanderthal" throughout the Hadon books. Hadon and Kwasin, so say the modern stylists, would have used a Khokarsan word, one that doesn't refer to a small valley in Germany. The idea being that the "modern" word pulls the reader out of the story. But Phil is writing in an entirely appropriate tradition which says that the writer is ultimately translating all the words from a dead language anyway, so why not use a word with which the reader is familiar? So I threw that modern convention out the window, along with a number of others, and used Phil's. (His are better anyway, in my opinion!) As much as possible, I wanted the book to read seamlessly as the third in a trilogy. This was complicated by the fact that I had to write it from Kwasin's point of view instead of Hadon's, and they are quite different characters. So the main tonal difference may be that we are seeing things through Kwasin's eyes, not the idealistic Hadon's. And what is in Kwasin's head may be quite different from what we see of Kwasin on the outside from Hadon's vantage in *Hadon of Ancient Opar*. In the new book we'll get to see a bit of what makes Kwasin tick, why he's such an outrageous bastard. The first book relates the story of how Hadon and Kwasin were raised together by their uncle Phimeth in the caves above the Kemuwopar, and we feel much sympathy for Hadon, who bears the brunt of Kwasin's bullying. Now we'll get a glimpse of that through Kwasin's eyes.

I also tried to sprinkle throughout the manuscript many of Phil's phrases and sentences that were taken verbatim from the outline. I think that lends to the genuine feel you are picking up on. And every scene from Phil's outline is in the book. I think one of the big reasons Phil granted permission for me to complete the book was that he knew I was a consistency hound and that I knew and loved the source material, as well as what I call the Farmerian Monomyth, the interconnected but often unspoken backstories in Phil's works. I promised him that I wouldn't stray from the outline and I didn't, although occasionally there were gaps I had to fill in or details I had to reconcile. But luckily I had Phil's notes and a lot of other sources that Phil himself drew upon to guide me. I'd never claim it's the same novel Phil—a Grand Master of Science Fiction—would have written, but I'm confident it's the same *story*. Right after Phil granted permission for me to complete *Kwasin*, he also gave me a general idea of how he felt the book should wrap up, since *Kwasin* wasn't originally conceived as the last in the series. And while he was also gracious enough to say I could end the book however I felt best, needless to say, Phil's advice was immensely helpful and I accepted it gladly. It was definitely the right way to end the book and the series as a whole.

Of course, I have to append here that this entire interview may be a smokescreen in which I am covering for the fact that ancient Khokarsa was a real civilization. In reality Phil gathered the stories of the heroes Hadon and Kwasin from his dealings with a certain Lord G. and his researches into the life of Allan Quatermain. You realize, don't you, that both Hadon and Kwasin are descended from Sahhindar, who we all know is the time-traveling Gribardsun from *Time's Last Gift*. So in reality both heroes are members of the Wold Newton family, even though they were born 12,000 years prior to the fall of the radioactive meteorite in Yorkshire in 1795. And that means that many, many more people living today than previously believed may potentially be members of the Wold Newton family. Further, the Wold Newton family hence extends to individuals who lived *before* 1795. Think on that.

F: What is the current status of the book right now? Has *The Song of Kwasin* found a publisher yet?

CPC: As of the time of this interview, June 2008, *The Song of Kwasin* is in the hands of Phil's agent. It's possible *The Song of Kwasin* will be published in an omnibus with *Hadon of Ancient Opar* and *Flight to Opar*, but we don't yet know for sure. But for now you can read the teaser excerpt that's being printed in this issue and rest reassured that at long last, after over thirty years in the making, the heroic ballad of Kwasin of Dythbeth, and the climactic conclusion to the trilogy, will at last be sung.

More Real Than Life Itself:
Philip José Farmer's Fictional-Author Period

First published in *Venus on the Half-Shell and Others*, ed. Christopher Paul Carey, Subterranean Press, 2008. Revised for publication as an afterword to *Venus on the Half-Shell* by Philip José Farmer, Titan Books, 2013.

"The unconscious is the true democracy. All things, all people, are equal."

—Philip José Farmer

By one count, Philip José Farmer, a Grand Master of Science Fiction, has written and had published fifty-four novels and one hundred and twenty-nine novellas, novelettes, and short stories. Creatively, Farmer's work is equally ambitious. In 1952, he authored the groundbreaking "The Lovers," which at long last made it possible for science fiction to deal with sex in a mature manner. He is the creator of Riverworld, arguably one of the grandest experiments in science fiction literature. His World of Tiers series, which combines rip-roaring adventure with pocket universes full of mythic archetypes, is said to have inspired Zelazny's Chronicles of Amber series and is often cited as a favorite among Farmer's fans. And in the early 1970s, he penned the authorized biographies of Tarzan and Doc Savage and inspired generations of creative mythographers to explore and expand upon his Wold Newton mythos. Yet among all of these shining minarets of his opus, Farmer has stated that he has never had so much fun in all his life as when he wrote *Venus on the Half-Shell*.

I believe it is no coincidence that this novel belongs to what

Farmer has labeled his "fictional-author" series. A fictional-author story is, as defined by Farmer, "a tale supposedly written by an author who is a character in fiction." Many of Farmer's readers are aware that *Venus on the Half-Shell* originally appeared in print as if authored by Kurt Vonnegut's character Kilgore Trout. However, most are not aware that Farmer, in league with several of his writer peers and at least one major magazine editor, masterminded an expansive hoax on the science fiction readership that spanned a good portion of the 1970s.

As with Farmer's usual *modus operandi*, the plan was ambitious. Beginning in about 1973–74, in true postmodern reflexivity, a whole team of writers acting under Farmer's direction were to begin submitting fictional-author tales to the short fiction markets. Farmer's files, to which the author kindly gave me access, reveal that his plan of attack was executed with focus, precision, and a great deal of forethought.

The authors queried to write the fictional-author stories were instructed that "the real author is to be nowhere mentioned; it's all done straight-facedly." Each story would be accompanied by a short biographical preface giving the impression that the fictional author was indeed a living person. However, all copyrights were to be honored; those who chose to write stories "by" the characters of other authors would need to contact those creators for permission. Sometimes Farmer himself wrote the creator and, having received permission, then handed over the fictional-author story to his fellow conspirator to complete. Authors were encouraged to submit their stories to whatever market they pleased, although the majority were to appear in *The Magazine of Fantasy and Science Fiction*, whose editor, Edward L. Ferman, was in on the joke. Once enough of the stories had been published in various markets, Farmer himself planned to take on the role of editor and collect them all in a fictional-author anthology.

Writing even before the fallout with Kurt Vonnegut (which is described in great detail by Farmer in his "Why and How I Became Kilgore Trout"), Farmer placed great emphasis on literary ethics during the execution of his hoax. Even authors

Venus on the Half-Shell

AT LAST! KILGORE TROUT'S epic science fiction saga

DELL · 6149 · 95¢

whose characters had lapsed into the public domain—and whom Farmer and his cohorts could have used legally without payment of royalties—were offered 50% of any monies made by the publication of a fictional-author story (a stipulation that appears to have been waved by all of those who granted Farmer permission). Provisions were made for the original authors and their agents to receive copies of the stories upon publication. And always, Farmer made clear that his request to write a story under the name of an author's character was his intimate tribute to said author.

While the vast majority of those queried for the use of their characters granted permission, a couple did not. Farmer wrote respectful, though clearly disappointed, replies to these authors, explaining again that he only meant to honor them with the stories, but that in deference to them he would withdraw his offers and pursue them no further. Most authors, however, reacted much differently and became infected by the passion that seemed to ooze from Farmer when he proposed to them his audacious hoax. Nero Wolfe author Rex Stout, besides granting permission to write the story "The Volcano" under the name of his character Paul Chapin, was tickled enough to suggest that Farmer should also author stories by Anna Karenina and Don Quixote. Farmer's correspondence indicates that he planned on doing just that. P. G. Wodehouse, author of the Jeeves and Blandings Castle stories, also tried to come up with alternative fictional-authors among his own works that could be used, and it is telling of the excitement surrounding Farmer's fictional-author conceit that multiple authors queried for permission enthusiastically consented by exclaiming the phrase "Of course" within the first paragraph of their replies. Occasionally, permissions went in the other direction. J. T. Edson, the author of many Westerns, sought permission to use Farmer's Wold Newton genealogy as the basis for his own characters' ancestry in his Bunduki series, a request Farmer happily approved; and while the Wold Newton genealogy was not exclusively related to the proposed fictional-author series, it remains clear that Farmer was pleased to interweave the two concepts in several instances.

As concerns those peers enlisted to write the fictional-author stories under Farmer's coordination, the list included (among others) Arthur Jean Cox, Philip K. Dick, Leslie Fiedler, Ron Goulart, and Gene Wolfe. Unfortunately, not all of these writers succeeded in completing their stories or having them published, though there were some notable exceptions. At Farmer's suggestion, Arthur Jean Cox tackled one of his own creations, writing "Writers of the Purple Page" by John Thames Rokesmith, published in the May 1977 issue of *The Magazine of Fantasy and Science Fiction*. Rokesmith was a character in Cox's novella "Straight Shooters Always Win" (*The Magazine of Fantasy and Science Fiction*, ed. Edward L. Ferman, May 1974). And Gene Wolfe—whose humorous "Tarzan of the Grapes" appears in Farmer's survey of feral humans in literature, *Mother Was A Lovely Beast*—wrote "'Our Neighbour' by David Copperfield," first published in the anthology *Rooms of Paradise* (ed. Lee Harding, Quartet Books, 1978), albeit under Wolfe's own name. But the fun did not end there. Author Howard Waldrop, although not enlisted by Farmer, sought out the author of *Venus on the Half-Shell* and joined in with the other conspirators, publishing "The Adventure of the Grinder's Whistle" as by Sir Edward Malone in the semipro fanzine *Chacal* #2, (eds. Arnie Fenner and Pat Cadigan, Spring 1977; reprinted in the collection *Night of the Cooters*, Ace Books, 1993, wherein Waldrop, in his introduction to the story, says, "Like with most things from the Seventies, this was Philip José Farmer's fault"). Harlan Ellison's "The New York Review of Bird" (*Weird Heroes, Volume Two*, ed. Byron Preiss, Pyramid Books, 1975), while not technically a fictional-author story, was tied in with Farmer's project, and served to turn Ellison's *nom de plume*, Cordwainer Bird, into a full-fledged fictional author. Bird went on to appear in Farmer's fictional-author tale "The Doge Whose Barque Was Worse Than His Bight" as by Jonathan Swift Somers III (*The Magazine of Fantasy and Science Fiction*, ed. Edward L. Ferman, November 1976; reprinted in *Tales of the Wold Newton Universe*, Titan Books, 2013). Farmer himself used the Cordwainer Bird pseudonym for his story "The Impotency of Bad Karma" (ed. Brad Lang, *Popular*

Culture, First Preview Edition, June 1977), which he later revised and had published, using his own name this time, under the title "The Last Rise of Nick Adams" (*Chrysalis, Volume Two*, ed. Roy Torgeson, Zebra Books, 1978), and integrated Bird into his Wold Newton genealogy in *Doc Savage: His Apocalyptic Life* (Doubleday, 1973; reprinted in a deluxe hardcover edition by Meteor House, 2013, and in paperback and ebook editions by Altus Press, 2013).

The failures—those fictional-author stories imagined but never written—are almost as compelling as the successes. Ed Ferman suggested that Farmer have Ron Goulart write a story as by his character José Silvera, and while Farmer did query him, there is no immediate evidence that Goulart pursued the matter. Farmer himself sought and was granted permission to write a story under the name Gustave von Aschenbach, the novelist from Thomas Mann's *A Death in Venice*; however, apparently overwhelmed by the large number of fictional-author stories he planned to write on his own, Farmer turned the idea over to writer and literary critic Leslie Fiedler. This story, too, seems to have fallen by the wayside; if it was ever written, it never saw print.

One of the first authors approached to join in the conspiracy was Philip K. Dick. Farmer trusted Dick with the secret of who had written *Venus on the Half-Shell*, and in the process discussed Dick writing a fictional-author tale for Ferman's magazine. Dick decided this would be a short story entitled "A Man For No Countries" by Hawthorne Abdensen, the writer-character from his classic novel of alternate history, *The Man in the High Castle*. No fictional alter ego could have suited Dick better for the undertaking, as Abdensen himself was the fictional author of *The Grasshopper Lies Heavy*, a novel that implied the existence of multiple realities. The Chinese-box scenario must have pleased Dick, who worked often with such themes; but it must also have pleased Farmer, who years later went on to write the similarly head-twisting *Red Orc's Rage*, a novel wherein Farmer's own World of Tiers series serves as the basis for a method of psychiatric therapy to treat troubled adolescents, and in which Farmer himself lurks just off screen as a character. Although "A Man For No Countries" never seems to have been written,

VENUS
on the Half Shell

PHILIP JOSÉ FARMER

27531-3 ★ IN US $3.95 (IN CANADA $4.95) ★ A BANTAM SPECTRA BOOK

Farmer's role in proposing that Dick pen a fictional-author story is important, for that unwritten story appears to have been the idea-kernel that led Dick to write the posthumously published novel *Radio Free Albemuth*, which itself was an aborted draft of his critically acclaimed novel *VALIS*. One must also ponder the timing of Farmer's proposal, in the spring of 1974, a period when Dick claims to have had a number of mystical experiences, including one in which his mind was supposedly invaded by a foreign consciousness.

While Farmer was by far the most industrious and successful of the group in executing the fictional-author ruse, many of his own plans had to be abandoned because of time constraints placed upon him by other writing obligations. Farmer's correspondence, notes, and interviews from the fictional-author period reveal a long and fascinating list of stories never written and those started but not completed:

- "The Gargoyle" as by Edgar Henquist Gordon. (Fictional title and author from Robert Bloch's short story "The Dark Demon"; permission for use granted by Robert Bloch.)

- "The Feaster from the Stars" as by Robert Blake. (This unfinished Cthulhu Mythos pastiche derives from a title and fictional author in H. P. Lovecraft's "The Haunter of the Dark." Lovecraft's story is a sequel to Robert Bloch's "The Shambler from the Stars," wherein Bloch kills off a character based on H. P. Lovecraft. Robert Blake, of course, is an analog for Robert Bloch, and is in turn killed off in Lovecraft's tale. A good friend of Farmer's, Bloch enthusiastically gave his blessing to this unfinished story about Haji Abdu al-Yazdi, a pseudonym belonging to one of Farmer's real-life heroes, who was also the main protagonist of the Riverworld series: Sir Richard Francis Burton. Robert Blake is also mentioned in Farmer's Cthulhu Mythos tale "The Freshmen," which was recently reprinted in the anthology *Tales of the Wold Newton Universe*, Titan Books, 2013.)

- "UFO Versus CBS" as by Susan DeWitt. (From Richard Brautigan's *The Abortion: An Historical Romance 1966.*)

- Untitled "Smoke Bellew" stories. (Continuation of the series by Jack London. Although the stories were in the public domain, permission was refused by London's literary executor and the stories went unwritten.)

- Untitled story as by Martin Eden. (From Jack London's *Martin Eden*; no record yet found of a permission query.)

- Untitled story as by Edward P. Malone. (The intrepid reporter from Sir Arthur Conan Doyle's *The Lost World*. As mentioned above, this fictional author was turned over to Howard Waldrop.)

- Untitled story as by Gerald Musgrave. (From James Branch Cabell's *Something About Eve*. Interestingly, Cabell used anagrams prominently in his work, as Farmer does in *Venus on the Half-Shell*.)

- Untitled story as by Kenneth Robeson. (Proposed second story of *The Grant-Robeson Papers*; the first was Farmer's "Savage Shadow" as by Maxwell Grant.)

- *The Son of Jimmy Valentine* as by Kilgore Trout. (Permission denied by Kurt Vonnegut after the fallout from *Venus on the Half-Shell*.)

- "The Adventure of the Wand of Death" as by Felix Clovelly. ("Felix Clovelly" is a penname of Wodehouse's thriller novelist Ashe Marston from *Something New*. Permission granted by Wodehouse.)

But however many ideas Farmer abandoned, his list of completed fictional-author tales is equally impressive. These tales are sly, tongue-in-cheek, sometimes shocking, and more often than not uproariously funny. The following list is a chronological bibliography of Farmer's published fictional-author stories:

- *The Adventure of the Peerless Peer* as by John H. Watson, M.D. (Aspen Press, 1974; reprinted as *The Further*

Adventures of Sherlock Holmes: The Peerless Peer, Titan Books, 2011. Dr. Watson, of course, is from the works of Sir Arthur Conan Doyle.)

● *Venus on the Half-Shell* as by Kilgore Trout. (*The Magazine of Fantasy and Science Fiction*, ed. Edward L. Ferman, December 1974–January 1975; reprinted in book form, Dell, 1975, and Titan Books, 2013. Kilgore Trout is the wildly imaginative, though sad-sack, science fiction author from the works of Kurt Vonnegut.)

● "A Scarletin Study" as by Jonathan Swift Somers III. (*The Magazine of Fantasy and Science Fiction*, ed. Edward L. Ferman, March 1975; reprinted in *Tales of the Wold Newton Universe*, Titan Books, 2013. Jonathan Swift Somers III appears as a fictional author in *Venus on the Half-Shell*, and is also the subject of Farmer's biographical essay "Jonathan Swift Somers III: Cosmic Traveller in a Wheelchair.")

● "The Problem of the Sore Bridge—Among Others" as by Harry Manders. (*The Magazine of Fantasy and Science Fiction*, ed. Edward L. Ferman, September 1975; reprinted in *Tales of the Wold Newton Universe*, Titan Books, 2013. Harry "Bunny" Manders is a fictional author from the Raffles stories of E. W. Hornung.)

● "The Volcano" as by Paul Chapin. (*The Magazine of Fantasy and Science Fiction*, ed. Edward L. Ferman, February 1976. Paul Chapin appears in Rex Stout's Nero Wolfe novel *The League of Frightened Men*.)

● "Osiris on Crutches" as by Philip José Farmer and Leo Queequeg Tincrowdor. (*New Dimensions 6*, ed. Robert Silverberg, Harper & Row, 1976. Farmer wrote of Leo Queequeg Tincrowdor in his novel *Stations of the Nightmare* and short story "Fundamental Issue.")

● "The Doge Whose Barque Was Worse Than His Bight" as by Jonathan Swift Somers III. (*The Magazine of Fantasy and Science Fiction*, ed. Edward L. Ferman,

November 1976; reprinted in *Tales of the Wold Newton Universe*, Titan Books, 2013. See the entry above for "A Scarletin Study.")

• "The Impotency of Bad Karma" as by Cordwainer Bird. (*Popular Culture*, First Preview Edition, ed. Brad Lang, June 1977; revised version published in *Chrysalis, Volume Two*, ed. Roy Torgeson, Zebra Books, 1978 as "The Last Rise of Nick Adams," now under Farmer's own name. Cordwainer Bird appears as a character in Harlan Ellison's short story "The New York Review of Bird" and in Farmer's "The Doge Whose Barque Was Worse Than His Bight.")

• "Savage Shadow" as by Maxwell Grant. (*Weird Heroes, Volume Eight*, ed. Byron Preiss, Jove/HBJ Books, November 1977. Maxwell Grant was the house penname used by the authors of The Shadow pulp magazine and paperback stories.)

• "It's the Queen of Darkness, Pal" as by Rod Keen. (*The Magazine of Fantasy and Science Fiction*, ed. Edward L. Ferman, August 1978; revised version published in *Riverworld and Other Stories*, Berkley Books, 1979 as "The Phantom of the Sewers." Rod Keen is a fictional author from Richard Brautigan's *The Abortion: An Historical Romance 1966*.)

• "Who Stole Stonehenge?" as by Jonathan Swift Somers III. (*Farmerphile: The Magazine of Philip José Farmer*, No. 2, eds. Christopher Paul Carey and Paul Spiteri, October 2005. Although this one-page fragment of an unfinished Ralph von Wau Wau story was published under Farmer's name, the original manuscript is attributed to Jonathan Swift Somers III; see the entry above for "A Scarletin Study.")

Farmer has cited Paul Radin's *The Trickster*, a book about the role of the mischievous archetype recurrent in mythology and folklore, as one of his influences; and among the stories at hand

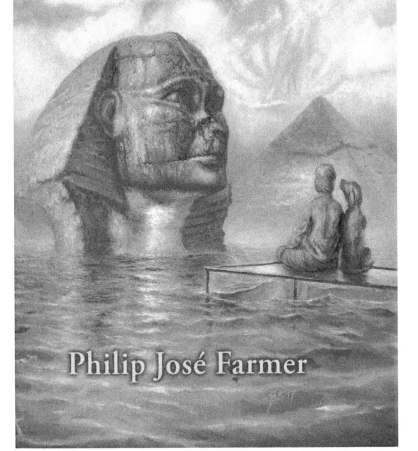

Venus on
the Half-Shell
and Others

Philip José Farmer

it is easy to see why. By assuming the role of a fictional author, Farmer dons a shamanic mask and enters the sublime creative world where fictional characters take on a life more real than our own.

A long-held theory goes that Farmer unconsciously hatched his fictional-author series, as well as penned his many pastiches, in an attempt to get over a period of writer's block which had descended upon him during the early to mid-1970s. I do not doubt it; although, if true, I—doubtless along with all of Farmer's readers—am grateful that his muse found such a scintillating, creative means to overcome its obstacle.

But there is another possibility, more fun to contemplate and more in tune with the spirit of the fictional-author concept: Perhaps Farmer's muse did not merely find a clever mechanism to jumpstart itself. What if the fictional-author period was not a hoax after all, but instead Farmer, donning his shamanic mask, did indeed glimpse into another universe? One in which William S. Burroughs wrote *Tarzan of the Apes*, and John H. Watson hobnobbed at the same gentlemen's club as A. J. Raffles and Edward Malone. Where Kurt Vonnegut may have asked Farmer's Riverworld counterpart, Peter Jairus Frigate, for permission to write a World of Tiers novel. A universe in which you and I are merely fictional characters in the works of a Grand Master of Science Fiction.

Yes, paging through this new edition of *Venus on the Half-Shell*, I think I too am getting a glimpse through the doors of perception.

Thank you, Philip José Farmer, for opening them.

In the Alien Corn:
Philip José Farmer and The Other

Introduction to *The Other in the Mirror* by
Philip José Farmer, Subterranean Press, 2009

Philip José Farmer has been described as a good-natured groundbreaker, whose classic 1952 novella "The Lovers," while tame by today's standards, shattered forever the taboo of addressing sex in science fiction. As his career progressed, Farmer pushed literary boundaries to a degree still regarded as shocking, most notably with such jocularly explicit tales as *A Feast Unknown*, *Image of the Beast*, and *Blown*. But overlooked by some critics is the fact that Farmer's exploration of iconoclastic themes is hardly limited to those dealing with sex. In the omnibus at hand the reader will find three novels which tackle head-on and with no apologies the explosive issues of race and religion. Although one of these novels is not science fiction, all three are united by one of sf's central tropes, that of The Other.

The concept of The Other can be traced as far back as the German philosopher Hegel and his dialectic method of solving conflict: thesis, antithesis, synthesis. Hegel saw all of human history as a progression from a condition of self-alienated slavery to a more rational state of self-unified freedom. In other words, by coming to understand The Other-that which is different from us-and incorporating a part of that Otherness within our own being, we become liberated from the slavery we have created for ourselves by our distorted perceptions of The Other. Following Hegel, the notion of The Other has been much explored in the realms of philosophy, literature, and psychology. Sartre proclaimed *"L'enfer, c'est les Autres"* ("Hell is Others"), while for Rimbaud it was *je est un autre"* ("I is another"). Ursula K. Le Guin, one

The
Other
in the
Mirror

PHILIP JOSÉ FARMER

of Farmer's literary peers, writes about the concept quite deftly in her short essay "American SF and The Other" *(Science-Fiction Studies* 7, 1975), pointing out the latent prejudices made apparent when the theme of The Other is more closely examined within the genre of science fiction. Le Guin makes her case that sexually, socially, culturally, and racially, American science fiction writers have had a tendency to illustrate Otherness utilizing unimaginative stereotypes: "The only good alien is a dead alien," or conversely, depicting the beneficent alien "up on a pedestal in a white nightgown with a virtuous smirk." It is exactly to shatter the mold of such immature renderings that Farmer has written the three novels which follow this introduction.

Although all three books—*Fire and the Night, Jesus on Mars,* and *Night of Light*—were written over a period spanning much of his career, Farmer vehemently criticized sf's underdeveloped, unexamined, and yawningly "safe" approach to The Other even earlier when, writing under the pseudonym Tim Howller in the Winter 1954-55 issue of the fanzine *Skyhook*, he stated the following in an open letter to *Astounding Science Fiction* editor John W. Campbell:

"Would *Astounding* dare to print a story which depicted a future Union of Colored People, an organization with principles like a labor union which struck against racial discrimination? Such a story would be science fiction because it would be concerned with a sociological invention, one which was an extrapolation from a present day institution. To me such a story would be far more fascinating than one about a star-begotten prisoner of Earth who subtly infects and overthrows his captors' barbaric government with a few well-chosen words.

"Would Mr. Campbell dare print such a work, one that might strike a spark in the mind of a Negro sf writer and launch such a movement? And would the many PhD's and technicians among his readers accept such a story? They applaud the narrative of the persuasive philosophical alien, and say yea to liberal and humanitarian views. But what if there is a real and very close danger that the dark-skinned alien who makes enough money to afford the high rents in Dr. Jones' neighborhood will move next door to him and there will be little Dr. Jones can do about it?

"What about it Mr. Campbell?"

It is telling that Farmer stepped outside of science fiction circles with the writing and publication *of Fire and the Night* (1962), his long-ignored mainstream novel about racial prejudice. From the letter in *Skyhook,* it is clear Farmer felt there would have been no market at the time daring enough to publish such a novel dressed in the cloak of science fiction. Indeed, even among mainstream markets the book only found a home at Regency Books, a publishing house whose advertising slogan was "REGENCY BOOKS MEAN CONTROVERSY."

Unlike many of Farmer's protagonists, *Fire and the Night*'s Danny Alliger is not a hero; though he thinks of himself as educated and open-minded, he quickly discovers much to his own horror that he is filled with much latent prejudice. It is moreover Danny Alliger's own guilt over his prejudice that impels him to approach The Other, as if his subconscious instinctively has made the decision to play out Hegel's dialectic. Guilt abounds in the novel, from both white and black perspectives. Danny Alliger's motivations are nearly identical to those of another character, David Virgil; both want to overcome their guilt by exchanging a part of their being with The Other. Ironically, it is their guilt which defines their mutual Otherness while at the same time revealing something of their Sameness.

It is interesting to note that guilt motivates the protagonists of all three novels in the present collection, that none of the protagonists are heroes, and that a case may be made that each is in fact a varying degree of antihero. Whether it be Danny Alliger from *Fire and the Night,* Richard Orme from *Jesus on Mars,* or John Carmody from *Night of Light,* each character is driven toward The Other by his guilt, while at the same time being separated from The Other either by perceptions created by guilt or, in the case of Carmody, by denial of guilt. Danny Alliger and Richard Orme are milder forms of antihero. Both have good intentions

Was the man who claimed to be Jesus Christ a spirit, a Martian, or a creature born in a star?

PHILIP JOSÉ FARMER

Jesus on Mars

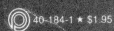

40-184-1 ★ $1.95

but find they must battle their own misperceived worldviews. If they do not succeed, they will never span the gulf between their distorted outlook and The Other. Carmody is the other extreme; consciously he cares for nothing but himself, while his subconscious hurls him unwittingly to face The Other. One way or another, the perceptions of all three characters will change.

While Danny Alliger fights to overcome his latent racial prejudices in *Fire and the Night,* Richard Orme in *Jesus on Mars* (1979) wrestles with his culture's perceptions of the past. Some of the beings Orme encounters on Mars are true aliens, while others are transplanted humans from ancient Earth; but it is the latter Martians, the humans, who are truly the most alien to Orme and his crew. The past, not their planet of origin, has made them so. Orme strives to deal in the objective present with the Martians but finds he cannot do so despite the fact that he shares their Judeo-Christian roots. In fact it is religious background that separates him from the Martians, for the Judeo-Christianity of Earth has been bundled with so much societal, cultural, and political baggage as to make it, while superficially similar, at heart substantively different from its Martian counterpart. "'It'd be easier, I think,'" Orme says when speaking to the Martian Jesus, "'to accept something totally alien to our beliefs.'" Consequently Orme agonizes over whether or not to convert to the Martian Judaism. Avram Bronski, one of Orme's fellow shipmates aboard the *Barsoom* and an agnostic Jew, faces the same dilemma, although he finds the Martian religion strangely compelling. Summoning an allusion from Keats' "Ode to a Nightingale," Bronski tells Orme, "'Still...here I am, like Ruth standing in the alien corn, and the corn doesn't look so alien.'" And so the characters in *Jesus on Mars* find themselves pulled apart at the core, both attracted and repulsed by the perhaps too familiar alien. Again, it is not the alien in itself that may be so different so much as the perception of the alien.

But while Orme is earnest in his desire to understand the Martians, he is also driven by a greed that thwarts his ability to break through their Otherness. "Though a devout Christian, he is out for himself, always looking for a way to make a quick

REGENCY
RB 118
50¢

what
did she
want him for?

FIRE AND THE NIGHT

PHILIP JOSÉ FARMER

dollar, even if that means exploiting his newfound Martian kin. By contrast, the alien Krsh and the human Martians value only "truth." Of course, Farmer is a keen enough writer not to make a judgment call for his readers on what that truth might be, and whether or not it precludes self-interest. It might he argued that leaving the individual to make that call is in fact Farmer's truth.

Orme's greed is but a faint reflection of John Carmody's in *Night of Light* (1966). Carmody is the true antihero, a man with no conscience, or at least none that he recognizes in his conscious mind. But Dante's Joy is a planet where the subconscious rules, at least during the seven-day-and-night-long Night. Carmody can deny feeling the guilt over murdering his wife, but the time of the Chance—in which the deepest currents of emotional repression are brought to light in the form of incredible physiological transformations—will force him to face his darkest fears head-on. In this tale, Otherness is something to be sought. The Kareenan inhabitants of Dante's Joy need Carmody for his Otherness. They seek to create a god from Carmody's own flesh, as well as his own twisted guilt a god who, because of his Otherness, will be able to transcend Kareenan provinciality and spread the religion of the winning faction, those loyal to either Yess or Algul, across the galaxy. The merging of the two Others, Kareenan and Carmodyan, creates a new thing, one so horrifying as to at last awaken Carmody's once dead conscience. By encountering The Other, as excruciating as that experience is for him, Carmody has again become a man.

In *Fire and the Night, Jesus on Mars,* and *Night of Light,* Farmer showcases the same boldness of vision and thoughtful probing of controversial issues as he has demonstrated in his most provocative work. And although these three novels do not by any means exhaust his literary examination of The Other, they represent three of his deepest excursions into one of science fiction's most compelling themes, an achievement for which Farmer has too long gone without recognition.

Philip José Farmer and the Cross-time Continuum

Afterword to *Two Hawks from Earth*
by Philip José Farmer, MonkeyBrain Books, 2009

It was on a pleasant spring evening in 2001 as I sat across from Philip José Farmer in an upscale restaurant that a stunning thought occurred to me. Phil's friends, family, and a spattering of fans from around the world had converged on the author's hometown of Peoria, Illinois, to celebrate what was perhaps the crowning achievement of his career as a writer: his recent induction into that elite group of individuals known as SFWA Grand Masters. I'd lucked out; I was sitting cater-corner to the Grand Master of Peoria himself. I'd been a longtime reader of Phil's works, and I had corresponded with and then met the man a few years earlier. Though I knew something about Phil's later years and his long and successful career as a writer, I had only the barest knowledge about Phil's time in the military, aware only that he'd served in the Army Air Force during World War II. Curious, I asked Phil about it. And it was after his answer that I had that stunning thought.

As Phil spoke, I learned that the future Grand Master had developed an enthusiasm for flying while taking a CCA course at Bradley University, and shortly thereafter—full of passion and derring-do, but probably just as much seeking a stable career after his recent marriage to his college sweetheart, Bette Andre—he had enlisted as an aviation cadet in the Army Air Force. Just after he arrived for preflight school at Kelly Field, Texas, Japan attacked Pearl Harbor and the United States found itself irrevocably drawn into World War II. As the world darkened around him, Phil moved on from primary to basic training at

Randolph Field, where fate gave him the luck of the draw in the form of an ill-tempered flight instructor. Though a fair pilot, Phil washed out of flight school and, as he had enlisted before the Pearl Harbor attack, he was allowed to be discharged. This was to be the end of Phil's dream to be a pilot.

There was certainly a degree of disappointment in Phil's tone as he told his story. I could tell that something of his longing for adventure as a young man remained with him, a disappointment not quite consoled even by his prestigious Grand Master Award. But Phil, while a Grand Master of the fantastic, is also a realist, and there was also resigned acceptance in his deep-timbre voice; he'd made his decisions in life, would live with them, and would keep on keeping on. *"I still live!"* as the immortal Tarzan and John Carter are wont to say.

But while that evening Phil might have conveyed some sense of failure at the memory of his bygone aviation career, the reading public certainly feels quite differently. For if young Phil Farmer hadn't drawn the misfortune of that irascible flight instructor, if the universe had split into another time stream and Phil had instead gone on to a successful military career— or, heaven forbid, had been shot down over the skies of war-torn Europe or the Pacific—then who would have written the groundbreaking "The Lovers" in 1952, the novella which broke down for all time the sex-barrier in science fiction? Who would have gone on to write the audaciously scaled Riverworld series? Or cued the world in to the fact that the great fictional characters of literature were part and parcel of the same genetic lineage known as the Wold Newton family? Or written the book that you now hold in your hands?

No one person in any universe could have done these things and touched so many people with his unique perspective. No one person but Philip José Farmer.

And that was the shocking thought that nearly knocked the wind out of me on that otherwise wonderful spring evening in Peoria.

Phil has stated elsewhere that he got the idea for writing *Two Hawks from Earth* after reading a book on the evolution of

TWO HAWKS FROM EARTH

PHILIP JOSÉ FARMER

horses in North America, but certainly his days as an aviation cadet during World War II must have been fresh on his mind as he began typing out the story of the courageous war hero Roger Two Hawks. In a way, the story permitted Phil a means to finally live out his dream of passing his flight test and soaring into the skies of, well, if not this Earth, then at least another.

It's fitting that MonkeyBrain Books is the publisher bringing *Two Hawks from Earth* back into print, located as it is in Austin, Texas, so close to the airfield where Phil once dreamed of adventure as he buzzed about the big Lone Star skies in his open-cockpit Stearman biplane. Perhaps some of Phil's psychic ectoplasm still lingers in the Texan air, raining down its creatively soul-gratifying, manna-like goodness on MonkeyBrain's headquarters. I'd like to think that had something to do with the new edition, and who can really prove otherwise?

Two Hawks from Earth is without a doubt a gem of a story, one that certainly deserves a place on the shelf of every lover of adventure-laced science fiction. When the original version of the novel was published by Belmont in 1966 under the rather misleading title *The Gate of Time* (so named by Belmont, much to the author's displeasure), Phil was deep in the development of the World of Tiers, his popular science fiction series about a family of immortal Lords fighting for dominance over a complex labyrinth of interconnected "pocket universes." In these bubble-worlds of Phil's new series, the Lords (or Thoan) engage in grand anthropological experiments, scooping up human guinea pigs from diverse cultures and time periods, transplanting them within a singularly constructed world, and-with a dash of Dr. Moreau-like genetic tampering and a lot of malevolent prodding-sitting back and watching the sparks fly. The millennia-old Lords are bored, after all, and who can blame them? Certainly not Phil Farmer, who seems to take a devilish pleasure in his literary manipulations of the Lords' creations. For Phil himself is a sort of literary Thoan, who-weary with the humdrum of the everyday world-delights in his mercurial experimentations upon vast universes of the imagination.

Phil has indulged in such speculative excursions into

speculative "applied" anthropology repeatedly throughout his five-decade-plus career as a writer, most notably with his award-winning Riverworld series, in which cultures from every time and place are resurrected with no overt explanation upon an alien world. Similarly, the theme may be seen in the synchronously existing, sliced-crosswise chrono-cultures of Phil's Dayworld series, and also in his Edgar Rice Burroughs-inspired Ancient Opar books in the mixing of the proto-Algonquin-speaking tribes of Central Asia with prehistoric Central African cultures-the fusion of these peoples being a pet project of a time-looped, incognito Tarzan, of course!

Two Hawks from Earth not only stands out among these examples of Phil's science fictional melting pot experiments; it also sparkles as a jewel of the entire alternate history genre. Of course, in one sense *Two Hawks* is not precisely an alternate history novel, for here Phil is too innately curious to craft an alternative timeline without having some scientific explanation for the mechanism that links his proposed parallel world to our own Earth-in this instance, a dimensional gate. But in another sense the novel exists within a subset of the alternate history subgenre generally recognized as the "cross-time" story, a name almost as equally deceptive as *Two Hawks from Earth's* original title, *The Gate of Time,* in that the subset has more to do with travel between synchronously developing parallel universes than it does travel across time. Still, misleading labels and quibbles about subgenres aside, *Two Hawks from Earth* clearly illustrates a type of alternate history with its story of "What if the American continents never existed?" And Phil's classic 1952 short story "Sail On! Sail On!"—an alternate history tale in which Columbus and his crew, instead of discovering America, sail over the edge of the world—shows that the author has been interested in the subgenre since the earliest point of his SF career.

While the mechanism of *Two Hawks'* premise is based upon the many-worlds interpretation of quantum mechanics formulated in the late 1950s and popularized in the alternate history subgenre since that time, the novel's influences may reach back much farther, to Phil's childhood immersion in pulp

165

BELMONT SCIENCE FICTION   B50-717 50¢

A Science-Fantasy of a man's return to
a world and time that could never be
...or could it?

the
gate
of
time

by Philip Jose Farmer

science fiction. The novels of one of Phil's longtime favorites, Edgar Rice Burroughs, without question echo throughout Roger Two Hawks' adventures on Earth 2. In an unequivocal tribute to the Master of Adventure, Phil opens his story with the same literary device that Burroughs uses to bookend his "alternate future" novel *The Moon Maid* (1923): that of a war correspondent interviewing the story's protagonist. This nod to ERB was made even more explicit in *The Gate of Time* version of the book, with its last chapter concluding the interview, following the same convention as *The Moon Maid*. And Phil grants further homage to Burroughs' Moon trilogy, in particular with regard to the concluding novel, *The Red Hawk* (1925), and its Native American-inspired protagonist. Although his writings have often focused on Burroughs' more popular Tarzan, Phil must have found ERB's Moon trilogy dear to his literary heart, as he also reportedly penned his 1962 novel *The Cache from Outer Space* as an homage to Burroughs' postapocalyptic *The Moon Men* (1925).

Moreover, *Two Hawks from Earth* follows in the tradition of another Burroughs novel, *Beyond Thirty* (1915), which relates an alternate future in which a denunciation of the horrors of World War I results in a neutral zone separating the Western Hemisphere from the Eastern for a period of two centuries. In a situation reminiscent of Roger Two Hawks' transposition to an Earth made vastly different by the absence of North and South America, Jefferson Turck, the protagonist of *Beyond Thirty*, finds himself crossing the thirtieth parallel to the forbidden hemisphere, which has developed into a much different Europe and Asia than those with which both he and the reader are familiar. Much like Roger Two Hawks finding himself betwixt the bloody war between the British-counterpart Blodlandish and the Axis-counterpart Perkunishans, Jefferson Turck leverages himself into the thick of a battle for Euro-Asian dominance. But the parallels between the two stories become even more specific: the protagonists of both books both share a love interest who hails from the royalty of a counterworld "England." Certainly this is Phil's homage to ERB.

Phil's writing and world building is, of course, more

sophisticated than that of Burroughs. Whereas Burroughs paints a simplistic caricature of medieval English culture in the Britishcounterpart society of *Beyond Thirty*, Phil scrutinizes the complex, realistic societal and linguistic roots and physical anthropology of his Blodlandish, as well as the other cultures he details. For anyone who has previously read Farmer this is not surprising, although it is probably one factor among many that makes revisiting a Farmer book such an enjoyably enriching experience. And while Phil has never shied away from tackling hard SF, he does fairly revel in social SF. This might be expected of one who, besides bearing a lifelong interest in anthropology, also worked out the phonetics and grammar of Quadling (the language of the country south of the Emerald City of Oz) and Khokarsan (the mother language of Tarzan's lost city of Opar), translated a good portion of *Tarzan of the Apes* into Esperanto, and came only a few credits shy of a Master's degree in linguistics. In *Two Hawks from Earth,* Phil puts his deep understanding of language to good use, extrapolating how English would have developed had the proto-Native Americans been unable to cross the land bridge to North America but instead headed back westward and collided with the prehistoric and historical populations of Europe. When Two Hawks asks Ilmika Thorrsstein, *"Hu fart vi thi, lautni Tva Havoken?"*—this is no hastily contrived pseudo-babble. Phil has done his homework and gone back to the English-precursor language of Wessex, factoring in the influences to which it had been subjected (for instance, Etruscan), in order to determine the proper phonemes and syntax of the Earth 2 Blodlandish. Phil's world building is gritted with authenticity and realism, but often in a way so effectively subtle that the reader only recognizes this subconsciously. And that is the mark of genius which expresses itself in a wide array throughout Phil's work.

This afterword would be remiss without addressing the differences between *Two Hawks from Earth* and its original publication as *The Gate of Time,* and indeed it is almost too fitting that a novel about two parallel Earths exists in two versions. So why did Phil decide to revise portions of the novel and carry on the story beyond its original conclusion?

For one, the editors at Belmont rewrote a torture scene in the book without Phil's permission, probably in reaction to the explicit realism with which the torture act was depicted. The altered scene in *The Gate of Time* is sloppy and ludicrous, with the victims being strung up by wires around their ankles and stretched on a rack until their feet promptly fall off, with no consideration of the anatomical realities of how hard it would actually be to sever an ankle joint with a wire in such a manner. Phil's original scene, restored in the current edition of *Two Hawks from Earth,* portrays a historical practice of Native American torture with an authenticity that leaves one sweating and cringing just to read it.

In the revised edition, Phil also took the opportunity to update the novel's world building with the knowledge he had garnered from his wide reading in history, anthropology, and linguistics in the intervening twelve or thirteen years since writing *The Gate of Time.* This is chiefly seen in the description of the differences between Earth 1 and Earth 2 at the end of Chapter 7.

Another reason for the novel's revision is that Phil had matured as a writer over the years. Thus, instead of the all-too-neat, practically Burroughsian happy ending of *The Gate of Time,* Phil adds an additional three chapters that unravel Two Hawks' relationship with Ilmika and send him back on his quest for a gateway home. Two Hawks finds the latter, although that "home" is not exactly what he expects. Then again, as Farmer-the-realist knows, it never is. Fortunately for Two Hawks, his biracial ethnicity has left him uncomfortable on his own world to begin with, and his new home looks like it will allow plenty of breathing room for his free-soaring spirit.

The novel abounds with the imagery of dualism: *Two Hawks from Earth* (symbolizing both the protagonist's name and the fact that the story is about two industrious war hawks from Earth, Roger and his slippery nemesis, the Nazi Raske), Earth 2; two nations at war; and even the fateful fact that the novel exists in *two* versions. Indeed, the novel's prevailing theme that "polarity equals strength" is illustrated in the contrast between Roger

Two Hawks and his fellow Earthman, O'Brien. Two Hawks is adaptable, a "quicksilver Proteus" like his World of Tiers counterpart Kickaha—whose middle name "Janus" refers not only to the Roman deity with two faces that look in opposite directions, but also to Janus' role as the god of gates, doors, and doorways. Both characters share the ability to transition easily from one world to the next without tripping as the pluriverse shifts under their feet, like Phil himself mischievously hopping between the fantastical literary universes of his own creation. But where the versatile Two Hawks thrives in his new situation on Earth 2, his comrade O'Brien finds his very soul fading out of existence due to his own rigidity.

Flexibility is life, stiffness is death: a lesson the creatively resourceful Grand Master from Peoria knows well... and for his readers, the reason why opening up a Philip José Farmer novel is a portal to unparalleled worlds of heart-pounding adventure and unbounded vistas of the imagination. *Two Hawks from Earth* is one such gateway.

As of writing this afterword, I have recently returned from another trip to Peoria to visit Phil and his lovely wife Bette upon the occasion of Phil's ninety-first birthday. During the visit, while contemplating writing this afterword, I again wondered about that fateful chain of events that led Phil from his, Stearman biplane and back to the typewriter. I didn't really come up with anything useful for the afterword. Only gratitude to the Great Whomever Who controls the quantum strings of the pluriverse that I've been blessed to exist in the same continuum as Philip José Farmer the Writer.

And you know, that's good enough for me.

Philip José Farmer:
A Remembrance

Locus, Issue 579, Vol. 62, No. 4, April 2009

I first met Phil Just over ten years ago, when he was 80 years old. We'd corresponded briefly about an article I'd written, which he'd called "stimulating." It was about enough to make my young writer self weep, having the man who'd written "The Lovers" and *Tarzan Alive* and *The Unreasoning Mask* write that to me in a letter. When, in 1998, l drove from eastern Pennsylvania out to Peoria, Illinois, to meet Phil at local library event in his honor, he thought I was crazy. "I don't know if it'll be worth the trip," he told me in a self-deprecating tone. But I think that secretly he was pleased. He'd never achieved the same breadth of fame as some of his luckier SF peers, but I think maybe he knew he had something better than that: the ability to make each of his readers, or at least the perceptive ones, think they'd been let in on a secret. Otherwise why else would he have planted such a wide array of esoteric "Easter eggs" throughout his writings? So many, in fact, that it'd be impossible for a single person to ever find them all.

At a dinner two or three years later, Phil—who often wrote about immortality—joked with some friends and me that he really had the physical build of a twenty-three-year-old but was hiding it behind a clever disguise. Then he grew deadpan serious and said that anyone who had the secret to immortality would have to be willing to kill to protect it. Phil often played his literary cards close. There are in-jokes people will be rooting out of his writings two hundred years from now, and probably just as many serious themes woven nigh invisibly throughout the dark web that is the Farmerian

PHILIP JOSÉ FARMER
DANNY ADAMS

THE City
BEYOND Play

With an
Introduction by Chris Roberson

And an
Afterword by Tracy Knight

Monomyth. And that is the sort of thing that will grant Phil a kind of immortality. And Trickster that he was, I think he knew that. Immortality's better than fame anyway.

I only knew Phil in his later years, so I don't know how he might have treated bright-eyed aspiring writers when he was younger. But I do know how he treated myself and my good friend Win Eckert, and his nephew Danny Adams, not to mention each of the post-Farmerian Wold Newton writers with whom he was acquainted who ran gleefully through the playhouse of his fictional Wold Newton genealogy. And that was respectfully, as peers. And for that, I know we were all as much shell-shocked as we were, and are, overwhelmingly grateful. And among the younger generation of writers, those who grew up reading the bloom of Farmer paperback originals and reprints in the 1970s and '80s—people like Chris Roberson and Rhys Hughes and Michael Carroll and Paul Malmont—Phil's legacy will go on. And that is another kind of immortality.

In a way, Phil wasn't joshing. With his two strains of immortality elixir, he'll outlive us all.

Philip José Farmer and Edgar Rice Burroughs:
A Shared Mythography

The Burroughs Bulletin, New Series, No. 81, Winter 2010

"When I was ten, I built my personal pantheon of heroes... Bright as these Greeks and Norse and Algonquins were, however, they were outshone by others, men and demi-gods who sprang, like Athena from Zeus' brow, full-grown from the mind of an American.

"This man was a modern. He was Edgar Rice Burroughs, a man as fertile in the making of modern myths as his middle name indicates."

These words, composed over a half century ago and first appearing in "The Golden Age and the Brass" in twelfth issue of *The Burroughs Bulletin* (First Series), mark one of the first known entries in the public record of Philip José Farmer's longstanding love and appreciation for the works of the Master of Adventure. It was to be among the first of many published expressions that illustrated the joy ERB's works brought to Phil, ranging from letters and articles in Burroughs fanzines to novels and stories set directly in—or sometimes at sly, oblique angles to—ERB's worlds.

While the above quote states that he was ten when he forged his heroic pantheon, Phil has elsewhere written that by 1925, at the age of seven, he had already read the Tarzan and John Carter of Mars books, first having encountered them in the McClure Library in Peoria, Illinois, sometime after his family moved there from Mexico, Missouri in 1923. "[W]hen I got to the adult section [of the library]," Phil once stated in an interview, "I just went ape. Literally, because I discovered the Tarzan books." Soon the young Phil's imagination transformed the local woods and creek banks where he played into John Carter's Barsoom and Tarzan's Africa. In childhood, as throughout the rest of his life, Phil wasn't shy about his enthusiasm for ERB's creations, and before long his schoolyard peers stuck him with the moniker of "Tarzan." Phil went on to save a portion of his allowance, and to ask for at least one Burroughs book as birthday and Christmas gifts, so that he eventually acquired a near-complete ERB library of his own. But Phil's love of reading did not end with Burroughs; he devoured everything, from *The Arabian Nights* and the Bible to the Doc Savage and The Shadow pulps. "Of course, in those days I had no literary discrimination," Phil once wrote. "They all read great to me, and many gave me some of the keenest pleasure I've ever had... [A]s I look back, the intimations of immortality, that blue-tinged, gold-shot thrilling and trembling-on-the-edge-of-revelation, that almost mystical feeling, came as much, perhaps more, from the pulps as from the classics I was reading." It was sometime during this golden age of his youth that Phil formulated his ambition to write and have published an Oz novel, a Doc Savage novel, and a Tarzan novel, a dream he would one day go on accomplish with the publication of *A Barnstormer in Oz* (1982), *Escape from Loki* (1991), and *The Dark Heart of Time* (1999).

Phil's literary explorations expanded as he grew into a young man and pored through the works of Dickens, London, Balzac, Rabelais, Goethe, Dostoyevsky, Joyce, Miller, and many other writers of classic literature. And while Phil matured and learned to discriminate between the classics and the pulps of his youth, to distinguish the merits of the former and the faults and frailties of the latter, he came to understand that some of the popular literature he loved as a child bore a mythic strength as prodigious as that of Hercules'. "The unconscious is the true democracy," Phil wrote in 1988 at the age of 70. "All things, all people, are equal. Thus, in my mind, Odysseus towered no higher than Tarzan, King Arthur was no greater than Doc Savage, and Cthulhu and Conan loomed as large on my mind's eye as Jehovah and Sampson."

Phil graduated high school in 1936 and went on to study

journalism at the University of Missouri, but soon financial problems at home forced him to withdraw to help pay off his families debts and save money for school. After working over a year and a half as a lineman for Illinois Power and Light, Phil returned to his studies, this time majoring in English literature and carrying a minor in philosophy at Bradley Polytechnic Institute in Peoria. Here, in the fall of 1940, Phil met the love of his life, a musical and science scholarship student named Elizabeth (Bette) Virginia Andre. When Phil saw Bette appear as the lead singer in a play at the school, it was love at first sight—at least for Phil, who decided he had to throw himself down a set of stairs, not once, but three times, to get the girl's attention. The stunt worked.

The following year Phil transferred back to the University of Missouri so he could take classes in classical Greek, but he so missed Bette that he cut his English class and hitchhiked back to Peoria to visit her nearly every Friday night. In April 1941, without notifying their families, the couple drove out to Boonsville, Missouri with friends and eloped. So began a marriage that would endure for over sixty-seven years.

In fall 1941, Phil enlisted in the Army Air Force just prior to the attack on Pearl Harbor. Though a fair pilot, he washed out of flight training due to an ill-tempered flight instructor, and was forced to return home to Peoria, where he worked for the Keystone Steel & Wire Company for the next eleven and a half years. His experiences in the steel mill would later inspire one of his finest and most overlooked novels, *Fire and the Night* (1963; recently reprinted in the omnibus *The Other in the Mirror*, Subterranean Press, 2009), a mainstream story about interracial relations in a small Midwestern town.

In 1942, Phil and Bette had a son, Philip Laird, and in 1946, a daughter, Kristen. As he continued to work at Keystone and struggled to support his new family, Phil began to write mainstream stories and submit them to the slicks without much success. (Many of these mainstream stories would later go on to be published in *Farmerphile: The Magazine of Philip José Farmer* from 2005–2009, with most of these being collected in *Up from* the *Bottomless Pit and Other Stories*, Subterranean Press, 2007). One exception was Phil's first published short story "O'Brien and Obrenov." The story was accepted by the prestigious *Saturday Evening Post* on the condition that the drunk scene be excised; but Phil, never one to bend easily to censorship, refused. The story, after being rejected by *Argosy* for being too long, appeared in the March 1946 issue of *Adventure*.

Phil must have believed himself on the verge of success, but such thoughts were soon to be tempered by a lack of further story sales. In fact, it would not be until 1952, when Phil turned his writing to the science fiction that he loved as a youth, that he would sell another story. The novella "The Lovers" is now a landmark in the history of science fiction literature, and back then the story took the science fiction community by storm. Letters poured into *Starling Stories* (where the story appeared) for well over a year after publication, with some readers praising its groundbreaking nature, and others clamoring for where they could get a back issue so they could read what all the fuss was about. Phil went on to earn a Hugo for Most Promising New Talent in 1953 mainly on the basis of "The Lovers," and the story made him a recognizable name in the SF field.

It is worthy to note that Phil and Bette struck up what would become a longtime friendship with *Burroughs Bulletin* and Burroughs Bibliophiles founder Vern Coriell in the same year that "The Lovers" was published. Bette Farmer wrote of their early friendship in the January 2006 issue of *Farmerphile*:

> In October, 1952, we received a phone call from Pekin, Illinois from Vernell Coriell. He had just read "The Lovers" and wanted very much to come up and meet Phil and bring a friend, Jack Cordes.
>
> Vern was a devoted Tarzan fan and at the time was editor of *The Burroughs Bibliophiles*. We kept up that friendship for many years, and after Vern passed away, Jack continued to come to our house... Vern was a member of the famous Coriell family acrobatic team for many years. After he retired from that, he did lectures and

demonstrations of acrobatic prowess for high schools. One day he came to our house with a unicycle, which he was learning to ride so he could take it with him on the tours of the high schools. At the same time, another friend of ours, Burke Martin, stopped by. He had taken a job with the Post Office for the Xmas holidays, so he came in with his mail bag to have a cup of coffee and rest and visit with us. Time flew by and suddenly Burke remembered his mail route. Vern said he had to go too, so we all went out on the porch and Vern did a double flip down the six steps from the porch, jumped on his unicycle, and rode down the street and back. Suddenly we noticed that many neighbors down the street were looking out for their mail. The saw all the "goings on" at the Farmer household, as Vern went by on his cycle. Their mouths dropped open...those kooky Farmers were at it again.

Phil would later pay tribute to his friend and fellow admirer of ERB by setting a violent shootout scene in his hardboiled Peoria P.I. novel *Nothing Burns in Hell* (1998) at the site of the Coriell family plot in North Pekin's Lakeside Cemetery.

Phil's meeting Vern Coriell just as he was beginning a career in science fiction somehow seems fitting, and one must wonder if their talks about ERB at this crucial time played any role in stimulating the Burroughs-inspired direction of some of the budding author's later works. While Phil certainly carved out his own distinctive writing style from the outset, Burroughs' stamp is clearly recognizable in some of his earlier stories. I believe it may have been Bob Barrett who pointed out that the post-apocalyptic *The Cache from Outer Space* (1962) could be read as a disguised sequel to ERB's *The Moon Men* (whether it was intended to be, I do not know). Similarly, *The Gate of Time* (1966), later revised as *Two Hawks from Earth* (1979; reprinted by MonkeyBrain Books, 2009), is framed with Burroughs-style narrative bookends, with the reader being drawn into the story by a faux-journalistic narrative, and the novel's fighter pilot hero passing into a parallel universe almost exactly the

BURROUGHS BULLETIN
NEW SERIES #81   WINTER , 2010

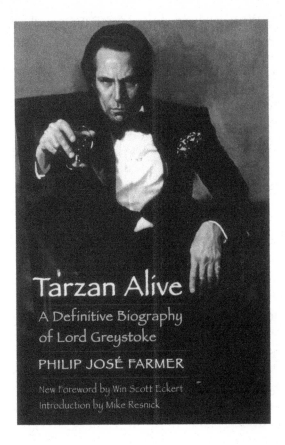

Tarzan Alive

A Definitive Biography
of Lord Greystoke

PHILIP JOSÉ FARMER

New Foreword by Win Scott Eckert
Introduction by Mike Resnick

same way that Tangor finds himself transported to Poloda in ERB's *Beyond the Farthest Star.*

Such apparent, if somewhat indirect Burroughsian influences in his fiction would only be the beginning of an ERB-spattered career for Phil. Soon he took on ERB directly. The first of his stories to do so was the audacious and brilliant "The Jungle-Rot Kid on the Nod" (1968), which asked the question, "What if William Burroughs instead of Edgar Rice Burroughs had written the Tarzan novels...?" That same year *A Private Cosmos*, Phil's third novel in the World of Tiers series, appeared, in which the hero Kickaha gets to have an adventure on a moon engineered to reproduce ERB's Barsoom.

With the publication of *A Feast Unknown* by the erotic publisher Essex House in 1969, Phil's literary excursions into the worlds of ERB took a strange turn that would have been impossible for anyone to see coming previous to its release. This underground classic of sexually explicit Tarzan and Doc Savage analogs is a love it or hate it book for ERB and Savage fans, with its decriers unable to get over seeing their childhood heroes in over-the-top depictions of sex and violence, and its supporters (yes, many of them ERB fans) recognizing the humor Phil expressed by exaggerating sex lives of the pulps' ridiculously sex-neutered heroes and also enjoying the immensely satisfying action-packed conspiracy plot looming behind the parody. This latter storyline continued in the markedly non-explicit sequels, *The Lord of the Trees* and *The Mad Goblin*, both published together in 1970 in an Ace Double. Bette Farmer once remarked to me that all the big names in SF were writing for the erotic presses at the time, but Phil was the only one of them to do so under his own name. When asked in an interview by David Pringle about how he responded to those who accused him of writing corrupting books, Phil replied, "I just tell them I'm doing it for fun. They don't realize what I'm actually doing. I never would have done it if I hadn't been asked. It just didn't occur to me, but as soon as I was asked to write something for [Essex House publisher] Brian Kirby all these ideas clicked out. They must have been lying fallow."

Next up for Phil's ERB inspired work was *Lord Tyger* (1970), and I won't spoil the big reveal in the novel for those who have not yet read it. Algis Budrys called it "a major novel," and *Locus* proclaimed that "this novel transcends the mythos that inspired it." I doubt Phil would have gone that far himself, but he did once tell me he regarded it as one of his better works. He once stated in an interview that

...sometimes in my books which are regarded as adventure stories there are deeper currents. I was very much disappointed at the reception of *Lord Tyger*—it's usually sloughed off as another Tarzan novel, but that's not true. The structure is based on Joseph Campbell's *The Hero with a Thousand Faces*, and anybody familiar with that book, reading *Lord Tyger*, can trace Campbell right on through. The cyclic adventurer, the heroes of classical mythology, primitive religion and so forth. There's a hell of a lot more in that book than most people realize.

The 1970s saw Phil becoming more active in Burroughs fandom, attending Dum-Dum conventions in Detroit in 1970 (Guest of Honor, banquet speaker), Toronto in 1973 (banquet speaker), and Kansas City in 1976 (banquet speaker). During this period he also penned a number of articles that appeared in various Burroughs fanzines: "The Arms of Tarzan" (*The Burroughs Bulletin*, Summer 1971, based on a speech presented at the 1970 Dum-Dum), "A Reply to 'The Red Herring'" (*Erbania*, No. 28, December 1971), "The Great Korak–Time Discrepancy" (*ERB-dom*, No. 57, April 1972), "The Lord Mountford Mystery" (*ERB-dom*, No. 65, December 1972), "From ERB to Ygg" (*ERBivore*, Nos. 6 and 7, August 1973), and "A Language for Opar" (*ERB-dom*, No. 75, February 1974). All of these articles are still available in the anthology *Myths for the Modern Age: Philip José Farmer's Wold Newton Universe*, ed. Win Scott Eckert (MonkeyBrain Books, 2005).

Work on *Tarzan Alive*, the monumental "biography" of Tarzan published by Doubleday in 1972, as well as his Ancient Opar/Khokarsa cycle, fueled Phil's enthusiasm for Burroughs throughout this part of his career. These were preceded, however, by *Time's Last Gift* (1972), a prequel of sorts to the Ancient Opar books that explains the means by which Phil's Tarzan analog, John Gribardsun, can conceivably appear 12,000 years beforehand in *Hadon of Ancient Opar* (1974) and *Flight to Opar* (1976) as Sahhindar, the Khokarsan god of plants, of bronze, and of time.

Phil put a great deal of time, work, and love into *Tarzan Alive: A Definitive Biography of Lord Greystoke*, the great tome that first proposed the expansive literary family tree known as the Wold Newton family, which is now back in print courtesy of Bison Books' Frontiers of Imagination series, fittingly the same imprint to reissue a host of quality ERB reprints in recent years. The unique angle of *Tarzan Alive*, of course, is that Lord Greystoke is a real person—and Phil had met him! An account of Phil's meeting with Tarzan appeared in the April 1972 issue of *Esquire* under the title "Tarzan Lives: An exclusive interview with the eight Duke of Greystoke" shortly after the biography's publication. The cognitive dissonance created by this claim has both puzzled and intrigued fans of the ape man ever since the book's release, and to my knowledge Phil never publicly tipped his hand with any indication other than that Tarzan was real and he had met truly him. In a letter in the Summer 1977 issue of *Erbania*, Phil wrote, "For me, it's not a game. I *know* that there was a real Tarzan and the he still lives. I'm dead serious, though not deadly serious, I hope." In the Summer 1985 issue of the same fanzine, he went on to tease, "Did you know that Tarzan's father's oil portrait hangs in the National Gallery in London?", and in an interview for a 1996 documentary titled "Moi, Tarzan," Phil practically tears up as he recalls in seeming earnest his meeting with the lord of the jungle.

On the heels of *Tarzan Alive* came *The Other Log of Phileas Fogg* (1972), revealing the secret history of the extraterrestrial conspiracy behind Jules Verne's classic *Around the World in Eighty Days* and interweaving its characters into the Wold Newton genealogy. Phil's second "biography," *Doc Savage: His Apocalyptic Life*, which expanded the Wold Newton family concept and detailed the life of Tarzan's famous crime-fighting cousin, came out in 1973, soon to be followed by *Mother Was a Lovely Beast*

(1974), an anthology of "fact and fiction about humans raised by animals," edited by Phil, that reprinted "The God of Tarzan" from ERB's *Jungle Tales of Tarzan*, as well published "Extracts from the Memoirs of 'Lord Greystoke'" based on manuscripts that the ape man allegedly passed on to the editor.

Over the period when these last several ERB-inspired works were written and published, Phil had already begun to think about the aforementioned Ancient Opar series set in Africa at the end of the last Ice Age. Phil's personal files indicate that he was in correspondence with ERB fan Frank Brueckel as early as 1971, and it was in fact a monograph by Brueckel and another ERB fan, John Harwood, that gave Phil the kernel of the idea for what was originally planned to be an ambitious series intended to span six to twelve novels. The heroes of the first few books were to be Hadon of Opar and his giant, herculean cousin Kwasin of Dythbeth. Unfortunately, only the first two novels, *Hadon of Ancient Opar* and *Flight to Opar*, were completed and published, although a third novel—not set in ancient Opar but rather in Phil's own creation, the island of Khokarsa—was outlined and begun. The series itself, while written in the spirit of epic heroic fantasy, was no mere Burroughs pastiche, but rather interwove the traditions of ERB with those of H. Rider Haggard, combined with rich, intricately designed world building that was Phil's own. The monograph by Brueckel and Harwood that inspired Phil's formulation of the Khokarsan civilization never saw print as expected in *The Burroughs Bulletin*, but was at last published decades later in a fascinating collection titled *Heritage of the Flaming God*, ed. Alan Hanson and Michael Winger (Waziri Press, 1999), which I heartily recommend to all fans of ERB and PJF.

In between *Hadon* and *Flight*, Phil made time for one more ERB-inspired work, *The Adventure of the Peerless Peer* (1974), a short novel "edited by John H. Watson, M.D." in which Sherlock Holmes meets Lord Greystoke. Out of print since the 1976 Dell edition, the novel finally available again in a collection of Phil's "fictional-author" stories titled *Venus on the Half-Shell and Others* (2008), along with a note of thanks from Phil to Danton Burroughs for his blessing to reprint the story.

Even after the heyday of his ERB-inspired works in the 1970s, Phil never lost touch with Burroughs fandom. On October 21, 1989, Phil joined a group of ardent Burroughs enthusiasts as they gathered at The Adventurer's Club in Chicago, Illinois to commemorate the 75th anniversary of the first hardcover publication of *Tarzan of the Apes* (see Phil's keynote speech, "I Still Live!", in *Farmerphile* No. 3, January 2006). Phil also continued to write letters into the Burroughs fanzines, dropping tantalizing lines about possible articles he'd like to write such as "Are you interested in such things as an article on the real barons of Greystoke, which also shows that George Washington was a direct descendant of them?" (*The Burroughs Bulletin*, New Series, No. 4, October 1990) or "By the way, has anyone published an article on the anatomical effects of egg-laying on the Martian human female?...Would a short article on this from me be welcome?" (*Burroughs Bulletin*, New Series, No. 31, Summer 1997). To the great regret of his and ERB's fans, he never did write these, but he did have one last major ERB project left in his creative arsenal: the fulfillment of his childhood dream to write and have published an authorized Tarzan novel.

Fans had been eagerly awaiting such a novel from Phil for many years, and Phil himself hinted at the Tarzan story he wanted to write in the chronology in Addendum 5 of *Tarzan Alive* when he made the entry for Aug., 1914, to Oct., 1918: "The events of *Tarzan the Untamed*. Also, a 'lost adventure,' during which Tarzan traced the route on the map of the dead giant Spanish soldier." *The Dark Heart of Time: A Tarzan Novel* was published in 1999, after being rescheduled from an earlier release to coincide with the new Disney Tarzan film and so as not to be associated with the box office failure of *Tarzan and the Lost City* in 1998. The novel was not only to mark the realization of Phil's childhood ambition; it would also be the last novel he would ever write.

Still, a ERB-related gems trickled in after Phil retired from writing. In 2006 *Pearls from Peoria*, a mammoth collection of Phil's rare and previously unpublished works came out from Subterranean Press and included the never-before-seen short story "A Princess of Terra," a recursive, parallel universe take on *A Princess of Mars* in the form of a review of "the great master of science fiction, Erb of Anazrat." The giant collection also presented for the first time "The Purple Distance," a foreword to a never-published edition of Longfellow's *The Song of Hiawatha*, in the form of an essay comparing Tarzan and Hiawatha.

In January 2009 I gathered with a group of Phil and Bette's friends and family at their home in Peoria, Illinois to wish Phil a happy 91st birthday. The bookshelves in the living room gave testament to Phil's diverse reading background, but there in a position of highest esteem up on the topmost shelf sat a first edition of *Tarzan the Invincible*, an old hardback edition of *Tarzan and the Jewels of Opar* resting only a shelf lower. I would be back in Peoria only a month later to attend Phil's memorial service, and again after a few short months just days before Bette's passing.

Phil is most widely known for his bestselling Riverworld series and his groundbreaking "The Lovers," but I think this article illustrates that a vast part of his opus—and an important part of it—owes much to one of his favorite childhood writers. Without ERB's influence, it's hard even to imagine what Phil's career would have been like. But one thing is for certain: while another era has now come to close, Philip José Farmer's works, like Edgar Rice Burroughs', still live.

Partial list of works cited:

Farmer, Bette. "The Roller Coaster Ride with Phil Farmer," *Farmerphile: The Magazine of Philip José Farmer*, No. 3, January 2006.

Farmer, Philip José. Foreword to *Philip José Farmer's The Dungeon, Volume 1: The Black Tower*, Bantam, 1988.

Pringle, David. "Philip José Farmer: Interviewed by David Pringle," *Vector* #81, June 1977

Bibo, Terry. "The Legacy Project: A Conversation with Philip José Farmer." *Peoria Journal-Star*, January 1999, http://www2. pjstar.com/index.php/legacy/article/a_conversation_with_ philip_jose_farmer/.

Philip José Farmer's Influence

Published online at *The Official Philip José Farmer Home Page*, June 2011

Michael Croteau: Tell us a little about yourself and how you first discovered Philip José Farmer.

Christopher Paul Carey: Well, from a young age I've been fascinated by science fiction and fantasy. I started out reading H. G. Wells. I had an omnibus—I think it was titled *The Complete Science Fiction Treasury of H. G. Wells*—that I devoured when I was in grade school. I also read and enjoyed Jonathan Swift, Jules Verne, and Tolkien at an early age, but it wasn't until I encountered Edgar Rice Burroughs that the dam broke and I knew I had to write. Right after that I discovered Farmer. The first books of his that I read were *The Maker of Universes*, *Hadon of Ancient Opar*, and *Tarzan Alive*, having been drawn to him by the intersection with ERB's worlds in the latter two works. I was spellbound straightaway with how Farmer had taken Burroughs' proclivity for linking his own series together and expanded it, so that all of literature seemed to exist in a meta universe that one could get access to by creative reading. We're so used to hearing the phrase "creative writing," but Farmer initiated his readers into the wondrous secret that reading itself can be an actively creative process. And as I devoured everything of Farmer's that I could find (after reading almost every ERB novel then in print), I was also reading a lot of the authors that influenced Phil, such as Vonnegut, Twain, London, and Doyle.

So I guess because of all of this exposure to the fantastic I ended up a writer and editor of SF/F. In my day job I work as an editor at Paizo Publishing, publisher of the Pathfinder Roleplaying Game and the Planet Stories science fiction and fantasy imprint. In the past few years I've also had some of my short fiction published in anthologies. In my free time I write.

And eventually, I should add, I got to meet and know Phil Farmer and his wife Bette, which I count as one of the great honors and experiences of my life. I was also fortunate to have had the opportunity to edit three Farmer collections for Subterranean Press (*Up from the Bottomless Pit and Other Stories*, *Venus on the Half-Shell and Others*, and *The Other in the Mirror*).

MC: Going back a bit, starting in 1996, you wrote a number articles about Farmer's Doc Savage origin story *Escape From Loki*, which were published in *The Bronze Gazette* and the anthology *Myths for the Modern Age: Philip José Farmer's Wold Newton Universe*. Phil was aware of these articles, you sent him copies, and you even corresponded with him about them. What made you so interested in this story in particular that you chose to examine it so closely?

CPC: I forgot—somehow—to add in the answer to the previous question that I obsessively read the Doc Savage series in the Bantam reprints beginning at age fifteen. It took me seemingly forever to track them all down, and I didn't finish reading them all until the 1990s.

In any case, after I read Farmer's *Escape from Loki* when it came out in 1991, I didn't even pause for a day before I picked it up again and started rereading it. And then I turned around and reread it yet again. Each time I did this, pieces of a Brobdingnagian jigsaw puzzle seemed to fall into place and I quickly became convinced Phil had laid a hidden backstory in the novel that could only be understood by someone who'd read certain of his other works, such as *The Other Log of Phileas Fogg* and his Sherlock Holmes/Raffles pastiche, "The Problem of the Sore Bridge—Among Others." One of my ideas was that Phil had taken one of Doc's nemeses from the original Doc Savage pulps and given him a female disguise in *Escape from Loki*. Phil was genuinely tickled by this when he read the article I'd written on it, comparing it to when Rex Stout scandalized the

Sherlock Holmes community by proposing that Watson was a woman. The theory really isn't as far out as it sounds. Anyone who's familiar with the novel *Venus on the Half-Shell* knows to what lengths Phil will go to play the trickster, and the theme of duplicitous sex change does appear elsewhere in Phil's work. Phil said he approved of my way of thinking.

MC: This leads us to one of the main reasons we were eager to interview you. Do you think all this attention to detail contributed to Phil allowing you to complete the third, and concluding, novel in the Khokarsa series (the first two novels being *Hadon of Ancient Opar* and *Flight to Opar*)?

CPC: I think it was probably a big factor, yes. He knew I wasn't just familiar with his own body of work, but also that I had a deep appreciation of the Burroughs and Haggard traditions that inspired the series. He also knew I had a degree in anthropology—one of his great lifelong interests—and was then working on my Master's in writing. By this time, Phil had stopped writing and was long into his retirement. But I think it nagged at him that the Khokarsa series was left unfinished, and when the original manuscript fragment and outline he'd written for the third novel turned up, I think he and Bette felt the stars had finally aligned. For myself, I was astounded, thrilled, and humbled all at once to be able to help complete the trilogy.

MC: Without revealing any spoilers, what's the novel about?

CPC: It's the story of the giant Kwasin's return to the civilization of Khokarsa after eight long years of exile in the Wild Lands. But on his return, Kwasin discovers that King Minruth has overthrown Khokarsa's matriarchy and seized control of the empire. Kwasin wants take up the fight against Minruth, but first he has to clear his name with the woman he wronged and the oracle who cast him out because of it. The novel picks up right after the events of *Hadon of Ancient Opar*, when Kwasin is last seen wielding his great ax in an epic battle with Minruth's soldiers, remaining behind to give his cousin Hadon and his companions a chance to escape.

MC: Where did the title *The Song of Kwasin* come from?

CPC: The novel outline by Phil that I worked from was originally titled "*Kwasin of Opar,*" but Phil was never really happy with the title since Kwasin was from Dythbeth, not Opar, and also because the novel is chiefly set on the island of Khokarsa, not in distant Opar. So when the chance to complete the novel surfaced, so did the opportunity to retitle it. "*Kwasin of Dythbeth*" (pronounced "Deeth-bayth" in Khokarsan) was too much of a mouthful, so we went for something that evoked Longfellow's poem "The Song of Hiawatha," since Hiawatha's strongman friend from that poem—Kwasind—was the inspiration for Kwasin's name. The title also evokes the ballads of the great Khokarsan bards, such as *The Song of Gahete* and *The Song of Kethna*, which were referenced in *Hadon of Ancient Opar*. To seal the deal, a song also plays a key role in the novel's plot.

MC: What were some of your biggest challenges when writing *The Song of Kwasin* and how did you overcome them?

CPC: I think one big challenge was to write a book that would read like it was written in 1976, the last time a book in the series was published. I felt it was important that all three books should as much as possible have a similar feel since it was likely they'd be collected in an omnibus, which was a bit of a trick since the third book is in a different voice—Kwasin's—than the first two, which are in Hadon's viewpoint.

Fortunately, Phil gives an idea of how Kwasin sees the world in his outline to the novel. Kwasin isn't quite as smart as Hadon, and in fact, like the classic trickster archetype, he sometimes does really stupid things that cause trouble for him and those around him. In the first two books, we see Kwasin from Hadon's point of view, but Hadon doesn't really know why Kwasin acts the way he does. That is, as a lout, a bully, and a larger-than-life trickster. So the third book gets to dig into Kwasin's past a bit and also shows something of how Kwasin viewed Hadon—not with simple hatred, although there was a fair degree of that, but more so with a deep jealousy.

So there's that—establishing Kwasin's viewpoint—and then

PHILIP JOSÉ FARMER

THE
MAKER OF UNIVERSES

"INCOMPARABLE."
—ROGER
ZELAZNY

ACE 51624-6/$2.25

SF

BORIS

absorbing the style of the first two books, and layering on the established world-building. Of course, Phil's world-building is extremely rich.

MC: What was it like writing in another author's world—in this case, the lost civilization of Khokarsa?

CPC: Also challenging, but I reveled in it because world-building is something I love. And I was fortunate to have Phil's extensive notes from the series: those concerning the culture and characters, as well as the maps, lexicons, and unpublished articles on the Khokarsan civilization, language, and syllabary. Regarding the latter, I was lucky to run across Phil's complete Khokarsan syllabary in his files after I'd already completed the book, so I was able to go back through it and make sure all of the names in the novel followed the rules of the syllabary. Phil had sometimes referred to what he called "interim" names in his original outline, which was his cue to go back and make sure the names corresponded with the linguistic rules for Khokarsan, which in many cases they didn't. So I was able to sync these up with the language rules.

MC: Did you find any other discrepancies in the outline?

CPC: I think it's pretty clear Phil was writing like a man possessed when he composed the original outline, and also that a little time had passed since he'd finished the first two books in the series. So he did make a few mistakes that he probably would have corrected later, like forgetting that in *Flight to Opar* he'd already established some of the characters and events surrounding Kwasin's arrival in Dythbeth, the names of the king and queen there, what happened the first night he got to the city, and so on. So I had to sync up those details. Charles Berlin, the artist who rendered the new maps, was also able to correct some minor errors that first appeared in the maps in the DAW edition of *Hadon of Ancient Opar*. These weren't Phil's mistakes, but rather errors introduced by the original cartographer, the SF artist Jack Gaughan.

MC: In your aforementioned essay in *Myths for the Modern Age*, you excavate some of the secret backstory of Farmer's work, just as he claimed to uncover some hidden storylines in the works of authors like Verne and Doyle. Does any of that sort of intrigue come into play in *The Song of Kwasin*?

CPC: Sure. But I think for the most part the reader will have to carefully parse the text to pick up on it. I tried not to browbeat the reader with that sort of thing, because Phil at his most intriguing was subtle. A hint here, a taste there. It's there in plenty in the novel, but readers are going to have to draw their own road maps to it, because that's what makes reading a Farmer novel fun.

MC: So you won't give us any hints?

CPC: Readers of Haggard should pick up on some interesting threads, beyond just the presence of Kwasin's ax, which appeared a number of Haggard stories. But that's all I'll say.

MC: Did you have much interaction with Farmer in regards to writing the story?

CPC: As late as 1999, Phil had been thinking of wrapping up the series himself in one final novel, and as I mentioned previously, I think it disappointed him to see the series languish unfinished. So when I was in the thick of writing the novel in 2007, Bette Farmer would read installments aloud to Phil as I finished them, and she would tell me how Phil would light up at hearing of Kwasin's adventures. They both said how pleased they were and that they really enjoyed the novel, which put me over the moon.

Phil did give me some input about how he wanted the novel to wrap up. This was back in 2005, shortly after the manuscript fragment and outline had turned up. I pointed out that the original outline stops abruptly just before the conclusion, and also presents a couple of alternate courses of action for Kwasin and Awineth. When I asked Phil for his advice, he specifically told me he wanted to abandon these options for the characters, and instructed me as to how he thought the book and trilogy should drop the curtain. So I took all of that to heart and put it in the novel.

MC: So is *The Song of Kwasin* the ultimate culmination of the series or is there yet more of the story to tell?

CPC: certainly stands as a conclusion to a trilogy. If any further books were to be written in the series, they would be part of a new sequence. Phil did leave a brief outline of events that would have transpired after the conclusion of the third novel, but as to whether that tale will ever be told, who knows?

MC: When will *The Song of Kwasin* be published?

CPC: The publisher has not officially announced the book yet, but in the Spring of 2012 Subterranean Press is slated to bring out an omnibus encompassing all three novels in the series: *Hadon of Ancient Opar, Flight to Opar,* and *The Song of Kwasin.*

MC: *The Song of Kwasin* is not the first thing you've written set in Khokarsa. You also wrote the short story "A Kick in the Side," which was published last year in *The Worlds of Philip José Farmer 1: Protean Dimensions.* What can you tell us about this story, and what prompted you to write it?

CPC: I actually wrote that story early on when I was working on *Kwasin.* I had been rereading *Flight to Opar* a number of times over, and each time I got to the part where Hadon's scribe Hinokly abruptly fell over the side of the ship into the sea and was never mentioned again, I couldn't help but wonder if that was the end of his story. I wrote "A Kick in the Side" to explore Hinokly's fate, and also as a tribute to anyone who's been bullied by a dullard. I admit, when I wrote it I was thinking of some of the trials and tribulations Phil went through in publishing over the years.

MC: You also coauthored a 20,000-word novella with Farmer called "Kwasin and the Bear God," which will be available in the anthology *The Worlds of José Farmer 2: Of Dust and Soul.* Can you tell us how this story came to be written and how the novella relates to the novel?

CPC: I was in Peoria in January 2009 to celebrate Phil's 91st birthday with a small group of friends. At the end of the weekend, most everyone who'd come from out of town had left except for [*Pearls from Peoria* editor and Phil's friend] Paul Spiteri and me, and a few hours before my flight Bette Farmer said we could go downstairs to browse Phil's files and look for anything that might have been overlooked for possible future publication. That's when I ran across a manila folder I'd never seen before labeled "Khokarsan Lore." Paul can probably attest that I blanched when I pulled from the folder a fragmentary alternate outline to the *Kwasin* novel, which I'd already completed months before using Phil's partial manuscript and a different outline. But on closer examination, a large portion of the alternate outline was unusable because it contradicted already published canon from the other Khokarsa books. Another portion told the same story as Phil's original outline, the one I'd used to complete *The Song of Kwasin*. But there were about two pages of outline that covered the story of Kwasin's adventures from the time he'd left the capital of Khokarsa to just after his arrival in the mountains near his birth city of Dythbeth. I was very excited to realize this part of the outline fit in neatly between the first and second chapters of *The Song of Kwasin*.

So when Meteor House began their *Worlds of Philip José Farmer* series of anthologies, they said they'd love to publish the unwritten story if I'd be willing to write it. I said of course I'd do it. The scene with Kwasin and the sloth of bears is probably one of the craziest, most over-the-top things I've ever written—and one of the most fun—and I have Phil to thank for that. I was also happy to be able to use a previously unpublished little piece written by Phil in the story, a Khokarsan creation myth that appears in the form of a priestess' dialogue. I think the novella, perhaps even more than the novel, captures the essence of Kwasin's trickster nature. Like *Hadon*, it also follows the classic structure of the Campbellian hero's journey, something I realized only when I was finishing up the story. Writing about heroes brings that out subconsciously, I suppose.

MC: Do you have any other projects in the works?

CPC: I'm currently writing a dark fantasy novel set in the year 1888. Since it's also a historical novel, I did a tremendous amount of primary- and secondary-source research for it, although it will bend the truth in that it's a secret history. It's not a Farmerian-inspired or Wold Newton-inspired novel, but readers of Farmer might appreciate its conspiracies and intrigues. After that, depending on what else might present itself, I'm hoping to write a novel set in the "Pluritopian" world of my novelette "Caesar's Children: A Tale of Pluritopia." But one novel at a time.

More immediately, I have a story titled "Devil's Dark Harvest" in the about-to-be-released *The Avenger: The Justice Inc. Files* edited by Joe Gentile and Howard Hopkins. It's sort of an *Island of Doctor Moreau*-type story, which I guess is fitting, since I first became interested in fantastic literature when I read Wells. And Richard Benson—The Avenger—is, of course, a Wold Newton family member. You'll find him on the family tree in *Doc Savage: His Apocalyptic Life* right next to his cousin, Paul Janus Finnegan, aka Kickaha from the World of Tiers series. That I've been fortunate enough to chronicle the story of Kwasin as well as an episode in the life of Richard Benson—both Wold Newton family members—is, I assure you, only a coincidence.

On Writing *The Song of Kwasin*

Published online at the *Philip José Farmer International Bibliography*, November 2011

Rias Nuninga: Hi, Chris, first my congratulations with the publication of *The Song of Kwasin*. When did you learn that it would be published? How could you keep it a "secret" all this time?

Christopher Paul Carey: I guess I first knew for sure that the book would be published in the fall of 2009, when the agent called and said Subterranean wanted to bring it out in an omnibus of the whole series. As for keeping it a secret, that's publishing. You get used to it.

RN: Will you tell us something more about yourself?

CPC: By day (and okay, sometimes on nights and weekends), I'm an editor for Paizo Publishing, the creators of the Pathfinder Roleplaying Game and publishers of the Planet Stories imprint. When I'm not editing, I'm usually writing or researching what I'm planning to write. Or reading old books.

RN: How did you first encounter Farmer's work? And when did you meet him in person?

CPC: I first read Farmer when I was twelve or thirteen, starting out with books like *The Maker of Universes*, *Tarzan Alive*, and, appropriately, *Hadon of Ancient Opar*. I think those were the first three books of his that I read.

The first time I met Phil was in 1998 when I drove out from eastern Pennsylvania to Peoria, Illinois to see him at the opening of the Philip José Farmer Odyssey. This was a month-long exhibit honoring his life and work showcased at the main branch of the Peoria Public Library. Phil already knew who I was because he'd read some articles I'd had published about his work and we'd corresponded. But he was surprised I'd come all that way. He said, "All the way from Pennsylvania? I don't know if it'll be worth the trip." But I knew it was and I told him so emphatically.

RN: What were your thoughts about the Opar novels when you first read them?

CPC: They were on fire for me. I was immersing myself in Burroughs' works at the time, so it was a natural transition. And also, like a lot of folks, I was frustrated because the series ended abruptly with only a tentative conclusion at the end of *Flight to Opar*. It was obvious that Phil planned more, but it was nowhere to be found. And back then it was hard to know if an author was planning to write more books in a series, or even if they had already been written. You just had to keep going back to the bookstore and looking. Usually, you came back home empty handed. But then, on rare occasions, you brought back a treasure. The good old days!

RN: When did you first learn about the unfinished third novel in the series? How did you get permission from Farmer to complete this novel? Did he ask you or did you make the suggestion to finish it?

CPC: I was editing *Farmerphile* at the time, back in 2005. Mike Croteau, Phil's webmaster and the publisher of *Farmerphile*, had just returned from visiting Phil and Bette Farmer in Peoria and had gone through the files looking for never-before-published material to print in the magazine. Since I was the editor, he sent me the list of what he'd found. And for one of the items he calmly stated something like, here's a partial manuscript and nine-page outline to *Kwasin of Opar* that I'm not sure what we should to do with. Of course, I told him to send it to me as quickly as he could photocopy it and get it in an envelope.

After I'd read it, I knew it couldn't languish. I wrote to Phil about it, and he eagerly agreed. Phil rarely used email, but after reading my proposal, he fired me back an email right away. He closed his reply with the imperative "forward it is." I almost couldn't believe it.

RN: What did you have at first from Farmer's archives to start writing? Could you start immediately or had you to do a lot of study before the writing? I think you first had to reread the first two novels in the series, *Hadon of Ancient Opar* and *Flight to Opar*.

CPC: At first, all I had were the published books in the series and Phil's manuscript fragment and outline. At the time, I was working on my Master's in writing, so, as I'd explained to Phil, I had to get my thesis written before I could work on *Kwasin*. But that delay also afforded me some research time. I went back and reread *Hadon* and *Flight* several times, underlining passages, taking notes, and creating a Khokarsan glossary and a timeline for the events in the series. Then, while visiting Phil, I came across his notes and outlines to the first two books, and Phil and Bette let me photocopy the material. This helped immensely. I was able to track down some of his original inspirations for the series, such as Weston's *From Ritual to Romance*, and also learn something about how he'd constructed the Khokarsan language. Or rather, how Phil had reconstructed it from records he had of the Khokarsan grammarians, since the series is, as everyone knows, based on real events.

Later, on another visit to Peoria after I'd already completed the first draft of the manuscript, I found another folder of Phil's notes, including several drafts of an article titled "The Khokarsan Language" as well as the complete Khokarsan syllabary. So I went back through the manuscript and was able to revise aspects of the novel to correspond with these.

RN: What was it like to write in someone else's world? Did you feel restricted? By Farmer or the pieces that were already written, like the outline?

CPC: I'm pretty much a purist about these things, and I love world-building, even if it's someone else's. So if there were restrictions, I more or less reveled in them, whether they were in the outline or in the established world of the series. Phil

Gods of Opar

Tales of Lost Khokarsa

Philip José Farmer
and
Christopher Paul Carey

and I both shared a love of and an academic background in anthropology, which the series is steeped in, so I felt at home in Khokarsa, especially having read the first two books so many times over the years.

RN: Did Phil and Bette Farmer see and read the finalized novel in 2008? What were their thoughts about it?

CPC: Yes, they did. As Phil's health began to decline, Bette read the novel aloud to him. She told me how Phil really lit up upon finally hearing Kwasin's adventures unfold. Both of them said how much they enjoyed it, and they were eager to have it see print.

RN: Are you yourself satisfied with the results of the novel you have finished? Was it hard work writing it, or just plain fun?

CPC: That's a devil of a question for a writer. I remember Phil himself once said that none of his stories ever turned out the way he'd envisioned them, none were ever quite as golden as he'd seen them in his mind's eye. What author is ever satisfied with his work? The temptation always lingers to go back and change a phrase here or a detail there. For me, writing is both soul-wrenching and ecstatic, often at the same time. It's a shamanic experience. Or something.

RN: I know that the publisher of DAW Books, Donald A. Wollheim, insisted that the name Opar was used with any title in the series. Farmer did not like that. Is that also the reason why the title of the novel changed from *Kwasin of Opar* to *The Song of Kwasin*, and the name of the series changed from Opar to Khokarsa?

CPC: Yes, that's right. That, and the fact that Kwasin is a native of Dythbeth and his adventures in the novel aren't set in Opar, but rather on the island of Khokarsa. And, other than briefly and at a distance in the opening paragraph, Opar doesn't appear in the first novel of the series either.

RN: You wrote two other Khokarsa stories. "A Kick in the Side" is your own, and "Kwasin and the Bear God" is written by Farmer and you. How did these come to be? And do you plan to write more Khokarsa stories?

CPC: I wrote "A Kick in the Side" in one sitting in a kind of mad, fevered fit of inspiration while I was deep in the midst of working on *The Song of Kwasin*. While rereading the series, whenever I got to the part in the second book where Hinokly literally drops out of the storyline, some part of me couldn't help but root for the poor guy. He was probably a lot smarter than Hadon—certainly more educated—but fate had dealt him a poor hand. So I figured he could have one more adventure that showed just how smart he was.

"Kwasin and the Bear God" came about after I'd found the folder containing Phil's detailed notes and articles on the Khokarsan language. Also in the folder was an incomplete alternate outline to the third novel in the series. Although it recapped some of Phil's more detailed outline, this alternate version was mostly unusable for the purposes of the novel due to various incongruities with the already published books. But about two pages fit in nicely with the continuity and detailed a lost adventure of Kwasin, so Meteor House asked me to write a story based on the outline for their *Worlds of Philip José Farmer* series. As for writing other stories set in the series, we'll have to wait and see.

Gribardsun and the
Prehistoric Wold Newton Family

Afterword to *Time's Last Gift* by Philip José Farmer,
Titan Books, 2012

Having just read the foregoing pages, some readers may be wondering in what manner Philip José Farmer's classic 1972 novel of time travel, *Time's Last Gift*, constitutes a Wold Newton novel. That is, how does the story fit into the author's overarching series chronicling the lives of heroes and villains from popular literature?

It is a natural question to ask, given the fact that on the surface the story reads quite well as an innovative, stand-alone work of science fiction, anticipating as it does the Novikov self-consistency principle of time travel. This theory, put forth by a Russian physicist over a decade after the novel at hand was first published, posits that time travel paradoxes— such as the old trope of traveling into the past and murdering one's parents before they conceived any progeny—cannot possibly occur; rather, anything the time traveler does while gallivanting in the past simply results in the natural unfolding of events as known and experienced before the present was ever left behind.

Those who have read Farmer's larger body of work, however, know that the author is not merely a novelist; he is a biographer, a chronicler of real-life heroes whose adventures have oft been mistaken as fiction. And so the question arises, who exactly *is* the hero of this novel, John Gribardsun?

Farmer leaves plenty of clues to Gribardsun's true identity within the preceding pages, although such hints are neither overbearing nor do they distract from the compelling, mind-bending narrative, and the reader should not feel embarrassed at having missed them. In fact, the author buried them deep for a reason. He could not risk the world knowing the truth, and, although he had come into an arrangement with "Gribardsun" to publish his memoirs in the guise of fiction, Farmer was honor-bound by the agreement to remain within certain very-well-defined parameters.

Clearly, Gribardsun was worried about more than just the feasibility of Novikov's self-consistency principle in authorizing the novelization of his future—and simultaneously past—self; Gribardsun had to ensure that the author would not reveal clues that might endanger him or his loved ones. For this reason, Farmer withheld publication of the novel's epilogue until the revised edition of *Time's Last Gift* appeared in 1977, by which time Gribardsun must have felt he had slipped far enough off the radar that no one could conceivably follow the clues to him or his family. This newly appended epilogue (also included in the present Titan Books edition) revealed that the jungle lord whom Farmer called Gribardsun was married to a beautiful blonde named Jane. And if that doesn't cinch the true identity of this novel's protagonist, the reader might do well to grab a vine and swing on back to Chapter 8, and peruse once more Drummond's account of the Duke of Pemberley, the British peer who was born in 1872 and "raised in indeterminate circumstances" in the jungles of West Africa, and whom Drummond believes is one and the same as his fellow expedition member John Gribardsun. Incidentally, the 1872 birthdate serves both as a red herring and a clue to Gribardsun's identity, as readers of Farmer's *Tarzan Alive: A Definitive Biography of Lord Greystoke* may well suss out.

But another set of questions arises. Novikov's self-consistency principle aside, how could Gribardsun have passed on to Farmer knowledge of the future? Did Farmer become privy to the events of the present novel from the original jungle lord, who had yet to embark on *H. G. Wells I*, and whom Farmer famously interviewed while conducting research for the aforementioned biography? Or did the author obtain this

Ballantine Books Science Fiction 02468•0•095

Time's Last Gift
Philip José Farmer

2780 A.D. held no secrets that did not exist in 12,000 B.C.

account of the future from the second jungle lord, who had already traveled back in time and then lived down through the millennia? Could Farmer have had contact with both men? Or did he instead reconstruct the events depicted in the novel from other sources?

For now, this mystery must be left to the reader's own speculation. The identification of Gribardsun with the jungle lord, however, does indeed establish that both "Gribardsuns" are members of the Wold Newton family, the origin of which dates back to the 1795 meteor strike near Wold Newton, Yorkshire. It was at this momentous time and place that two carriages of travelers were exposed to the meteor's ionized radiation, resulting in what Farmer called "a nova of genetic splendor"—a family tree of great detectives, scientists, explorers, heroes, and villains descended from the carriages' occupants.

It is important to note that while the above statement is true—that the Wold Newton family originated in 1795 with the meteor strike in Yorkshire—it is not correct to state that the Wold Newton family did not exist before the falling star of 1795. This seeming paradox follows from the fact that Gribardsun—a Wold Newton family member—traveled back to 12,000 B.C. and conceived a number of offspring who passed on the mutated genes he had inherited from his ancestors to pre-1795 generations.

And thus the Wold Newton family enters prehistory.

Fortunately, information about some of these early, prehistoric members of the Wold Newton family, including its progenitor, has been preserved in the archaeological record, as well as in other sources. Perhaps the first mention of such findings is related in Sir William Clayton's now hard-to-find travelogue *Gold and a Lost Love in Africa*:

> For a long while we stood thus, awestruck to have happened across evidence of such a high civilization in these remote parts. The stelae among the moldering ruins—in the few places they jutted from the scape in a manner such that we were able to clear away the encroaching vegetation and examine them—bore

engravings both symbolic and aesthetic. The low relief on one such monument appeared in a series of images depicting a great, half-naked warrior, inexplicably European in countenance, nocking an arrow upon the string of a stout longbow. If I followed the story aright, the warrior seemed to have been cast out from his people by a large, bare-breasted goddess with the head of an African water-eagle. A grand motif of the sun and the moon spiraling backwards repeated many times in this most curious of picture-tales, although what the motif could mean and what profane taboo the warrior might have broken to gain the wrath of the hideous divinity I could not gather from the scenes.

Little more of value can be garnered about these vaguely located African ruins from Sir William's travelogue, and if he had anything more to say in print about the matter, it would surely have been in his multivolume autobiography, published in Paris in 1888 under the title *Never Say Die: The Memoirs of One Who Always Heard the Distant Trumpet*. And although one may certainly muse upon the marked resemblance between the mysterious exiled warrior engraved upon the stela and John Gribardsun, any hope of uncovering further information from the Baronet's writings about either the ruins or the low relief upon its monuments is unfortunately now a moot point. Sir William's scandalous, erotically tinged memoirs were suppressed by his nephew, and the only known extant copy, once in the possession of Farmer, seems to have gone missing.[13]

As luck would have it, however, a young Professor George Edward Challenger, many years before his famed expedition to Maple White Land,[14] once cornered Sir William at a dinner engagement and spoke with him at length on the matter. The conversation left such an impression upon Challenger that,

13. For more on General Sir William Clayton and his nephew, see Philip José Farmer's *Tarzan Alive: A Definitive Biography of Lord Greystoke*, Doubleday & Co., 1972; University of Nebraska Press Bison Books, 2006.
14. See Sir Arthur Conan Doyle's *The Lost World* for a popular account of the professor's expedition to this singular South American plateau.

decades later, he embarked upon his own African expedition, the findings of which led him in his elder years to privately publish a slim volume titled *The Sahhindar Cult in Pre-Diluvian Khokarsa*,[15] the abstract of which I quote from here:

> In which I attempt to illustrate the existence of a widespread Cro-Magnon cult, centered near the Hoggar and Tibesti massifs in sub-Saharan Africa and dating to the extreme terminus of the Pleistocene epoch; and further, that said cult persisted amidst an expansive Bronze Age civilization which arose upon the coastlines of two great primordial landlocked seas, flourished over a period of less than two thousand years, and was destroyed in what may be the greatest catastrophe man has ever known....

The names "Sahhindar" and "Khokarsa," not to mention the professor's hypothesis, are sure to stir up some recognition, if not excitement, in readers of Farmer's *Hadon of Ancient Opar*.[16] In that book—and in the two other novels that complete the trilogy, *Flight to Opar* and *The Song of Kwasin*—Farmer relates the saga of the grand empire of Khokarsa, which existed on the shores of two Central African seas beginning in approximately 11,800 B.C. In this series, Sahhindar is a mysterious man who appeared among the pre-Khokarsan tribes somewhere around the time they settled along the shores of the northern inland sea. Over a period of fifty years Sahhindar made many visits to these tribes, teaching the locals how to cultivate plants and animals, and how to mine copper and tin, and thereby make bronze tools—in short, advancing this culture of hunter-gatherers almost instantly from the Old Stone Age to the Bronze Age in an unprecedented case of applied anthropology. Further, the Khokarsans regarded

---

15. According to *The Evil in Pemberley House* by Philip José Farmer and Win Scott Eckert, a copy of Professor Challenger's monograph was once to be found in the library at the Pemberley estate in Derbyshire, although for reasons of the current owner's privacy the head steward declines to confirm whether the volume is at present part of the collection. Fortunately, the author of this afterword was able to consult a rare extant copy of this work on file in the Charles Bluepress Reading Room at Shomi University, where it may still be examined by appointment.
16. Look for this novel in Titan Books' ongoing Wold Newton series.

Sahhindar as the god of Time, bronze, and plants. Their legends tell of how he stole Time from the Great Mother Goddess Kho, and that because of this transgression, Sahhindar was banished from the land. In the addendum to *Hadon of Ancient Opar,* Farmer writes of Sahhindar, "Undoubtedly he was a time traveler from the twenty-first century who had been stranded in 12,000 B.C. (See my *Time's Last Gift.*)"

This admission by Farmer, in conjunction with the revelation of Sahhindar's exile by Kho in the myths of the ancient Khokarsans, immediately sheds new light on how one might interpret the low relief described by Sir William in his travelogue. Surely the "grand motif of the sun and the moon spiraling backwards" upon the stela depicts the *H. G. Wells I* traveling back into the past, and who can deny the resemblance between the bow-wielding warrior and both Sahhindar and Gribardsun, or between the water-eagle-headed goddess and the Bird-Headed Mother Goddess Kho?

Of course, it is in Farmer's *Hadon of Ancient Opar* where one learns that another spinner of popular tales had privileged knowledge of about lost Khokarsa. Here I refer to the British author H. Rider Haggard, biographer of the adventures of that most intrepid of hunters and explorers, Allan Quatermain. In his extensive travels throughout Africa, Quatermain ran across traces of the lost Khokarsan civilization upon more than one occasion, whether it was the ages-old massive stone road leading to Kukuanaland; the lost land of Zu-Vendis, whose residents were descended from immigrants from the Khokarsan city of Wentisuh (note the transposed syllables); the Pompeii-like, lava-encrusted ruins of the ancestors of the Walloos; or the mountain fortress-city of Kôr, founded by Hadon's son after a great calamity threw down from its foundations almost the entirety of the Khokarsan civilization. I say almost, for while the grand empire was no more, Khokarsan culture did linger on in these and other lost cities and peoples; and while Haggard often attempted to explain their presence by claiming they were survivals of ancient Egyptian culture and other civilizations well known to historians, these editorial insertions in Quatermain's

PHILIP JOSÉ FARMER

JOURNEY 15,000 YEARS BACK IN TIME... TO KEEP AN EXTRAORDINARY DATE WITH THE FUTURE.

TIME'S LAST GIFT

51440-8 ★ $3.95 (CAN $4.95)

memoirs were certainly either mere speculations on Haggard's part or clever misdirection to prevent the foolish from trying to retrace Quatermain's footsteps to these fragile, dying cultures. If the latter, one can be assured that Haggard's obfuscation of facts did not always work, as evidenced by the Great Detective himself tracking down the surviving descendants of Zu-Vendis in John H. Watson's *The Further Adventures of Sherlock Holmes: The Peerless Peer*, as edited by Farmer (Titan Books, 2011).

While research into lost Khokarsa has been generally overlooked by modern historians, archaeologists, and anthropologists due to the paucity of verifiable source material, there are notable exceptions to this rule. Frank J. Brueckel and John Harwood's monograph, posthumously published as *Heritage of the Flaming God* (eds. Alan Hanson and Michael Winger, Waziri Publications, 1999), explores the latter-day remnants of a lost Central African civilization that the authors call "Atlantis." The similarities between the pre-cataclysm African culture that Brueckel and Harwood extrapolate in their monograph and that of Challenger's and Farmer's Khokarsa are striking, and any serious researcher would do well to seek out that work, as Farmer himself did during his own investigations.

I have digressed somewhat from the subject of the prehistoric Wold Newton family to give the reader some sense of the extensive and complex scope of Gribardsun's interference in our planet's timeline. Also, without an understanding of the Khokarsan civilization, one cannot comprehend to what extent Gribardsun's lineage survived in the descendants of that mother country, some of whom lived into the nineteenth and early twentieth centuries, if not beyond. It is known, for example, that the giant Kwasin, a descendant of Sahhindar, had intimate relations with many women during his exile in the Western Lands. In all likelihood, some of Kwasin's offspring in West Africa survived the great catastrophe that decimated his culture.[17] Further, the native city of the hero Hadon, Kwasin's cousin and also a descendant of Sahhindar, was spared utter destruction by the catastrophe, and the high priestess whom the jungle lord

---

17. Farmer's notes, which the author graciously provided to me while I was completing *The Song of Kwasin*, the third novel in the Khokarsa series, cite an unwritten novel about Kwasin's West African progeny that would have been titled *Sons of Kwasin*.

found reigning there in the early twentieth century was only the latest member of a long-lived dynasty of high priestesses who could trace their descent in a direct line back to Hadon and his wife Lalila. Wold Newton researcher Chuck Loridans has extended this lineage even further, speculating that in his pre-time-travel youth, Gribardsun and this same high priestess had a liaison resulting in a daughter who would grow up to be as prone to adventure as her biological parents and become known to the world as none other than Modesty Blaise.[18]

It is Gribardsun's far-flung travels in lands beyond Khokarsa, however, that produce the greatest impact on our world. His exploits throughout history in such diverse locales—Mesopotamia, Sumeria, Egypt, Greece, Rome, China, Gaul, the British Isles, and the Americas, to name but a few—ensure that his descendants thrive to this day in great numbers across the globe.

But I shall go even further than that bold notion in closing out this afterword and state that it is likely that every reader of this book, if one deigns to search the family tree back far enough, may be descended from the man known as John Gribardsun.

Of course, if that is true, we may all be members of the Wold Newton Family, which is why *Time's Last Gift*, long regarded as a minor classic of the time travel subgenre, may in the end be the most important Wold Newton novel of them all.

---

18. See Loridans' "The Daughters of Greystoke" in *Myths for the Modern Age: Philip José Farmer's Wold Newton Universe*, Win Scott Eckert, ed., MonkeyBrain Books, 2005.

Collaborating with a Grand Master

Published online at *SF Signal*, June 2012

This month sees the release of *Gods of Opar: Tales of Lost Khokarsa*, my collaboration with Hugo and World Fantasy Award-winning author and SFWA Grand Master Philip José Farmer. Yeah, those honorific titles leave me humbled and in awe too, and they're enough to make my inner voice frequently exclaim, "Whoa, wait a minute, how did this happen? How did I end up working with the Wizard of Peoria to complete the long-awaited-and long feared to be forever stalled-conclusion to his Khokarsa series?"

The answer, as is often the case with big inner-voice questions, varies wildly depending on how far back you want to trace it. You could say it began in the early 1970s when I was four years old and over at my grandfather's house for Christmas, as my older brother tuned in a snowy, barely discernible image of Mr. Spock on a UHF channel. It might have been when, in grade school, I picked up and started reading a giant tome titled *The Complete Science Fiction Treasury of H. G. Wells*. Or when, between the ages of twelve and fifteen, I obsessively read every single novel then in print by Edgar Rice Burroughs. (I would have read them all in only a few months but it was the pre-Internet Age and the books were so hard to track down-but boy did I have fun searching them out!) Quite early in that latter period I picked up three books by Philip José Farmer: *The Maker of Universes*, *Tarzan Alive: A Definitive Biography of Lord Greystoke*, and, fatefully, *Hadon of Ancient Opar*, which I regarded as the best of the lot. Other Farmers, of course, quickly followed, such as the Riverworld series; the rest of the World of Tiers books; the other Wold Newton "biography,"

Doc Savage: His Apocalyptic Life (which led to many more hours of reading during the lengthy hunt to complete my Bantam Doc Savage collection); *Time's Last Gift* (a new edition of this classic novel of time travel is now available from Titan Books, with an afterword I've written to explain how this novel serves as a sort of prequel to *Gods of Opar*); *Venus on the Half-Shell* by "Kilgore Trout"; and on and on until, still in my teenage years, I had almost all of them.

Early on I knew there was something different about Farmer. He had this funny way of planting little magic seeds in his writing. Seeds that, if nurtured by the water of attention, would sprout into the most fantastically bizarre trees of the imagination. These seeds were little, seeming irrelevancies in his novels and short stories—here, an arcane factoid; there, a character that seemed a little off but who was so tantalizingly familiar; and over yonder, a genealogical incongruity that appeared undermined the storyline. But if you took notice of these disparate "mythemes" (to borrow anthropologist Claude Levi-Strauss' term for the smallest bundle of meaning in a narrative), and if you held them in your awareness as you read more of Farmer's work, these seeds squirmed and wriggled, sprouting roots and branches and then entire trunks, until you eventually had a whole Brobdingnagian World Tree rising up out of your imagination—a grand meta-story that suddenly made you feel like you yourself were a character in the Grand Adventure. And the weird thing, the gratifying thing—and I believe, the enduring thing—about Farmer's palimpsest method of writing was that it was for the self-initiated only. You couldn't sit there and read passively or you missed half the fun.

Farmer, above all, is a Trickster. He knew some people would grok the seeds, understand they were a doorway, a pocket-universe-hopping "gate" that opened the way so that the normally too-passive reader could step through to discover a new kind of experience—not an inactive one, but rather one that can only be called creative reading. An opportunity not only to share in the writer's experience, but to take the story beyond it until it seems like a living thing in your mind...

and sometimes out of it. Farmer makes his readers pause on a mystical brink—sometimes with skepticism, other times with the sheer joy of faith—and consider that Kilgore Trout might really have written *Venus on the Half-Shell*, or that the identity of Tarzan of the Apes just might actually be discernible if you spent enough time poring over the dusty pages of *Burke's Peerage*. When Farmer makes deadpan statements such as Doc Savage is "a man as real as you or I, and perhaps even more real," his initiated readers understand this in a unique way. It's a shared, knowing look between the author and the reader, a secret handshake of sorts.

Why do I think he did all this? For one, because it's the way his mind worked. To cite another term used by Levi-Strauss, Farmer was a *bricoleur*. That is, someone skilled in taking what's at hand regardless of its intended purpose—whether that be, in Farmer's case, a rich background in pop lit (i.e., pulp, SF/F, children's, etc.) as well as classic literature; or his Renaissance man's knowledge of anthropology, or linguistics, or religion; or the love he had for lighter-than-air craft, or Sir Richard Francis Burton, or Krazy Kat, or you name it—and crafting it into a new thing that often transcends the original. Farmer created bricolage because that's how his deep love for knowledge imprinted him—he couldn't help but plant the seeds in his work because that's how he saw the world. You can see this bricolage clearly at work in his merging of the peoples of different ages and cultures in the Riverworld series; or in how he took hundreds of literary characters and ingeniously linked them all together to form the Wold Newton family; or in the many backbiting and closely related Lords of the World of Tiers series, who formed pocket universes of their own, all of them linked via cleverly booby-trapped gates, but which somehow could never manage to keep the other Lords out. All of these examples are metaphors for how Farmer couldn't prevent the neural pathways in his brain from finding ways to connect seemingly disparate bundles of information (quite appropriately, Joe Lansdale once called Farmer "the Man with the Electric Brain").

Philip José
FARMER
& Christopher Paul CAREY

OPAR

INTÉGRALE

MNÉMOS

Of course, just as often, I think Farmer sowed his magical seeds throughout his bricolage simply because he wanted to laugh his ass off. I did say he was a Trickster, after all.

In any case, if I had to provide a single answer to the question of how I came to coauthor a novel with Philip José Farmer, it would be because of those seeds, those mythemes, that were planted in my imagination so long ago. Without them I never would have begun writing articles about his work in the early 1990s (the one I'm most proud of having been reprinted in revised form in Win Scott Eckert's 2005 Locus Award Finalist anthology *Myths for the Modern Age: Philip José Farmer's Wold Newton Universe*). Nor would I have begun corresponding with Farmer in 1997, or a year later hopped in my car and drove halfway across the country to just meet him and listen to him talk about his work. Eventually, Phil Farmer and Michael Croteau called on me to serve as editor of *Farmerphile*, a digest magazine dedicated to printing rare and previously unpublished works by Farmer. And it was while working with these materials that Mike uncovered in Phil's files the partial manuscript and outline to what would eventually be titled *The Song of Kwasin*, the final installment of the Khokarsa trilogy. (Incidentally, these papers were found on the same trip during which Mike Croteau and Win Scott Eckert discovered the materials relating to *The Evil and Pemberley House*, which Win would later go on to complete with Phil's permission.)

In the next few weeks after the find, I carefully drafted a proposal and sent it off to Phil. It was one of the gutsiest things I've ever done. Phil, who by this time had retired from writing and was experiencing a declining health, wrote back with great enthusiasm, saying he approved of my proposal and wanted me to complete the novel. As late as 1999, Phil himself had been considering writing the conclusion of the trilogy, and I think the unforeseen prospect of making good on his intentions excited him. We discussed some details about the novel's close, and Phil told me what he had in mind now that *The Song of Kwasin* would be the conclusion to a trilogy rather than a novel in the middle of a longer series. I was attending graduate school for writing at this point, and needed to finish my thesis before I could break ground on Kwasin, but Phil and his wife Bette were firmly supportive of this and wanted me to hold off until I'd earned my degree.

I completed the first draft of *The Song of Kwasin* in early 2008. Phil wasn't doing so well now, but Bette Farmer read the novel aloud to him, telling me how Phil lit up at hearing of Kwasin's adventures, which made me very happy to say the least. Then, in January 2009, while visiting Phil about a month before he passed, I uncovered another trove of Khokarsa materials in the files (in addition to another assortment of Khokarsa files I'd found in 2006 and to which Phil graciously gave me access while I was writing the novel). These newly found papers included the complete Khokarsan syllabary and several drafts of an article on Khokarsan linguistics as well as other addenda— the best sense I can give you of Phil's world building is to say that it's truly Tolkienesque in its breadth and detail. In any event, it was a lucky find. I used this new information to make some adjustments to the final draft of the novel, which is at last seeing print *Gods of Opar: Tales of Lost Khokarsa*, an omnibus of the series now available from Subterranean Press.

The road to Khokarsa has been a long, strange, and winding one for me, and it's not a path that I could ever walk again if I tried. But I'm glad I did, just as I'm glad for all those seeds Philip José Farmer planted in my imagination so many years ago. I know I wouldn't—and couldn't—have written *The Song of Kwasin* without them.

The Literary Archaeology of Khokarsa

Introduction to *Hadon of Ancient Opar*
by Philip José Farmer, Titan Books, 2013

Welcome to the lost civilization of Khokarsa.

You are about to embark on one of the most epic journeys of heroic adventure in the annals of history. Philip José Farmer's *Hadon of Ancient Opar* is a tale of a nigh-forgotten age, when heroes and giants—and perhaps even a god—walked the earth, and when swordplay and prophecies weren't merely the stuff of legends, but rather a fact of everyday experience.

Sounds a lot like fantasy, or perhaps sword and sorcery, doesn't it? Of course, readers of Philip José Farmer's larger body of work know that the author is not merely a novelist; rather, he is a chronicler of real-life heroes whose adventures have oft been mistaken as fiction. Namely, many of his "stories" record the factual exploits of members of the Wold Newton Family, the origin of which dates back to the famed meteor strike near Wold Newton, Yorkshire on December 13, 1795. It was at this momentous time and place that two coaches full of travelers were exposed to the meteor's ionizing radiation, which mutated the genes of the travelers and resulted in what Farmer called "a nova of genetic splendor"—a family tree of great detectives, scientists, explorers, heroes, and villains descended from the coaches' occupants.

Philip José Farmer's Khokarsa trilogy—comprising the present work, *Hadon of Ancient Opar,* as well as the novels *Flight to Opar* and *The Song of Kwasin*—is no exception to the above: the Khokarsa tales also recount the real-life histories of members of the Wold Newton family.

But how can this be? If the meteor strike at Wold Newton occurred in 1795 A.D., how could members of the Wold Newton family possibly have been present circa 10,000 B.C., when the Khokarsa series takes place?

The answer to this question can be found in Farmer's *Time's Last Gift*, now available from Titan Books in their ongoing Wold Newton series. In that novel, a man named John Gribardsun travels back in time as a member of an anthropological expedition from the year 2070 A.D. to 12,000 B.C. He appears in *Hadon of Ancient Opar* under the identity of Sahhindar, the Gray-Eyed Archer God, also known as the god of plants, bronze, and Time. As a member of the Wold Newton family, Gribardsun introduced the mutated genes of his lineage to the prehistoric peoples of Khokarsa and other lands, and since both Hadon of Opar and Kwasin of Dythbeth—the heroes of the Khokarsa trilogy—can count him as an ancestor, this means they themselves are both members of the Wold Newton family despite having been born 12,000 years before the meteor fell to earth near Wold Newton, Yorkshire in December 1795.[19]

Where Farmer learned of the stories of the heroes Hadon and Kwasin is still a matter of debate. Did he get wind of their great deeds while conducting research for his groundbreaking *Tarzan Alive: A Definitive Biography of Lord Greystoke*? Or did he perhaps learn of their adventures from Sir Beowulf William Clayton, Baronet?

Readers of Philip José Farmer's *The Other Log of Phileas Fogg* (also available from Titan Books) will doubtless recall Sir Beowulf was the noted linguist of the University of Oxford who provided Farmer with a partial translation of Phileas Fogg's enciphered diary, which related the secret history behind Jules Verne's *Around the World in Eighty Days*. Recent evidence has surfaced that Sir Beowulf had access to a tremendous trove of materials relating to lost Khokarsa, and that he shared these with Farmer in their mutual correspondence. These include copious

---

19. Further details about Sahhindar's role in the history and culture of Khokarsa can be found in Addendum 2 at the back of this book. Inquisitive readers will also want to consult my afterword to *Time's Last Gift*, Titan Books, 2012, which hints at John Gribardsun's true identity.

rubbings from ancient tablets of unknown origin, all inscribed in the syllabic glyphs of the Khokarsan civilization, as well as translations of some of these records by Sir Beowulf in various stages of completion.

Whether Farmer obtained his intimate knowledge of Khokarsa from Sir Beowulf or from another source, it is clear he knew that other authors of popular fiction were also aware of the lost civilization, and upon several occasions left veiled references to it in their work. Of course, Opar—that shining "city of granite and little jewels"—appears in the works of Edgar Rice Burroughs. Or rather, what is left of that once grand queendom of Khokarsa, for in Burroughs' tales the city is in ruins, albeit still inhabited in the early twentieth century by a few savage descendants of Hadon's native city.

Perhaps no author has made such copious reference to the latter-day survivals of the Khokarsan civilization as Sir Henry Rider Haggard, biographer of the adventures of that most intrepid of hunters and explorers, Allan Quatermain. It was in Haggard's classic *King Solomon's Mines* that Quatermain encountered a massive, ages-old stone road leading to Kukuanaland. While one of Quatermain's traveling companions, Sir Henry Curtis, speculates that this wonder of ancient engineering might be the handiwork of the ancient Egyptians or Phoenicians, he surely would not have been so hasty in his attribution had he known of the advanced road-building skills of the late-Pleistocene Khokarsans.

In his travels throughout Africa, Quatermain continued to run across numerous traces of a lost civilization that modern researchers can now confidently link to Khokarsa. Perhaps the most famous of these encounters is told in Quatermain's final adventure, edited by Haggard under the title *Allan Quatermain*. In this adventure, our daring hunter enters the strange land of Zu-Vendis. Quatermain himself admitted that "the origin of the Zu-Vendi is lost in the mists of time," and went on to muse as follows:

> Whence they came or of what race they are no man
> knows. Their architecture and some of their sculptures
> suggest an Egyptian or possibly an Assyrian origin; but

it is well known that their present remarkable style of building has only sprung up within the last eight hundred years, and they certainly retain no traces of Egyptian theology or customs... Still, for aught I know, they may be one of the lost ten tribes whom people are so fond of discovering all over the world, or they may not. I do not know, and so can only describe them as I find them, and leave wiser heads than mine to make what they can out of it, if indeed this account should ever be read at all, which is exceedingly doubtful.

But Quatermain's account was published after all, and a wiser head did, in fact, read it. Farmer's personal papers relating to the Khokarsa series—to which the distinguished author, then retired, graciously granted me access while I was completing *The Song of Kwasin* based on his outline and partial manuscript—reveal a direct correlation between the Zu-Vendi and the inhabitants of Khokarsan queendom of Wentisuh. First of all, the reader should note the transposed syllables: *Wen-ti-suh* > *Ven-di-zu* > *Zu-ven-di*. Farmer indicates that "Wentisuh" means "Yellow Land" or "Yellow Country" in the Khokarsan language, the same meaning attributed to "Zu-Vendis" by the locals in Allan Quatermain's autobiography. Further, the city that Quatermain visits in Zu-Vendis is called Milosis, which means "Frowning City" in both the language of the locals he encounters and the Khokarsan tongue.

Farmer's papers reveal that when the great calamity that destroyed the Khokarsan civilization struck, the survivors from the city of Siwudawa fled into the mountainous area in or near Uganda and founded the land that was later called Zu-Vendis. The Siwudawa people, being of the Khokarsan ethnicity known as the Klemsuh, had yellowish skins, and for this reason they called their country the Yellow Land. Soon thereafter, however, other refugees from the cataclysm who were of Khoklem stock—the darker-skinned, most populous ethnicity of Khokarsa—entered the region and the Siwudawa genes were diluted. With the passage of several millennia, the Zu-Vendi of Quatermain's time could no longer recall that their country was named after the once dominant ethnicity of the region.

FANTASY

Philip José
FARMER

LE CYCLE D'OPAR I

UN TRÔNE POUR HADON

POINTS

Of course, there is a more direct link between Quatermain's African adventures and Farmer's Khokarsa: the legendary artifact known as the Ax of Victory. This ax, crafted out of meteoritic iron by the dwarf Pag (called Paga in the present novel), makes its first chronological appearance in Haggard's *Allan and the Ice-Gods*, a tale set just before the events of *Hadon of Ancient Opar* and witnessed firsthand by Quatermain after he partook of the mystical *taduki* herb. Here the reader learns not only Paga's backstory, but also that of the beauteous Lalila (rendered "Laleela" in Haggard's novel), and her lover Wi, the first wielder of the ax. In *Hadon of Ancient Opar*, the reader learns to whom the ax passes after Wi, and as the Khokarsa trilogy progresses, the ax changes hands yet again, then makes its way down through the ages until it one day passes to the mighty Zulu warrior Umslopogaas in Haggard's novel *Nada the Lily*. The Ax of Victory next appears playing a very important role in Haggard's *She and Allan*, in which Umslopogaas accompanies Allan Quatermain to the lost city of Kôr to assist the immortal Ayesha in her battles against the giant, self-proclaimed god Rezu. This is a strange tale for a number of reasons, not the least of which is the uncanny physical resemblance between the character Rezu and Hadon's giant cousin Kwasin, as noted by Wold Newton scholar Rick Lai in his article "Astar of Opar: The Secret Origins of Sumuru" (*Rick Lai's Secret Histories: Criminal Masterminds*, Altus Press, 2009). Ayesha admits that Rezu drank from the same Cup of Life as she did and so "lives on unharmed by time," but whether Rezu and Kwasin are indeed the same individual is a topic beyond the scope of this introduction. Readers should, however, note the similarity between the name Rezu and the name of the Khokarsan sungod, Resu, taking into account that the Khokarsan consonant "s" is pronounced more forcefully than it is in English.

But Burroughs and Haggard were not the only authors to write of the lingering traces of lost Khokarsa in the modern age. A clear correlation exists between the surreal land of Gondoroko in French author J. H. Rosny's novel *L'Étonnant voyage de Hareton Ironcastle* and the demon-haunted wilds near the Khokarsan city of Mibessem (see Farmer's *Flight to Opar* for more on the strange happenings in the vicinity of this city). Farmer's English-language translation and retelling of the novel under the title *Ironcastle* (DAW Books, 1976) appends an extra chapter to the novel not extant in Rosny's original text, giving a scientific—albeit extraterrestrial—explanation to the eerie landscape of the region. My novella *Exiles of Kho* (Meteor House, 2012), a tale reconstructed from Sir Beowulf's notes on a mysterious tablet detailing the history of the priestess-heroine Lupoeth, connects the land of Gondoroko with mysterious events important to the history of the Khokarsan civilization.

I would be remiss without mentioning two other authors who have touched on Khokarsa in their writings, although each was perhaps unaware he was doing so. One of these was Pierre Benoit, a French author and reputed literary nemesis of H. Rider Haggard, whose novel *L'Atlantide* (published in English as *The Queen of Atlantis*) tells of the remains of the lost city of "Atlantis" located in the Hoggar Mountains of the Sahara. Antinea, the queen who rules over this fortress-city, bears a striking similarity to Haggard's Ayesha, enough so that Benoit's novel gave rise to accusations of plagiarism. The resemblance between the two characters, however, was perhaps not so much literary as it was cultural, for Antinea and Ayesha both rule as supreme matriarchs, perhaps a testament to their common immersion in the ancient matriarchal traditions of Khokarsa. Interestingly, authors Frank J. Brueckel and John Harwood, with whom Farmer was in correspondence during the conception of his Khokarsa series, link the motherland civilization of Opar with the African model of Atlantis in their monograph *Heritage of the Flaming God: An Essay on the History of Opar and Its Relationship to Other Ancient Cultures* (Waziri Publications, 1999).

Lastly comes the American author Ambrose Bierce. Many scholars now accept Farmer's own claim that Bierce, when he wrote of that ghostly city described in his classic tale "An Inhabitant of Carcosa," merely transposed and modified the spelling of the syllables *Kho-kar-sa* so that they were rendered into *Car-co-sa*. Whether this spoonerism resulted from linguistic distortion over the passage of several millennia, or rather from the faulty transmission of the spirit-medium Bayrolles who channeled Bierce's narrative, is yet unknown. That the monoliths erected to the dead heroes of the Great Games in *Hadon of Ancient Opar* might indeed be akin to the "weather-worn stones" that were "broken, covered with moss and half-sunken into the earth" and were "obviously the headstones of graves" in Bierce's tale is truly a tantalizing speculation.

By now the reader should have a sense that *Hadon of Ancient Opar* is not just any old fantasy or sword and sorcery novel. Rather, it is a tale with rich literary and historical roots that burrow down deeply into the fertile soil of the Wold Newton mythos.

The latter, of course, is a skein that needn't be unwound to enjoy and appreciate the novel. And yet, as those familiar with Philip José Farmer's work are well aware, one of the greatest and most rewarding joys of reading his stories is sussing out the subtext beneath the tightly plotted, fast-moving surface adventure—and often not being able to tell quite where reality ends and the fictional begins...

An Archaeology of Dreams

Afterword to the Limited Edition of
Doc Savage: His Apocalyptic Life by Philip José Farmer,
Meteor House, 2013

It's a warm, overcast summer day in 1997 as I tear up the asphalt heading south on Missouri's Route 63. I've just made what in all likelihood is the worst decision of my life, forsaking a hard-won career in archaeology for what is surely a pipe dream. My future looks as stygian as Cthulhu's dark maw. I have no idea how I'll earn a living, much less make a success of myself. But my trunk is full of dog-eared Philip José Farmer paperbacks and the green sign that flashes by says it's only seven miles to La Plata, Missouri, home of Doc Savage author Lester Dent.

This pipe dream feels *right*.

It's a few days earlier and I've been working for the past couple weeks as an assistant site director at an archaeological site in western Illinois. It's my dream job, everything I've spent the last few years of my life striving for. I'm out in the field balancing transits and laying out excavation grids, exactly where I want to be, and yet something sticks in my craw: the creeping feeling that no matter how much I love digging into the past, I have something else I'm supposed to be doing. What that calling is, I'm not exactly sure, but a spectral voice from somewhere deep inside whispers that it has something to do with writing and literature. I know too that the eerie susurration probably has something to do with the letter I'd received shortly before I left my home state of Pennsylvania to take the job in archaeology.

The letter is from Philip José Farmer. I've brought it along with me as a talisman of sorts, tucked carefully in a folder between several layers of papers so it won't get damaged. When my spirits sink especially low, I take out the letter and read it. It's Farmer's response to an article I wrote for the Doc Savage fanzine *The Bronze Gazette* on the deeper currents in his novel *Escape from Loki*. In his letter, Farmer writes that he finds my article ingenious, that he believes it might cause as much uproar among the Doc Savage fan community as Rex Stout's essay "Watson Was a Woman" did among the Shelockian aficionados of the Baker Street Irregulars.

I don't know it yet but this letter is some kind of mystical chisel, one that's already split the fabric of space and time and shunted me off into another universe.

I'm back on Route 63. A sign says I'm entering La Plata as I ease my way betwixt cornfields. If there's a town here, I don't see it yet.

And then, there it is on my right. No, not the town. It's The Sign. In this pastoral Midwestern setting—with its farmhouse, grain bin, and outbuildings looming in the distance—the white blocky lettering against a background of blood red spells out an unlikely message:

DOC SAVAGE
COUNTRY
HOME OF LESTER DENT
LaPlata, Mo.

Arriving at The Sign, even as dilapidated as it is, is too much for words. I recognize in my gut that it presages something big. I can feel it palpably in the humid air. I park my 1984 Plymouth Reliant along the hayfield, get out, and just gaze, knowing this is a Moment I'll revisit many times in the years to come, no matter how far away life's current carries me from this magical place.

I'm fourteen years old and piling into the back seat of my dad's 1974 Plymouth Valiant. It's a school day, but my brother and I have been granted the day off for a family trip to Hershey Park, Pennsylvania. I've brought along my brand-new Playboy Paperback edition of Farmer's *Doc Savage: His Apocalyptic Life*. As a hardcore Edgar Rice Burroughs enthusiast, I've already read Farmer's other biography, *Tarzan Alive*, but I'm unfamiliar with Doc. I prop my knees up against the black vinyl seat back and read.

I've never been to Hershey, PA. When we arrive, I find the street lamps are shaped like Hershey's Kisses and the air literally smells like chocolate. But it's no big deal. I'm already longing for the two-and-a-half-hour drive back home. I'm eager to read more about the Revelator from Missouri, the Son of Storm and Child of Destiny, supermachine pistols, glass knock-out grenades, autogyros, the "eighty-sixth" floor headquarters that's really located on a lower floor. And I'm even more eager for the weekend to come. I'm pretty sure I recently saw a copy of the first Doc Savage supersaga in the 50-cent stripped-cover bin at the local farmer's market and I'm determined to get it if it's still there.

Content that I've permanently imprinted the image of The Sign onto my soul, and also feeling a bit self-conscious at the local traffic passing by, I hop back in my car and drive on, turning west onto Route 156 and setting off for La Plata's town center.

I don't find much there besides a road running between some houses and buildings, but I spy a small grocery store on the right and stop to get directions to Lester Dent's house. The woman I speak with in the store is perhaps eighteen or twenty years old—she has no clue who Lester Dent is. Yes, I know: THE

SIGN. But this is small-town America and I'm sure there are plenty of things I never noticed in my hometown even though they were right in front of me for more than twenty years. Luckily, the young woman *does* know where the local cemetery is and gives me directions.

I find the cemetery on the opposite end of town, turn in, and proceed to drive slowly down the gravel road that loops between the gravestones. It's then that a cemetery caretaker notices me. He rides his lawnmower up to my window and asks me if I'm looking for somebody. The man is Hispanic, his deeply tanned, leathery skin showing he's spent a lot of time out in the sun during his sixty-odd years. I tell the man that I'd like to see the Dent plot. He immediately kicks his lawnmower into gear and waves me to follow.

A largish, upright tombstone bearing the name DENT looms before us. I pull over on the side of the driveway and get out, again feeling that palpable something in the air. The caretaker jumps off his vehicle and points to the big headstone. "Dent," he says. I smile widely, but by then I've noticed that it's Bernard and Alice's grave, not Lester and Norma's. I tell the caretaker I'm looking for Lester Dent, and he replies, "You his grandkid?" I laugh at the thought, and have a momentary fantasy of posing as Dent's grandson or great-grandson. Speaking in a literary sense, there could be a grain of truth in answering yes to the question, though if that's so, then Dent has many thousands of grandchildren. But I shake my head, and say, "No, I just like to read his books and wanted to pay tribute." He doesn't seem to make the connection that Dent was an author.

Though in afterthought, I think he might have been playing me.

I'm lying on my bed on a hot, muggy night in August 1991. I've just finished reading Philip José Farmer's latest novel, *Escape from Loki*. The book has hit me harder than Renny Renwick's quart-sized milk-bottle fists, but instead of being knocked out cold, I feel like a Zen master has struck me with his bamboo stick and jolted my consciousness into satori. In the flash of that metaphysical lightning bolt, I see myriad tentacles writhing

229

··· HUGO AWARD WINNER ···

PHILIP JOSÉ
FARMER

THE BRONZE SUPERHERO OF
TECHNOPOLIS AND EXOTICA
DOC SAVAGE
HIS APOCALYPTIC LIFE

up from beneath the novel's surface, though I can't discern the exact form of the beast they're connected to.

I turn back to the first page of *Escape from Loki* and begin reading it again. And then, in the days that follow, I read the novel three more times, back to back. I've got an idea for an article. I wonder if the editor of that Doc Savage fanzine I recently subscribed to might be interested in it.

I call up my friend Karl and ask him is he's interested in taking the bus with me up to New York City for another visit to Doc's HQ. He tells me he is.

After I get off the phone, I fire up my Smith-Corona word-processor and start typing.

The cemetery caretaker asks me where I'm from, and I say Pennsylvania. This results in a raised eyebrow from the man, who seems to think I'm rather odd for coming all this way. I neglect to tell him about my recent fallout with archaeology and that I've had a layover in Illinois.

The man points to the grave right behind Bernard and Alice's plot, a long, flat headstone flush with the grass. He'd known right where it was all along.

Suddenly sensing the man knows more than he's let on, I ask him what he knows about Lester Dent. He still pretends (?) not to know Dent was a famous writer, but says he knew Dent personally.

Actually what he says is, "Yeah, I know 'im. He full o' shit!"

I am, needless to say, somewhat taken aback by this sudden vociferation. What could this fellow possibly mean? I press him, and I get two or three more variations on his prior statement. Coupled with the fact that the man's English is not perfect, I am quite puzzled. Determined to understand, I throw out some guesses as to what he means. Finally, I venture to ask, "You mean to say that he told lies?"

He nods vigorously, laughing. "He tell stories! Make up stories. You run into him on the street an' he pull your leg."

"Ah!" I say, laughing with the fellow. "He was a trickster, a jokester!" The man agrees, smiling because I understand him at last. The man tells me his father knew Dent, but that he, the caretaker, had only encountered Dent occasionally about town (and had tried to avoid Dent because of his prankster nature).

With his story told, the man jumps back on his lawn mower and leaves me alone at the gravesite. I snap some pictures and spend some time absorbing where I am, standing at the grave of a man who was a link in a literary chain that, I hope, I will one day also be a part of.

I return to my car and retrieve my dog-eared copy of Farmer's *Doc Savage: His Apocalyptic Life* from the front seat. As a bookmark in the "biography," I have a ticket stub from one of my several trips to the eighty-sixth floor of the Empire State Building. I pull this stub out of the book and leave it on Lester's grave. I think he'd probably have gotten a good laugh out of that, jokester that I've just been told he was. Then I'm off to hunt down the Dent home.

I can't find it. But while I'm searching I stop by the local library and discover a Lester Dent collection tucked in a nook in the back of the small building. An elderly librarian is kind enough to give me an overview of the library's Dent holdings, which, in addition to what I believe is a complete run of Doc Savage pulps from the 1930s and '40s, also includes a number of Doc Savage and general pulp fanzines. It's here that I first encounter Rick Lai's wonderful and classic Wold Newton article "The Secret History of Captain Nemo." This is the first glimmer I have that someone else is analyzing and expanding Farmer's Wold Newton concept with the same degree of care and intensity that I've striven for in my own work. Though I've seen Win Scott Eckert's groundbreaking *Wold Newton Universe* site by this time, it's yet in its infancy, and I am awestruck as I sit in the little nook and devour Rick's article.

And then I come across a folder, meticulously preserved by Norma Dent, that includes correspondence between her and Philip José Farmer. One item is a postcard Farmer sent to Norma while he was in New York City researching *Doc Savage: His Apocalyptic Life*. Farmer writes that he's just been to the Empire State Building, and though he circled all around it, he saw no sign of Doc, Monk, and the gang. Another item in the folder is Farmer's business card, listing his occupation as an "Unreal Estate Agent and Baroquer" representing choice lots in Ruritania, Poictesme, Ilium, R'lyeh, Barsoom, Middle Earth, Hallamshire, and Oz, as well as holding premium shares in the Hidalgo Trading Company. And then there's the copy of the first edition of the Doc Savage biography, inscribed from Farmer to Norma. It's a magical treasure trove. I use what little change I have on me to make as many Xeroxes as I can. When I get home to Pennsylvania, I'll make duplicates and mail them off to Win Eckert and Farmer's webmaster, Mike Croteau.

I'm sitting in Philip José Farmer's basement having a good conversation with Jack Cordes. It's the summer of 2006, and around us swirls the blissful festivity of the first-ever FarmerCon. Jack, of course, is Phil's longtime friend, who loaned him a complete run of Doc Savage pulps during the writing of *Doc Savage: His Apocalyptic Life*, and who accompanied Phil on his visit to Norma Dent as mentioned in that book. A twinkle in his eye, Jack has just revealed to me that Phil Tuckerized him in *Escape from Loki* as the character named Private Hans Kordtz.

Only a few hours ago, before the gathering, I was sitting upstairs talking with Phil about my progress on *The Song of Kwasin*, the third novel of the Khokarsa series. Phil had started working on the manuscript over thirty years ago and then abandoned it in lieu of a host of other pressing writing projects. Now Phil would like to see the novel finished, but since he's long into his retirement and has had a number of health setbacks, he's counting on me to see the book through to completion.

My life has become surreal.

In my excitement over the library's treasures, I decide it's best to leave La Plata on a high point and abandon my quest for Lester Dent's house. Besides, it's getting late in the day and I have a long drive ahead of me. What's more, I've now met someone who personally knew the Revelator from Missouri. Or at least who claimed to. But in the strange alternate universe I've slipped into, it's enough.

I head back onto the highway. The future is still uncertain, but something has changed this day in La Plata. A shifting of soul-stuff, a tilting of the planet's alchemical axis, a splintering of the pluriverse, something . . . I can *feel* it.

For some, it's a burning bush. For others, a bodhi tree.

For me, it's a beat-up paperback copy of *Doc Savage: His Apocalyptic* at my side, baking in the summer heat as I speed down a Missouri highway toward destiny.

A Carmody-Raspold Chronology

The Worlds of Philip José Farmer 4: Voyages to Strange Days,
edited by Michael Croteau, Meteor House, 2014

Philip José Farmer's Father Carmody stories represent some of his most compelling short fiction. With one exception noted below, they all debuted in issues of *The Magazine of Fantasy and Science Fiction* published over a nine-year period spanning 1953 to 1961. The stories were later collected in two books: *Night of Light* (Berkley Medallion, 1966) and *Father to the Stars* (Tor 1981). The latter is an interesting collection in that it presents the Carmody stories in chronological order from the viewpoint of the characters. Its only failing is that it does not include the second part of *Night of Light*, which was first published in the 1966 paperback. For purposes of this chronology, I have split *Night of Light* into two parts, although the second part was never published separately on its own.

The Detective Raspold stories, which occur in the same continuity as the Father Carmody series, are "Strange Compulsion" (in which Raspold appears as a major character, though not as the protagonist) and "Some Fabulous Yonder." "Strange Compulsion" first appeared in *Science Fiction Plus* in October 1953 and was reprinted in 1960 under the title "The Captain's Daughter" in Farmer's anthology *The Alley God* (Ballantine Books, 1962). Although "Strange Compulsion" is an intriguing story of alien biology much in the vein of his acclaimed "The Lovers" (*Startling Stories*, August 1952), due to its general lack of availability over the years, few have read it. Similarly, until the version restoring Farmer's original text of the story was published in the collection *Pearls from Peoria* (Subterranean Press, 2006), "Some Fabulous Yonder"

48-504-2 ★ A PINNACLE / TOR BOOK ★ $2.75

JIM BÆN PRESENTS:

PHILIP JOSÉ FARMER

FATHER TO THE STARS

FIRST BOOK PUBLICATION!

had only appeared twice, in its original magazine publication in the April 1963 issue of *Fantastic Stories of Imagination* and in a 1969 magazine collection of Hugo Award Winners, *Strange Fantasy #8*. Raspold also appears in both parts of *Night of Light*, but only as a minor character. Thus, many of those who have read a large body of Farmer's work do not realize that he had begun to flesh out this fascinating detective—referred to by Carmody as "the galactic Sherlock Holmes"—in other stories.

It should also be noted that Farmer's stories "Mother" (*Thrilling Wonder Stories*, April 1953) and "Daughter" (*Thrilling Wonder* Stories, Winter 1954) are set on the planet Baudelaire; a mention of the "molluscs" or "land-oysters of Baudelaire" in "Father" and a reference to "the Baudelairean Gang" in "Some Fabulous Yonder" place the events of "Mother" and "Daughter" in the same fictional universe as Carmody and Raspold. It is possible that Farmer conceived of the majority of his early science fiction tales—including "The Lovers," "Moth and Rust" (*Startling Stories*, June 1953), and "Rastignac the Devil" (*Fantastic Universe*, May 1954)—as having been set in the same continuity, albeit sometimes at different points in the future, but this topic is beyond the scope of the present chronology.

While rereading the Father Carmody and Detective Raspold stories, I discovered several inconsistencies that I believed needed some explanation. The major one involved the Federation's titanic protein computer. In some stories, it was referred to as "Og Boojum," or simply "the Boojum." In "Some Fabulous Yonder," however, it was called "ATHENA." Arranging the chronology, I discovered this pattern: in the beginning of the series the supercomputer is called Og Boojum, in the middle of the series the name is changed to ATHENA, and in the last part of the series the name is again restored to Og Boojum. I used my own story, "The Goddess Equation" (which fits into the chronology shortly after the events of "Some Fabulous Yonder"), to explain this seeming discrepancy. It should be noted that in the last chronological story, Part Two of *Night of Light*, the half-mile-wide cube that makes up the Vatican also houses a supercomputer, which is "second in size only to the Federation's Og Boojum."

Another inconsistency is the name given to the organization of planetary systems of which Earth and humanity is a part. In some instances it is referred to as the Commonwealth and at other times as the Federation. As both words are similar in meaning, it may be that they are interchangeable. It may also be that there was a renaming or reorganization at some point. If so, it changed from a Federation to a Commonwealth and back to a Federation. While the latter is possible, I have come to the conclusion that the words are interchangeable or function as nuanced terms with only slightly different meanings.

There are other errors which are probably typographical in nature. For instance, the planet Wildenwooly is also sometimes spelled Wildenwoolly. The frontier planet Diveboard from "Some Fabulous Yonder" is possibly meant to be the planet Springboard, where Carmody mentions in "The Night of Light" that he "made a fortune smuggling sodomspears" and was almost captured by Raspold. In another case, one of the stories states that it takes place in the twenty-second century. As exact dates are given elsewhere, however, it is clear that the series really occurs in the twenty-third century.

Other seeming inconsistencies are technology-based. It is curious to read the stories from our present vantage point in time, many years after they were written in the 1950s and 1960s. There are phones, screens, even T.V. We may have these today, but by current visions of the future they now seem obsolete. Be advised, however, that the series does not reveal much about the past and how Earth society has gotten to be where it is in the twenty-third century. Humanity could have gone through any number of upheavals that stunted technological development. Technology, and the human response to it, does not always progress at a constant rate. Further, terms like T.V. may not have the same meaning as in our time. There are plenty of words that we use today that have changed their meanings significantly in the course of a couple hundred years. This would seem to be the case in the two series, as in the second part of *Night of Light*, Carmody dons a visor-like device called a 'ducer to view a "letter" from Raspold, which takes the form of a personal video recording.

F 588 **BB** AN ORIGINAL BALLANTINE BOOK 50¢

THE ALLEY GOD

*3 extraordinary novelets of fantasy and science
fiction—by the author of "The Lovers."*

PHILIP JOSE FARMER

I have created the following chronology, and the above rationalizations, to help readers understand these two wonderful series in a new way, which have been made a bit confusing by their publishing history. I encourage Philip José Farmer enthusiasts to read the Father Carmody and Detective Raspold stories in the order that the characters experience them. Doing so opens up a whole new Farmerian universe.

Chronological order:

"Strange Compulsion" (aka "The Captain's Daughter")—Raspold is on Luna trying to transfer to Wildenwooly. That the town of Optima was "founded in the reclaimed Gobi Desert several hundred years before" is hard to reconcile with the dates mentioned later in the series and is probably merely an exaggerated claim by the Remoh zealots. Note that the character Rhoda Tu is likely some relation to Captain Tu in "Father."

2256 A.D.—Carmody is incarcerated at Johns Hopkins (see *Night of Light*, Part One).

Night of Light, Part One (aka "The Night of Light")—Carmody is a criminal. The Boojum is the supercomputer.

"Some Fabulous Yonder"—Raspold is on Wildenwooly. Carmody surrenders and is incarcerated again at Johns Hopkins (this is a separate incarceration from the one mentioned in *Night of Light*, Part One because reference is made to Carmody's experiences on Dante's Joy; according *Night of Light*, Part Two, Carmody stayed at Johns Hopkins for a year after his surrender. ATHENA is "the skyscraper-tall computer." The government is referred to as "the Federation."

"The Goddess Equation"—Raspold is on Earth after the events occurring in "Some Fabulous Yonder." ATHENA is the supercomputer, while Og Boojum has been retired.

"A Few Miles"—Carmody is being sent to Wildenwooly. This story occurs in 2260 A.D. or later. Carmody is a monk, not yet a priest.

PHILIP JOSÉ FARMER

HIS CLASSIC NOVEL OF THE ULTIMATE RELIGION

NIGHT OF LIGHT

0-425-06291-0 · $2.50 · BERKLEY SCIENCE FICTION

"Prometheus"—This story is a direct continuation of the events occurring in "A Few Miles."

"Father"—Carmody is a priest. The government is referred to as "the Commonwealth."

"Attitudes"—Carmody is "Father John" and has developed PK (psychokinesis). It is possible this story occurs after *Night of Light*, Part Two, but I have placed it here so it would not interfere with the dramatic impact of that story, which makes a fitting, if unsettling, conclusion for the series.

Night of Light, Part Two—This story occurs twenty-seven years after the events of *Night of Light*, Part One. Carmody is to become bishop of Wildenwooly. Og Boojum is the "Federation's titanic protein computer." Carmody receives a letter from Raspold, who is living in an apartment on the sixtieth level of the city of Denver. Some of Raspold's history of chasing Carmody is given.

Publication order:

"Attitudes" in *The Magazine of Fantasy and Science Fiction*, ed. Anthony Boucher and J. Francis McComas, Vol. 5. No. 4, October 1953.

"Strange Compulsion" (later retitled "The Captain's Daughter") in *Science-Fiction Plus*, ed. Hugo Gernsback, Vol. 1, No. 6, October 1953.

"Father" in *The Magazine of Fantasy and Science Fiction*, ed. Anthony Boucher, Vol. 99, No. 1, Whole No. 50, July 1955.

"The Night of Light" (novella) in *The Magazine of Fantasy and Science Fiction*, ed. Anthony Boucher, Vol. 12, No. 6, Whole No. 73, June 1957. (This story later appeared as Part One of the 1966 novel version of *Night of Light*; see below.)

"A Few Miles," *The Magazine of Fantasy and Science Fiction*, ed. Robert P. Mills, Volume 19, No. 4, Whole No. 113, October 1960.

"Prometheus" in *The Magazine of Fantasy and Science Fiction*, ed. Robert P. Mills, Volume 20, No. 3, Whole No. 118, March 1961.

"Some Fabulous Yonder" in *Fantastic Stories of the Imagination*, ed. Cele Goldsmith, Vol. 12, No. 4, April 1963 (rewritten without Farmer's permission) and in *Pearls from Peoria*, ed. Paul Spiteri, Subterranean Press, 2006 (Farmer's original text restored).

"*Night of Light*, Part Two" in *Night of Light*, Berkley Medallion Books, 1966. (This story was published alongside the original novella, "The Night of Light," to form a single novel.)

The Foundation of Kôr

FarmerCon IX Convention Program, Meteor House, 2014

Meteor House is excited to announce a brand-new cycle in Philip Jose Farmer's Khokarsa series, the Foundation of Kôr, a trilogy of novellas written by Farmer collaborator Christopher Paul Carey (*Gods of Opar: Tales of Lost Khokarsa*). The first volume in the new cycle, *Gates of Kôr*, releases in 2015, and will be followed by *Scourge of Kôr* and *Fires of Kôr*.[20]

Christopher Paul Carey: The new trilogy focuses on the hero Hadon's son, Kohr, who leads a large group of followers to found a new city in a strange, faraway land.

It's some fifteen to twenty years after the great calamity that destroyed the Khokarsan civilization. As far as Kohr is aware, his home city is the only queendom of the once grand empire that survived the cataclysm. But a great civil war—much like that which threatened to sunder the Khokarsan Empire—has left the city forever changed. The followers of Kho, the Great Mother goddess, have been defeated and a compromise religion has been established to finally put an end to the ages-old conflict. Now, the city is ruled by the followers of the sungod Resu, but they are presided over by a priestess—a high vicar of Resu—who at present happens to be Kohr's younger half-sister. Kohr and his

20. On the very afternoon before FarmerCon IX commenced, my publisher received the green light to publish stories set directly in the city of Opar, as opposed to the larger empire of Khokarsa that was Farmer's creation. Because of this opportunity, I decided to postpone writing the Foundation of Kôr trilogy and instead write *Hadon, King of Opar* and *Blood of Ancient Opar*, two tales set directly before the events of the proposed *Gates of Kôr*. I still plan to write the Foundation of Kôr trilogy, if permissions are still in place when my schedule clears.

followers, disgusted by the new religion, have left their home city, heading south on a great pilgrimage to found their own settlement. That's the setup for the trilogy.

MH: What are some of the inspirations for the Foundation of Kôr trilogy?

CPC: The idea for this cycle of the Khokarsa series comes directly from Philip Jose Farmer himself. The entire setup I just described is detailed in Phil's notes, as well as in a 1977 interview with Phil in *Vector* #81 in which he expressed his desire to write about Kohr taking his great Ax of Victory with him to eventually found Kôr, the lost city from H. Rider Haggard's classic novel She: A History of Adventure.

MH: Will Haggard's work influence the new trilogy?

CPC: Very much so. In fact, the way I'm planning it, the new trilogy—*Gates of Kôr, Scourge of Kôr,* and *Fires of Kôr*—will be as much inspired by H. Rider Haggard's novels as Farmer's *Hadon of Ancient Opar* and *Flight to Opar* were inspired by those of Edgar Rice Burroughs. In particular, the trilogy is going to draw heavily on Haggard's *She* and *She and Allan*, the latter being a novel about Allan Quatermain's encounter with the immortal Ayesha in the lost city of Kôr.

Kohr's Ax of Victory, obviously, derives from Haggard's work, having been crafted by the dwarf Pag (called Paga in the Khokarsa series) in *Allan and the Ice-Gods*, and later inherited by the Zulu warrior Umslopogaas in *Nada the Lily*, one of Philip Jose Farmer's all-time-favorite novels. Farmer's Khokarsa series filled in the gaps left by Haggard concerning the ancient history of the ax, and that tradition continues in the Foundation of Kôr cycle.

Of course, the setting of trilogy will be the same as that in *She* and *She and Allan*, but it will be twelve thousand years in the past. The city of Kôr has yet to be founded circa 10,000 B.C., and the basin of the massive volcanic mountain that will one day be home to Kôr was at that time filled with water—a miles-wide crater lake. Haggard speculated in *She* that the inhabitants

FARMERCON IX

Held in Conjunction with PulpFest 2014 · August 7–10

A Meteor House Publication

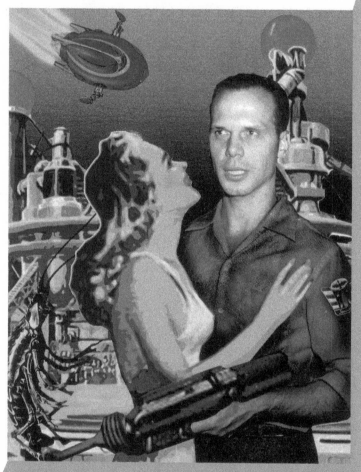

Announcing **THE MONSTER ON HOLD** *by Philip José Farmer & Win Scott Eckert*
and **THE FOUNDATION OF KÔR TRILOGY** *by Christopher Paul Carey*

of ancient Kôr or must have drained the lake via a great canal, thereby creating the nearly impassible swamp that circles the mountain and makes Kôr all but inaccessible to outsiders. In the Foundation of Kôr trilogy, we'll see how—and perhaps more importantly, why—that happens.

MH: You mentioned Kohr's ax, which readers of the Khokarsa series know once belonged to Hadon's mad herculean cousin, Kwasin. *The Song of Kwasin* drops curtain on Kwasin's storyline in a literal cliffhanger, with the character's fate uncertain. Will we find out what happened to Kohr's giant uncle in the Foundation of Kôr trilogy?

CPC: Farmer scholar and creative mythographer Rick Lai published a fascinating article in which he speculated that the character Rezu—Ayesha's giant sun-worshiping antagonist in Haggard's *She and Allan*—is actually Kwasin, who has somehow been made immortal. In fact, Haggard himself said that Rezu had become immortal by the same means as Ayesha. Readers of *The Song of Kwasin* might recall that King Minruth claimed to have received a vision about Kwasin's dark, long-lived future when his eye was gouged out by the Ax of Victory. Will that vision be borne out, and will Kwasin be back in the Foundation of Kôr trilogy? Readers will have to wait for the new series to find out.

On Writing *Hadon, King of Opar*

Published online at the *Philip José Farmer
International Bibliography*, June 2015

Christopher Paul Carey is a writer and editor. Three of Farmer's
story collections from Subterranean Press (in 2007–2009) were
edited by him. He is the coauthor with Philip José Farmer of
the third Opar/Khokarsa novel, *The Song of Kwasin* (2012). We
never thought to see this novel, after the publication of the first
two. These two were published in 1974 and 1976. A third was
announced then, but never published until Christopher finished
the novel with Farmer's permission.

In addition to writing and finishing *The Song of Kwasin*,
Christopher also wrote some other Opar stories, three novellas.
One together with Philip José Farmer, two others of his own,
based on notes from Farmer.

These novellas are "A Kick in the Side" (published in *The
Worlds of Philip José Farmer Volume 1: Protean Dimensions*, 2010),
"Kwasin and the Bear God" (written with Farmer, published in
The Worlds of Philip José Farmer 2: Of Dust and Soul, 2011), and
Exiles of Kho (published by Meteor House in 2012).

But Chris wasn't finished with Opar it seems. His publisher
announced two new novellas *Hadon, King of Opar* and *Blood of
Ancient Opar*, volumes 4 and 5 in the Opar/Khokarsa series.

Both will be published in limited editions by Meteor House:
Hadon, King of Opar in August this year, and *Blood of Ancient Opar*
in 2016.

Rias Nuninga: First, please tell us a bit about how and why did you come to write *Hadon, King of Opar*? What gave you the idea? Has Farmer infected you with the Opar virus?

Christopher Paul Carey: Thanks for having me back, Rias. I'm not sure I'd describe it with the metaphor of a virus. It's more like it's in my literary DNA. I grew up reading Farmer and Burroughs and Haggard. I've been writing since I was a young child, and I very much like the idea of working within a tradition. With the Khokarsa series, there's a very clear chain of transmission running from Haggard to Burroughs, and then from both of those authors to Farmer. Exploring that chain, and then carrying it forward, gives me a tremendous amount of satisfaction. That's the "why." As for the "how," that's simply a matter of making sure all of the interested parties have given their permission or blessings for new works set in Opar to be written. That was the breakthrough that happened last year, and so I went to work and wrote the book, which was dream come true for me.

RN: You finished the third and as I thought conclusive Opar novel, *The Song of Kwasin*. But the story wasn't finished? You had more to tell? Or was it original Farmer's idea to write more?

CPC: When I was working on *The Song of Kwasin*, I had access to Philip José Farmer's notes on the Khokarsa series, including two drafts of his outline for *Flight to Opar*. In one of those drafts, Phil mentioned that the next two books in the series after Flight would be titled *The Siege of Opar* and *Hadon, King of Opar*, respectively.

Ultimately, Phil changed his mind about *The Siege of Opar* and decided to write a novel about Hadon's giant cousin, Kwasin, and his struggles to unseat King Minruth from the throne of Khokarsa. So *The Siege of Opar* in the end became *The Song of Kwasin*. A bit later in that particular *Flight to Opar* outline, Phil stops outlining the novel and begins trying to figure out what would come later in the series. It's clear he was trying to work this out so he would know how to wrap up the plot of *Flight to Opar*, and all the implications that ending would hold for the unfolding series.

HADON, KING OF OPAR

KING OF OPAR

Christopher Paul Carey

So there is a brief sub-outline within the outline for *Flight to Opar* detailing what would have happened in Ancient Opar in the years following the great calamity that shatters the Khokarsan Empire, and even a hint of what would have happened after that period. So Phil was absolutely planning to write more in the series that would have been set after the cataclysm.

RN: Is the new novella completely of your own, or based on Farmer's notes? What did you have to do or study before you started writing this novella?

CPC: *Hadon, King of Opar* is based on Phil's synopsis of future events in the series, although since that outline only focused on major events, there were a lot of blanks I had to fill in on my own. I extrapolated several major plot points from the already written novels. So it's a combination of Farmer and Carey that sets the scene for more ideas outlined by Phil for the continuing series.

To prepare for writing the book, I did a lot of rereading of the Khokarsa series, and reread a lot of Burroughs and Haggard for inspiration. There was one classic fight scene in Haggard's *Nada the Lily* that I consulted, since I had a similar scene in the novella. I wanted to deconstruct how Haggard could write a passage so vivid that would stick with me for so many years. Turns out, the scene was much shorter than I'd remembered, and he'd made the scene memorable with a combination of crisp prose and mythic imagery. So I tried to learn from that. I also dipped back into *Heritage of the Flaming God*, the original monograph written by Frank J. Brueckel and John Harwood that inspired Phil to write the Khokarsa series.

RN: What is the story about? Can you tell us a bit about the storyline?

CPC: The story picks up about fourteen years after the great earthquake that destroyed all of the queendoms of Khokarsa except for Opar. Hadon is now king of his city of gold and jewels, tasked with keeping his people alive in a changing and hostile world. While his wife, the queen and high priestess Lalila, is conducting a ritual ceremony of the priestesses on the sacred

Isle of Lupoeth, a mysterious force invades the valley of Opar. There is a lot of intrigue in the story, and not a few surprises, so I don't want to go into much more detail than that.

RN: You wrote one novella and a second one to come, as volumes 4 and 5 in the Opar/Khokarsa series. Why novellas and not full length novels?

CPC: The publisher has an agreement with the Farmer estate that allows for the publication novellas set in Philip José Farmer's worlds written by other authors. Under those terms, I can write novellas set in Khokarsa and Ancient Opar, whereas novels are reserved for works written wholly by Farmer or coauthored by him. Therefore I'm writing two novellas back to back that will tell the story arc of a full-length novel. *Hadon, King of Opar* is the first, which will be followed next year by *Blood of Ancient Opar*. Both works will be at the upper end of the word count for what constitutes a novella—about a quarter longer than my first novella, *Exiles of Kho*. There's a lot of story to tell in this arc.

RN: I read the following in a review of the novella: "When reading *Hadon, King of Opar*, it felt like I was reading a lost work of Philip José Farmer himself. Carey's talent as a writer, knowledge of the works of Burroughs, Haggard, and Farmer, his education in anthropology, and interest in linguistics has allowed him to continue the Khokarsa series with the same skill and passion as Farmer." What are your feelings about this compliment?

CPC: The words are too kind. Phil was a real Renaissance man and his knowledge was much broader and deeper than mine. I do admit to being well read in Burroughs, Haggard, and Farmer, and I hold a bachelor's degree in anthropology. But Farmer was a Brobdingnagian, whereas I'm a Lilliputian by comparison..

RN: What will the next novella, *Blood of Ancient Opar*, be about? Who will be the protagonist?

CPC: The novella will pick up directly after the tumultuous events of *Hadon, King of Opar*. The city and the characters have undergone some major changes, and the wheels of intrigue continue to churn in unexpected ways. Hadon will continue to be the protagonist, although his daughter La will play a major role, as will his son Kohr and his stepdaughter Abeth.

RN: Blood of Ancient Opar was also announced for publication this year. The date changed to 2016. You did not have enough time to write both for publication this year?

CPC: The press release announcing the two novellas was written from the convention hall floor at PulpFest, and if I recall correctly, I don't think we meant for it to say that both novellas would be released in 2015. In any case, soon thereafter, Meteor House secured the rights to publish a Restored Edition of *Flight to Opar* in 2015, and since I was to be the editor of that novel, it quickly became apparent that it would be impossible for me to write both books, edit a novel, and have them all be ushered through the production schedule in the same year. So I'll be writing *Blood of Ancient Opar* this fall, and it should be available sometime in 2016.

RN: In an earlier interview I asked you if you planned to write more Khokarsa stories. Your answer then was: "we'll have to wait and see". I ask the same question again this time. Farmer's original plans were to write a series from nine to twelve books. Have you adopted these plans?

CPC: Right before I received the greenlight to write *Hadon, King of Opar* and *Blood of Ancient Opar*, I was gearing up to write a trilogy of novellas about Hadon's son, Kohr. This new cycle would again be based on an idea from Farmer's notes, and would be as inspired by H. Rider Haggard as the original Ancient Opar books were inspired by Burroughs. I will probably work on a non-Khokarsa project after the two Ancient Opar novellas are completed, but I do hope to be able to write that new trilogy someday sooner than later if the stars align and Great Kho gives me her blessing.

RN: Thank you very much for the interview, Chris!

On Restoring Farmer's *Flight to Opar*

"Preface to the Restored Edition" in *Flight to Opar*
by Philip José Farmer, Meteor House, 2015

Those who have never before read Philip José Farmer's *Flight to Opar*, or who have read it so long ago they forget most of its particulars, should at this time turn past this section and enjoy the novel on its own merits before returning to read the remainder of this preface. Readers well acquainted with the story at hand, however, should feel free to continue reading the following commentary on this new Restored Edition of Farmer's second installment in the Khokarsa series.

The existence and provenance in a university collection of Farmer's original manuscripts of *Flight to Opar* first came to my attention in 2012. This was around the time of the publication of *Gods of Opar: Tales of Lost Khokarsa*, an omnibus I edited for Subterranean Press that collected the novels *Hadon of Ancient Opar*, *Flight to Opar*, and *The Song of Kwasin*. At that time, I made a mental note that should *Flight to Opar* be reprinted in the future, I would consult the original manuscripts to assess how they might differ from the first edition, published in June 1976 by DAW Books, and provide that information to the new publisher. As it turned out, *Gods of Opar* sold out shortly after publication, and so the opportunity to examine Farmer's manuscripts for a new edition of *Flight to Opar* came only a couple years later, when Michael Croteau of Meteor House contacted me to let me know his press would be bringing out a new edition of the novel.

Two manuscripts of *Flight to Opar* were consulted in the preparation of the present Restored Edition. One is presumably Farmer's first draft, with many corrections made in pencil in the author's own hand. The other is a retyped version of that first draft, a typescript with a multitude of line edits and excisions made in red ink by the copyeditor at DAW Books, as well as a number of corrections made in pencil by Farmer himself. To the layperson, the copyeditor's line edits might seem to be a case of overreaching, or "red-pen syndrome," such as when an overeager novice editor unnecessarily "rewrites" an author's work. This is certainly not the case with the line edits made to the typescript submitted to DAW Books, which overwhelmingly are well informed and serve to considerably improve and tighten the original text without compromising Farmer's prose; such line edits have not been "undone" in this Restored Edition.

It may be relevant to observe here that the manuscript of *Flight to Opar* submitted to DAW Books is less polished than perhaps any of the several dozen Farmer typescripts I have examined over the years. This could very well be the result of tight deadlines and a busy work schedule during this period of the author's career, especially considering that Farmer's translation and retelling of J. H. Rosny's *Ironcastle* appeared in print from DAW Books only three months prior to the publication of *Flight to Opar*.

Many of the editorial excisions from Farmer's submitted typescript are of a different nature from the typically beneficial line edits, and they provide the rationale for the novel's Restored Edition. It is telling that the excisions become more frequent as well as encompass larger portions of text beginning about halfway through the typescript. While some of these cuts clearly were made to tighten pacing, this is not always the case, and one quickly begins to suspect that many passages were removed to effect a reduced page count purely for the sake of the economics of printing a shorter book.

The present edition of *Flight to Opar* restores numerous passages, both lengthy and brief, that serve to strengthen what is already an excellent novel of high adventure and meticulous world building. In total, these amount to nearly four thousand words of narrative and dialogue missing from the first edition and the various reprints of the novel published before Meteor House's Restored Edition.

So what exactly is new to this edition? To begin with, a number of lines and passages have been restored that exemplify Farmer's exceptional skill at world building. For instance, one line restored from Farmer's typescript reveals that the robes of the priests of Resu are "tasseled, bright-yellow, scarlet slashed"—in other words, their clothing is symbolic of the sun they worship. Similarly, another restored line observes that the bronze helmet of a lieutenant of the guard of the Temple of Resu is decorated with a "sunburst just above the bird's-beak visor" and has "seven fish-eagle feathers projecting from the top." This is not merely a hastily conceived description, but rather a meaningful and subtle one; in the Khokarsan language, which is detailed by Farmer in an article that appears in Addendum 1 of this book, the syllabary glyph for res can mean "sun," "sungod," or "eagle," and the components of the guard's helmet are emblematic of each of these meanings.

Other restored passages show how Farmer was building on the mythology of Edgar Rice Burroughs' Tarzan series, a fact doubtless missed by the copyeditor who struck them out. Typical of this is the following paragraph:

> Hadon understood. C'ak'oguq"o was an aboriginal deity, and this stone had probably been erected in her honor centuries, or even a thousand years ago, before the Khoklem had conquered the K'ud"em'o area. The conquerors had absorbed the indigenes, who must have been Klemqaba, the half-neanderthal people. That accounted for the short stature, heavy bones, and chunkiness of this tribe. Their language had probably been a sort of pidgin, a fusion of Klemqaba and Khoklem with some later additions of Klemsaasa vocabulary. And only Kho knew what else. They must have had, and might still have, contact with the Nukaar, the hairy subhumans of the forested interior. They might even have borrowed words from them. After all, the Oparian dialect contained loanwords from the local Nukaar.

This is a reference to the fact that in Burroughs' *The Return of Tarzan* (1915), La of Opar (not to be confused with the character of the ancient La created by Farmer, who was meant to be an

FLIGHT TO OPAR

Philip José Farmer

ancestor of Burroughs' La) is able to communicate with Tarzan only because they share a common language, that of the great apes. Farmer's Nukaar are meant to be Burroughs' Mangani, and the restored paragraph illustrates how loanwords of the "hairy subhumans" slipped into the local Oparian dialect, thus allowing for Tarzan and La to be able to make themselves understood to one another in Burroughs' novel. This topic was of such interest to Farmer that he even made it the subject of an article titled "A Language for Opar," which was first published in the Edgar Rice Burroughs fanzine *ERB-dom* in February 1974.

Similarly, a description of the gold ingots that Hadon, the hero of *Flight to Opar*, discovers in a vault deep beneath his home city ("shaped like two V's back to back") has been restored because it echoes a description of ingots Burroughs' ape-man discovered in the darkness of the very same vault in *The Return of Tarzan* ("they felt not unlike double-headed bootjacks").

The following paragraph restored from Farmer's original typescript further illustrates how the author was aligning his own series with the works of Burroughs, whose famous ape-man stumbled in the darkness down countless secret passageways beneath lost African cities during his many adventures:

> The situation reminded Hadon of a similar setup in the palace of Minruth. When he had escaped from the underground prison with Kwasin and the others, he had climbed just such a shaft to get through a secret passage to the apartment where Awineth was imprisoned. He wondered how many of the ancient cities had just such hidden tunnels and passageways? How many kings and queens had prepared escape routes, only to find that what can let some out can also let others in?

This again is a subtle and playful nod by Farmer, indicating that his ancient Khokarsa is the mother civilization of the many lost cities discovered by Tarzan in the first half of the twentieth century. A myriad of secret tunnels are found in both the bustling, thriving cities of Khokarsa and the ruined, timeworn cities of Tarzan's Africa because they are quite literally based on the same blueprints, if not the very same tunnels. This is classic Farmer, winking slyly as he makes connections that stir just beneath the surface of the reader's awareness.

Beyond such homages to Burroughs, multiple passages giving original flavor to Farmer's Khokarsa also appear for the first time in this edition, such as this description by Hadon of the mythology behind the Strait of Keth:

> "...It is in fact a chasm, a deep splitting of the mountains some time in the past, perhaps during the creation of the world. It is said that the earth split open there to give birth to M'agogobabi, the mosquito demon, after the Flaming God had lain with the mountain, which was at that time a giant goddess. She was turned to stone by mighty Kho immediately after giving birth to the demon..."

And when Queen Phebha of Opar orders Hadon to remain in the Temple of Kho while his brother is outside being held hostage by King Gamori's forces, Farmer's hero contemplates the archaic custom of fraternal sacrifice and its mythological origins in this restored passage:

> "...But still, people will think I am a coward, though there will be no logic to that thought. The custom that a younger brother should sacrifice himself for his older brother no longer lives. That died out hundreds of years ago, though the stories about such brothers as Desweth and Noqawi are still taught to schoolchildren."

In addition to having cut such meaningful text from Farmer's typescript, the novel's original copyeditor introduced a number of minor errors that altered details of the author's world building. For example, the term "hibiscus-coffee" was changed to "hibiscustea," probably because of the line "he purchased a cup of hot hibiscus-steeped water," as well as the fact that hibiscus tea is a common beverage in our modern age. However, Farmer's article "The Plants of Khokarsa" (which was probably extant in manuscript form in 1976, but only first appeared in print in 2012 as a bonus feature in the limited edition of *Gods of Opar: Tales of Lost Khokarsa*), includes the following entry in its list of plants introduced to Khokarsa from West Africa:

Hibiscus esculenta, known more familiarly as gumbo or okra. Its partially ripened fruit can be cooked like asparagus, pickled, or cut up for soups and broths. Its seeds can be cured and dried to make a sort of coffee bean.

This entry from Farmer's article makes it clear that the three references to Hadon's "hibiscus-steeped water" as a type of coffee were intentional, and so they have been restored for this edition.

Another minor alteration of Farmer's intent and meaning by the original copyeditor was the change in one line of the typescript from "on the tenth day of the week" to "on the tenth day." While this change might be considered trivial, it does alter the novel's timeline, as the Khokarsan week is ten days. Thus, "on the tenth day of the week" might be translated in Khokarsan as "on Saturday," a reference that does not indicate the passage of a specific period of time, whereas "on the tenth day" would indicate that ten days have transpired since the beginning of this stage of Hadon's journey. Further, the copyeditor changed another reference in this same passage from "a week" to "over a week." These seemingly harmless line edits had the potential to create far-reaching continuity errors. *The Song of Kwasin*—the third novel in the Khokarsa series, which I coauthored with Farmer—takes place in part concurrently with the events of *Flight to Opar*. Therefore, when I was preparing to complete Farmer's manuscript of *The Song of Kwasin*, it was necessary to add up all references to the passage of time in *Flight to Opar* so that I might draw up a timeline that would encompass major events from both novels. In this way, I hoped to ensure that specific happenings mentioned in both novels did not create contradictions in terms of when they occurred in relation to one another. However, because of the copyeditor's changes to Farmer's typescript, a large portion of the events in the timeline I created are off by a few days. Fortunately, the shift in the timeline was minor enough that it did not wreak havoc on the unfolding of events in *The Song of Kwasin*, but it very well could have. Therefore, Farmer's original text in this regard has been restored for the present edition.

Along the same lines, nine very important words have been restored to the end of the following passage in Chapter Twenty-Five (italics added for emphasis):

"...Klyhy is a capable woman, a strong one, but she needs a good man to lead her forces. You are the man. You can't marry her, since you are the husband of the violet-eyed woman from beyond the Ringing Sea. Of whom there is a prophecy, by the way, *but no man has known this—until this moment...*"

What Farmer apparently meant to convey by this struck-out line is that there is a *second* and possibly *older* prophecy about Lalila that is different from the one revealed by the oracle to Hadon and Lalila in Chapter Twelve of the novel. This second prophecy has far-ranging implications for the unfolding series, and so the copyeditor's change has been overturned.

Other passages have been restored to this edition simply because they exemplify good writing. Take for example the two paragraphs of poignant internal monologue in Chapter Eighteen wherein Hadon ponders the trauma that Abeth, Lalila's daughter with the hero Wi, has experienced as a result of being dragged along on her mother's adventures. The absence of this passage leaves the reader with the impression that Hadon is coldly oblivious to the child's struggles; its presence reveals just the opposite, adding an extra dimension to the two characters that cultivates sympathy in the reader for both of them.

Further, two scenes of explicit violence were toned down by the novel's original copyeditor from their appearance in Farmer's original typescript, and have been restored here. These are the attack by the soldiers of King Minruth on the priestesses during their ceremony on the Isle of Karneth in Chapter Six and the mob's attack on the guardsmen of the Temple of Resu at the end of Chapter Twenty-Four. Always one for raw realism in his fiction, Farmer himself once restored scenes of similarly explicit brutality to his novel *Two Hawks from Earth* (1979), which was a revised and expanded version of his bowdlerized novel *The Gate of Time* (1966).

The above examples are just a taste of what is new to

Meteor House's Restored Edition of *Flight to Opar*. Other restored passages include a lesson for Hadon in the use of the fore-and-aft sail under the tutelage of young Captain Ruseth; a discussion of naval strategy in Khokarsa's civil war; dialogue between Hinokly and Ruseth on the science of astronomy and the changing climate of Central Africa; an attempt by Hadon to get Lalila to explain why she believes she is cursed; Hadon's musings on the healthfulness of sexual fantasies; humorous exchanges between various characters; dialogue by Sahhindar; and much more.

In addition to these and other restorations, a number of typo graphical changes have been made for the sake of consistency, syncing up the present edition of the novel with those stylistic conventions employed by Farmer in his typescript that also appear in the published editions of *Hadon of Ancient Opar* and *The Song of Kwasin*. These are of a minor nature, such as lowercasing the words "emperor," "empress," "king," and "queen" when they do not precede a character's name or are not used as a title of direct address. Additionally, Farmer's use of the serial comma has been restored here, as it was also employed in the other published Khokarsa novels, and more importantly, because the arbitrary decision to strike out serial commas sometimes caused the original copyeditor to impose awkward and unnecessary rewordings of Farmer's prose in the attempt to avoid grammatical ambiguity.

Early in his career, Farmer suffered rewrites without his permission of three of his stories—"The Biological Revolt" (1953), "Rastignac the Devil" (1954), and "Some Fabulous Yonder" (1963), all of which he considered, in his words, "ruined." Other times, passages from his novels were altered against his wishes, such as when sex scenes were cut from *Flesh* (1960) and scenes of explicit violence were toned down in the aforementioned *The Gate of Time*. Farmer did not shy away from publicly decrying these alterations and rewrites. While it is probably unfair to proclaim that the text of *Flight to Opar* in editions prior to this one was similarly ruined—Farmer's typescript was, after all, expertly copyedited for the first edition and the story makes sense without the excised material—Meteor House's Restored Edition is clearly closer to Philip José Farmer's original vision for the novel.

As Farmer's longtime readers well know, it is often the interjection of the author's idiosyncratic phraseology, his sly references, and his characters' unique and oftentimes startling perspectives on society, technology, and the human condition that set his work apart from those of his colleagues in the field of science fiction and fantasy. There was something *different* about Farmer's approach, something so unique that only a single adjective is fit to wholly sum it up: Farmerian. And for this reason, Farmer's readers can join me in rejoicing at the publication of Meteor House's new Restored Edition of this classic novel, which scintillates all the brighter with a singular Farmerian light.

A History of *The Song of Kwasin*

"Preface to the Meteor House Edition" in
The Song of Kwasin by Philip José Farmer and
Christopher Paul Carey, Meteor House, 2015

For a period of almost thirty years, it became increasingly unlikely the novel you now hold in your hands would ever be written, let alone published. Even after the manuscript fragment and outline were discovered in Philip José Farmer's filing cabinet in July 2005, the odds were stacked against the third volume of the Khokarsa series ever being completed and seeing print. Farmer had retired from writing after the publication of *The Dark Heart of Time: A Tarzan Novel* in 1999 and was in declining health, so who would complete the manuscript? And then there was the even more daunting challenge: who would be willing to publish a new installment in a heroic historical fantasy series whose last chapter had been published in 1976, and that had been out of print in the author's native country for nearly twenty-five years?

The first volume of the Khokarsa series, *Hadon of Ancient Opar*, first landed on the bookstore shelves in April 1974. Its sequel, *Flight to Opar*, followed in June 1976. When a third "Ancient Opar" novel (a misnomer, as soon will become apparent) was announced in May 1975 in *Science Fiction Review* #13, it appeared as if the Khokarsa books were well on their way to becoming one of Farmer's major series.

Farmer discussed the forthcoming novel in a letter dated November 26, 1976 that was published in *Science Fiction Review* #20 (February 1977), stating that he was "busy with the 330,000-word draft of the third Riverworld novel," though he was in the meantime trying to come up with a suitable title for the third "Opar" novel. But there was a problem, as Farmer went on to explain in the letter:

> Don Wollheim insists that "Opar" be in the title of every one of the series. What do you do when the action takes place nowhere near that fabled city? Or if Hadon isn't in the tale? I'm planning on devoting the third book to the mighty Kwasin, and all events take place on the island of Khokarsa. How about *Far from Opar*?

Science Fiction Review editor Richard E. Geis wrote back to Farmer suggesting the title *Kwasin of Opar*, to which Farmer replied in a letter dated December 3, 1976:

> Actually, Kwasin was born in the city of Dythbeth, but he is a cousin of Hadon's, and he did spend almost all his early life in the Opar area. So, *Kwasin of Opar* is a title stretching the truth only a little bit...
>
> I look forward to writing *Nowhere Near Opar* some day. Let Don Wollheim chew on that.

Over the next few years, projects that were both higher profile and higher paying kept Farmer from writing the third novel of the Khokarsa series. These included the aforementioned third Riverworld novel, *The Dark Design* (1977), as well as *Dark Is the Sun* (1979), *Jesus on Mars* (1979), and *The Magic Labyrinth* (1980). During this same period Farmer also wrote two drafts of the ecological disaster novel *Up from the Bottomless Pit*, which went unpublished until its serialized appearance in *Farmerphile: The Magazine of Philip José Farmer* (Nos. 1–10, July 2007–October 2007), a fanzine dedicated to bringing into print the author's rare and unpublished work.

But the busy schedule did not mean Farmer had lost interest in the sequel to *Flight to Opar*, and he in fact outlined the novel and began writing the manuscript; this was likely around late 1975, when the novel was contracted with DAW Books. In 1978, the novel's contract was renewed, showing clearly that Farmer still had plans to continue the series.

Disagreements with the publisher, however, led to a parting of ways, and rights to the Khokarsa series reverted to Farmer in October 1983, leaving the third book without a publisher. Meanwhile, Farmer continued working on his more popular properties, wrapping up the Riverworld and World of Tiers series, and launching a new major series with the Dayworld trilogy.

Even so, Farmer continued to express interest in completing the Khokarsa series over the years, such as in this excerpt from an interview conducted by Michael Croteau and Craig Kimber in September 1997 for *The Unofficial Philip José Farmer Home Page*:

> I have thought about finishing [the Khokarsa series]. But instead of the proposed five or seven books, I'd just try to finish it in one book. I knew the final cataclysmic ending right from the beginning. A huge earthquake wrecks the civilizations and opens the inland sea to flow into the Congo. The dry spells were just starting then, before the Sahara became a desert. 12,000 years ago there was a lot of water there; it was the end of the Ice Age.

As late as January 1999, Farmer was still tossing around the idea of writing the third book, as illustrated in the following passage from a letter to Alan Hanson that appeared in *Heritage of the Flaming God: Ancient Mysteries of La and Savage Opar* (eds. Alan Hanson and Michael Winger, Waziri Press, 1999), a collection that at long last saw the publication of the monumental study on Opar and its motherland civilization that inspired the Khokarsa series:

> If I were to write the final book now, and this is important, where would I find a publisher? The old days are gone. Nowadays, all the major publishers are part of a conglomerate, and the driving motive is in big money. BIG. Not a modest profit. BIG profits. The first two books would have to be reprinted so that the reader could get reacquainted with the Opar books.

Wouldn't work. No publisher would want to reprint them and then print a new one.

Yet, on skimming through these Opar novels, *Hadon* and *Flight*, I'm tempted. Could I find a small publisher to invest in the novels? Would it be worth my time? I'm aged eighty-one, and I have left writing science fiction for the crime novel. Well, we'll see.

Despite such teasing statements to his readers, Farmer never returned to the series before his retirement, leaving *Hadon of Ancient Opar* and *Flight to Opar* appearing as if they would join the ranks of hundreds of other yellow-spined DAW original paperbacks from the 1970s in literary oblivion. And yet the "Ancient Opar" novels continued to be reprinted and popular among Farmer's fans the world over. *The Philip José Farmer International Bibliography*, a website that catalogs every known appearance of Farmer's work in print, records that *Hadon of Ancient Opar* saw at least eight printings by DAW Books in the years spanning 1974 to 1983, as well as eight foreign editions published outside of the United States. The exhaustive bibliography also lists five printings of *Flight to Opar* published by DAW Books from 1976 to 1983, and seven foreign editions. Clearly, there was an audience for the series, but with only two novels published in the cycle, the great Khokarsan revival seemed at best unlikely, and at worst doomed to obscurity.

But fortunately, good ideas never die; they only lie fallow for a season waiting to be cultivated.

So it was that in July 2005, Michael Croteau—now Farmer's official webmaster and the publisher of *Farmerphile*—was given permission by Phil Farmer and his wife Bette to go on a treasure-hunting excursion through the author's files looking for material to use in the fanzine. This was the same trip during which Mike and our good friend Win Scott Eckert uncovered several other unpublished gems written by Farmer, including the outline and partial manuscript of The Evil in Pemberley House. At the time, I was serving, along with my colleague Paul Spiteri, as *Farmerphile*'s coeditor. Upon his return from Peoria,

THE SONG OF
KWASIN

Philip José Farmer &
Christopher Paul Carey

Mike emailed me with the discoveries in order to discuss which pieces we might want to run in *Farmerphile*, casually listing the following item among the other finds: "*Kwasin of Opar*. Not sure what to do with this. Need to read it and see if it is compelling enough to either put in *Farmerphile* or sell photocopies [on behalf of Phil on his official website]."

To say that I was stunned by this last discovery would be an understatement. I instantly fired off an email to Mike requesting photocopies, which he promptly mailed to me. I received them a few days later just as I was heading out to an author reading at the Science Fiction Museum in Seattle. I brought the photocopies along with me to the reading and, having arrived at the museum early, read the novel's entire outline while I sat in the theater. That evening I barely listened to a word of the speaker, who was quite well renowned, and to whom, under other circumstances, I would have paid attention quite intently. But I was off in another world of "gold, and silver, ivory, and apes, and peacocks." The outline galloped along at the pace of a charging Cape buffalo, and Farmer's enthusiasm leaped from every line. Here at last was the story of what happened on the island of Khokarsa after Hadon flew with Lalila and their companions to distant Opar—the long and bloody war with King Minruth in its entirety!

I knew then and there that the story had to be told. That same month I drafted a proposal for how I would complete the novel, and sent it off to Phil Farmer. I had first corresponded with Phil in 1997 and met him in person the following year, later visiting with him and his lovely wife Bette at their home in Peoria. I had written over the years a number of articles on his work, which (much to my astonishment) Phil had told me and others were among his favorites. Like Phil, I also had a background in anthropology, which was the field of my undergraduate study, and a longtime love of all things Edgar Rice Burroughs and H. Rider Haggard, the two main inspirations for the Khokarsa series. To round it all out, I was currently working on a master's degree in Writing Popular Fiction. Phil knew all of this. Still, I had no expectation of a positive response.

Phil's reply, however, was warm, enthusiastic, and encouraging—and to my great surprise, he said yes to my proposal, closing out his email with the morale-boosting imperative of "forward it is." I think my letter had rekindled Phil's excitement to see his epic saga of Khokarsa through to its completion—if that happened by his hand or another's mattered less at this point in his life than whether the story would be told at all.

As soon as my proposal was accepted, I drafted a new outline in accordance to Phil's express wishes and comments, now that the novel was to be repositioned as the climax of a trilogy. Then, at Phil and Bette's recommendation, I stopped work on the novel and continued my master's program, which I completed in January 2007.

The delay turned out to be fortunate. While I was working on my degree, I was able to visit Phil at his home in Peoria and examine his extensive notes on the Khokarsa series. I had discovered a partial Khokarsan syllabary in his files that made the names I needed to coin for the new novel that much more authentic. I also reread *Hadon of Ancient Opar* and *Flight to Opar* more times than I can remember, as well as a number of Burroughs and Haggard novels for inspiration. Further, I created a glossary of names and terms from the books that I was able to fill in and expand with the help of Phil's original Khokarsa notes.

In early 2008, I completed the first draft of the novel, which was accepted by Phil's agent and began to make the rounds with prospective publishers. Now that Phil did not have to bow to Wollheim's demand to use "Opar" in the title, we decided to retitle the novel *The Song of Kwasin*. Opar simply did not figure into the plot, and Kwasin was not, in fact, from Opar. *The Song of Kwasin* made a fitting title for a number of reasons. First, it indicated that the novel was a departure from the first two books in that it concentrated on Kwasin's epic struggle against Minruth rather than Hadon of Opar's adventures. Second, the title evoked the great ballads of the Khokarsan bards. In the Khokarsan language, the title would be rendered *Pwamwotkwasin*, or "The Song of the Hero Kwasin."

And finally, the title was a play on "The Song of Hiawatha," the poem that inspired Phil to create the character of Kwasin in the first place. In Longfellow's poem, the character Kwasind is Hiawatha's giant strongman friend. For all of these reasons, we knew we had the right title.

By this time, Phil's health had worsened, but Bette Farmer read the novel aloud to him, and told me how Phil lit up at hearing of Kwasin's adventures. I will always regard the moment I learned this as a touchstone in my career as a writer.

Then, in January 2009, while visiting Phil on the occasion of his ninety-first birthday, I unexpectedly uncovered another trove of Khokarsa materials in the files. These newly found papers included the complete Khokarsan syllabary and several drafts of an article on Khokarsan linguistics, as well as other addenda and, perhaps most interestingly, an aborted alternate outline fragment to "*Kwasin of Opar*." The best sense I can give you of Phil's world building is to say that it's truly Tolkienesque in scope and detail. Or perhaps Farmerian is a better term for it, as it is wholly unique in its anthropological and metafictional approach. In any event, the new papers were a lucky find, and I was able to use the complete syllabary to revise a number of names and terms in the novel to fully line up with the linguistic rules of the Khokarsan language.

As fate would have it, Phil passed away only a month after I discovered the new materials. Although he did not live to see the novel published, I take some solace in the fact that he was able to see it completed in manuscript form and put on the market to publishers. I will never be able to thank Philip José Farmer enough for the opportunity he gave me as a younger writer trying to break into the field. I'm both a better writer and a better person for having known him.

In October 2009, I signed the contracts for *Gods of Opar: Tales of Lost Khokarsa*, an omnibus to be published by Subterranean Press that would collect *Hadon of Ancient Opar*, *Flight to Opar*, and *The Song of Kwasin*. However, due to the vagaries of publishing, *The Song of Kwasin* ended up waiting in the wings for another two and a half years while a different Farmer collection made it through the publisher's pipeline. As Philip José Farmer had passed in February 2009, this later led to the mistaken belief by many that *The Song of Kwasin* was completed by me after Phil's death. *The Song of Kwasin*—the plot, the characters, the mythic structure—is ultimately Philip José Farmer's tale; I just helped get the words on paper.

While I waited for *The Song of Kwasin* to be published, I studied Phil's alternate outline fragment for the novel. It became apparent almost instantly that the outline, while unusable in terms of the novel for a host of continuity reasons, told a lost adventure of Kwasin that fit seamlessly between the first and second chapters of *The Song of Kwasin*. Mike Croteau, now the publisher at Meteor House, urged me to do something with the idea, and so, using the outline, as well as some text from Phil's notes, I proceeded to write a 20,000-word novella titled "Kwasin and the Bear God."

I wrestled with the notion of incorporating the tale into the body of the novel. However, Phil had already put his stamp of approval on *The Song of Kwasin*, and was now no longer with us. Further, I worried that inserting the novella would create an imbalance in the dramatic unfolding of the novel's opening. For those reasons, I ultimately decided the novella should stand on its own. "Kwasin and the Bear God" first saw print in *The Worlds of Philip José Farmer 2: Of Dust and Soul* (Meteor House, 2011), almost a full year before *The Song of Kwasin* was published in *Gods of Opar* in June 2012. "Kwasin and the Bear God" has been included in this new definitive edition of *The Song of Kwasin*. Readers may now decide for themselves whether they wish to read the first chapter of *The Song of Kwasin*, flip to the back of the book to read "Kwasin and the Bear God," and then turn back to the second chapter of the novel to resume Kwasin's adventures in chronological order—or whether they instead wish to read *The Song of Kwasin* in its entirety before returning back in time to read an earlier adventure of Kwasin.

When *Gods of Opar* was published in 2012, I felt vindicated in the face of all the naysayers who had believed a thirty-year-old series inspired by a hundred-year-old series could never be revived. The book was a resounding success, received high praise from critics, and sold out almost immediately upon publication. But that success and the quick sellout also left *The Song of Kwasin* out of print for a number of years, a deficiency I am pleased Meteor House has been able to rectify with this handsome new edition.

So now that the third novel of the series is again in print, where does that leave Khokarsa and its far-flung queendom of Opar? While *The Song of Kwasin* closes out one chapter of ancient history, Farmer left a large part of the tale untold. After all, he once said he meant for the series to encompass anywhere from five to twelve volumes. Therefore, I am using Farmer's notes, as well as translations of ancient inscriptions by the late great linguist Sir Beowulf William Clayton, to continue the saga in a new cycle about Hadon and his son Kohr and daughter La, in addition to writing an earlier cycle that records the history of Opar's founder, the priestess-heroine Lupoeth.

Where will the grand adventure of Khokarsa end? Who can say? Perhaps like any good story, it won't, so long as there's someone around to tell the tale and someone to listen to it.

Let's Go...

Introduction to *Man of War* by Heidi Ruby Miller, Meteor House 2017

Philip José Farmer once speculated in one of his novels about the existence of what he called the "human magnetic moment," that is, "a quality, or 'field,' which pulls events together." This field, he said, "slightly distorts, or warps, the semifluid structure of occurrences, of space objects intertwined with the time flow." In other words, it is the quantum effect that explains what the ancient Greeks called the three Moirai, or Fates; what Carl Jung called synchronicity; and what we of the modern age are apt to dismiss rather blandly as mundane coincidence. Looking back, I believe a human magnetic moment of sorts occurred when Heidi Ruby Miller and I ended up in the same writing critique group in graduate school a decade and some change ago.

When we met, Heidi and I were both intent on writing science fiction novels for our graduate theses (which we accomplished—hers, *Ambasadora: Marked by Light*, went on to be published to much critical acclaim, while mine, *Soundstorm*, an invaluable practice run for my later published fiction, gathers dust in the trunk until I find the time or inclination to rewrite it whole cloth). Together, reading and commenting on one another's manuscripts as we wrote them, we plumbed the umbral depths of the craft of writing fiction in all its perplexing and frustrating, wondrous and rewarding glory. In our exploration, a synergy of consonant factors helped guide us: we both held undergraduate degrees in anthropology, shared a deep appreciation for the subgenre known as social science fiction, and clung ardently to the belief that high adventure and good literature are not mutually exclusive, whether in SF or any other genre.

Man of War exhibits all of these influences and more, and it is fitting it does, as all of these interests and worldviews are also exemplified throughout Farmer's body of work. In particular, they are on display in his *Two Hawks from Earth,* the novel that serves as the basis for *Man of War.* Anyone who has read *Two Hawks* (and if you haven't, go read it now) can glean something of the meticulousness with which Farmer researched his world building, such as extrapolating how the lack of horses and camels would have affected Western civilization, or how the English language would have developed had the proto-Native Americans been unable to cross the land bridge from Siberia to North America and instead headed back westward to collide with the prehistoric populations of Europe. For a detailed look at Farmer's process of world building in *Two Hawks from Earth,* I highly recommend a transcription of a talk he once gave titled "Creating Artificial Worlds" (this originally appeared in the fanzine *Pulsar,* 1979, and was reprinted in Farmer's collection *Pearls from Peoria,* ed. Paul Spiteri, Subterranean Press, 2006).

In *Man of War,* Heidi Ruby Miller illustrates her own knack for anthropological world building in the collision of three alternate Earth cultures, all quite distinct from one another. I won't go into detail about this clash of cultures except to say I'm particularly struck by the author's use of literary viewpoint to bring it all alive for the reader. For instance, Roger Two Hawks' culture is closest to our own and thus serves as a touchstone so we may understand the other two. But equally important is the viewpoint of Dakota Cummings, who, caught in the web of her own caste-based cultural biases, often seems to struggle with her predisposition to romanticize Two Hawks, even going so far on occasion as to regard him as something of a *bon sauvage.* Adding another layer of complexity, some of the cultural miscommunications in the story are reminiscent of Barry B. Longyear's "Enemy Mine"—but with a quite different outcome.

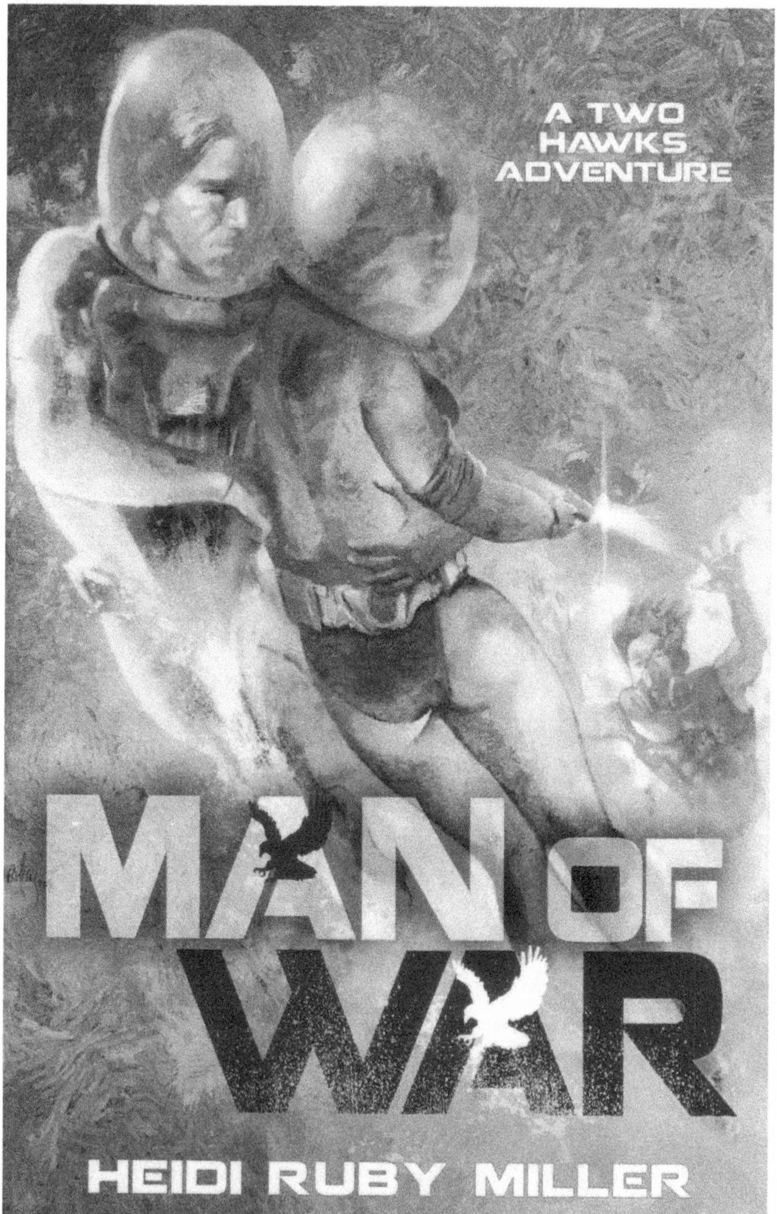
A TWO HAWKS ADVENTURE
MAN OF WAR
HEIDI RUBY MILLER

Above all, *Man of War* demonstrates the type of adventure fiction Heidi and I often discussed back in graduate school—it's a fast-paced, entertaining tale that dives down into the deeps of psychology and culture one moment, only to breach the surface into exhilarating, heroic exploits in the next. In this way, it embodies two grand pillars of Farmerian fiction—the grit of realism and the driving beat of fantastic adventure.

When Heidi and I first met, neither of us had any idea we would both one day expand upon the worlds and works of a grand master of science fiction. But then, perhaps it's not so surprising. In my experience, if there is a human embodiment of the quantum-entangling magnet that pulls events together, it is Philip José Farmer himself; once one falls within the sphere of his literary influence, the semifluid structure of occurrences is bound to warp a bit and open up a dimensional gate or two.

And now it's time for Heidi Ruby Miller to tell us what she found on the other side of the gate emblazoned with the words *Man of War*. In the immortal words of e. e. cummings (who, in another strange Farmerian convergence, shares a surname with Dakota, leading me to wonder if he is perhaps a relative in the know):

"Listen: there's a hell of a good universe next door; let's go."

Postscript
Philip José Farmer: The Next Hundred Years

Now that the Philip José Farmer Centennial—and this book—is drawing to a close, the natural, science-fictional question to ask is what the next hundred years will look like for Farmer's works. Will they stand the test of time?

According to Farmer, there might not be much of a future ahead for anyone, let alone the body of literature that he has bequeathed to fickle posterity. In a 1999 interview with Michael Croteau and Craig Kimber, Farmer stated that "the continuing overpopulation and the dwindling of our natural resources, including water, farmland, and so forth, are going to meet in the next century. Maybe in 2020 or 2050, I don't know. Then there is going to be a collapse of civilization, at which everyone laughs. They can't conceive it, but they don't have the imagination."

If civilization collapses, will the written word survive, and even if it does, will it play any significant role in human society?

As the aforementioned interview continued, Farmer stated that he would write "a hell of a novel" about civilization's downfall, if it weren't such a pessimistic idea. Then, in a classic Farmerian turnabout, he added, "Well, actually it's not, it'd be optimistic, because I don't look for the whole human race to become extinct. I look for the world population to dwindle considerably... There would be a big mad scramble, and a bloody mess battling for food, water, and so forth. It'll settle out and the tribes that are left will start again. Maybe they will have learned their lesson."

The tribes that are left will start again.

The sentiment reminds me of Farmer's novel *Dark is the Sun*, set fifteen billion years in Earth's future. Humanity has been reduced to a tribal state and has created a mythology around

PHILIP JOSÉ FARMER
DARK IS THE SUN

AN EPIC ADVENTURE BY
THE AUTHOR OF THE
AWARD-WINNING **RIVERWORLD** SERIES

surviving technology from the past that is no longer understood. Post-apocalyptic tribal humanity is similarly depicted in a much earlier novel by Farmer, *The Cache from Outer Space*. This also reminds me of his prelude to the Ancient Opar series, *Time's Last Gift*, in which John Gribardsun—the time traveling jungle lord who would become known as the god Sahhindar, among other identities—goes back to the late Pleistocene and shepherds an ice age tribe that will later change the course of humanity's future. Further, I can't help but think of Farmer's idealized alter ego, Kickaha, shedding his twentieth-century veneer and taking up the life of a warrior of the Hrowakas, the Bear People tribe, on the Amerindian level of the *World of Tiers*.

It's clear that Farmer had a fondness for so-called "primitive" societies. And that's appropriate, given that his fiction thrums deeply with the beat of mythic storytelling found in the oral traditions of such cultures.

And there, perhaps, lies the answer to how the literature of today and yesteryear might survive into the future, if Farmer's prognostication does indeed come true and civilization reduces itself to a state of tribalism. For while the written word might not survive such a tumultuous transition, oral traditions likely will. And do not Farmer's tales abound with mythic archetypes, heroes and villains and tricksters and godlike beings, and ordinary people caught up in their midst—that is, the very stuff of folklore? Are his stories not perfectly suited to serve as the basis for a new mythology in an age when the printing press and computers and ebook readers no longer exist?

And even if Farmer is wrong, if civilization does not fall, might not the Wold Newton family—that "nova of genetic splendor," as he called it—take a meaningful place in the collective unconscious of future generations? I honestly don't know. Perhaps the specific characters from that illustrious, and sometimes nefarious, lineage won't even be remembered a hundred years from now. But I do know that mythological pantheons have continued to arise among our species in every age after bygone age since the dawn of humanity. Are we moderns so arrogant to think it won't happen again?

I wonder...who's to say Philip José Farmer won't have a hand in it?

And who's to say he already hasn't?

Acknowledgments

My sincere thanks to James Goddard at Leaky Boot for his support of and hard work on this book; Michael Croteau, Win Scott Eckert, and Paul Spiteri for their help over the years while I was writing many of the pieces collected herein; Karl Kauffman for our many talks that came to fruition in the second article in this collection; Charles Berlin for his wonderful cover art; Charles N. Brown, Michael Croteau (again), John DeNardo, Win Scott Eckert, Henry G. Franke III, William H. Horner, Tony Lee, Zacharias Nuninga, Chris Roberson, William Schafer, Cath Trechman, and Howard Wright for originally publishing these articles, essays, and interviews; Heidi Ruby Miller for her friendship and encouragement; and Philip José Farmer and Bette Virginia Farmer for opening the door and allowing me to enter a pluriverse both wonderful and strange.

About the Author

Christopher Paul Carey is the coauthor with Philip José Farmer of *The Song of Kwasin*, and the author of *Exiles of Kho*; *Hadon, King of Opar*, and *Blood of Ancient Opar*, all works set in Farmer's Khokarsa series. He has edited four collections of Philip José Farmer's work—*Up from the Bottomless Pit and Other Stories, Venus on the Half-Shell and Others, The Other in the Mirror*, and (with Win Scott Eckert) *Tales of the Wold Newton Universe*—and he was the coeditor of *Farmerphile: The Magazine of Philip José Farmer* from 2005–2007. Carey is also the author of *Swords Against the Moon Men*, an authorized sequel to Edgar Rice Burroughs' classic science fantasy novel *The Moon Maid*, and he has scripted two comic books from Dynamite Entertainment featuring Burroughs' iconic characters: *Pathfinder Worldscape: Lord of the Jungle One-Shot* and *Pathfinder Worldscape: Dejah Thoris One-Shot*. His short fiction may be found in anthologies such as *The Avenger: The Justice, Inc. Files*; *Doc Ardan: The Abominable Snowman*; *Ghost in the Cogs: Steam-Powered Ghost Stories*; *The Many Tortures of Anthony Cardno*; *Tales of the Shadowmen*; *Tales of the Wold Newton Universe*; and *The Worlds of Philip José Farmer*. Carey is a senior editor at Paizo—working on the bestselling Pathfinder and Starfinder roleplaying games—and he has edited numerous collections, anthologies, and novels. He holds a master's degree in Writing Popular Fiction and resides in the Pacific Northwest. Visit him online at cpcarey.com.

CPSIA information can be obtained
at www.ICGtesting.com
Printed in the USA
BVHW08s1538250618
519958BV00002B/164/P

9 781909 849617